Amy –

What
Lies
Inside

Hope you enjoy the book!

What Lies Inside

A Novel
by
Nicholas H.

Harrowood Books

2021

First Book Printing: June 2021
    Trade Paperback Book Edition
    ISBN-13   978-0-915180-69-1
    ISBN-10   0-915180-69-3

10 9 8 7 6 5 4 3 2 1

First e-Book Publication: September, 2017
    eBook Edition
    ISBN-13   978-0-915180-57-8
    ISBN-10   0-915180-57-X

Harrowood Books
3943 N Providence Road
Newtown Square, PA 19073
800-747-8356

PRINTED IN CHINA

This novel is dedicated to the writer, director and composer
John Carpenter

It is published under the pen name Nicholas H.
To find more novels that feature drama, mystery and intrigue,
please visit the website for Nick Allen Brown at:
nickallenbrown.com

Chapter 1

1983 St. Clair, Pennsylvania

The tan-colored, rotary-dial telephone inside the Adler family home, rang and rang without an answer. Friends and family members would call and let it sometimes ring into the 40s before hanging up. The phone sat on a small table near two chairs in the living room. Directly underneath the phone was a perfectly placed, handmade lace doily.

After two days of neighbors and friends calling the Adler family and not getting an answer, they expressed their concerns to the sheriff's office. Deputy Barnes drove down Peach Mountain Road toward their farm to perform a routine wellness check late one evening before sunset. He had his AM radio tuned to a country station and was singing along as he came up over a hill and saw the Adler Farm up ahead. Every so often, Deputy Barnes would catch a glimpse of his hairline in the rearview mirror, which would force him to consider the possibility that it was receding. Nearing the Adler home, he applied the brake as he combed his hair forward with his fingers, trying to improve his masculine appearance.

Thinking the Adler family had just been traveling for an

extended period of time, he became concerned after pulling into their driveway. He could see the barn in the back of the house with their red Ford F-150 inside. It was their only means of transportation as Mr. Adler spent a good amount of his money on John Deere tractor parts, fuel and oil.

Deputy Barnes looked around the exterior of the house trying to find an unlocked door. He knocked on windows and yelled out while peering inside, leaving his handprints on the glass. The interior of the home looked desolate and straightened. While all of the windows were a simple, glass pane, the windows on the front door were beveled with frosted sections making it difficult to see the wide trail of brown, dried blood that ran up the entire length of the stairs. With all doors locked, he returned to his car. Before breaking into a resident's home, Deputy Barnes grabbed the handset of his CB radio and asked permission from the Sheriff. After a few questions were asked and answered, Sheriff Haydon finally replied with a voice of authority and irritation.

"The smallest pane you can find. If we have to end up paying for it, I don't want it to cost much."

Deputy Barnes bent down to pick up a rock that was lying on the unruly grass. His tan uniform was restrictive, and the unforgiving fabric limited his movements. With a faint grunt caused by the momentary discomfort in his crotch from bending over, he wrapped his thin, wiry fingers around a rock the size of a baseball. Keeping the damage to a minimum, he broke an eight-by-eight pane of glass near the doorknob and carefully reached his hand through the opening.

Upon entering, the odor of decay hit him in the face causing him to wince and cover his nose with his tan colored sleeve. The wide trail of brown, dried blood that ran up the staircase caused him to pause before hurrying upstairs, careful not to step on the blood trail to see if someone was injured. After spending less than thirty-seconds inside, he ran down the stairs, his state-issued patrol boots now trampling on the crime scene trail, dashing out of the house and off the front porch. Barnes dove into his car and grabbed the handset to his radio.

"Sheriff! Get over here! Get over here now. I am not saying anything more on the radio. This is an emergency."

Once Sheriff Haydon arrived, the magnitude of the scene prompted him to call the state police. Within the hour, the front lawn was covered with cruisers sporting flashing blue lights along with two coroners from two different counties. The murder of the entire Adler family was the biggest thing to happen in St. Clair since the opening of a McDonald's fast food restaurant years before.

Edward Adler farmed wheat and corn and mostly kept to himself unless he was down at the barbershop. His wife was a bookkeeper's assistant at the county co-op and had no enemies to speak of. Their eight-year-old son, Scott, was in grade school and loved basketball, while their daughter, Tilly, was thirteen and loved driving the family truck around the farm helping her dad. They were an American family who worked hard and were well known in the small town of St. Clair.

Years passed and the house never went up for sale.
Volunteers helped clean the blood off the floors and walls as
best they could. The hardwood had soaked up so much of the
blood; it was now stained dark brown with a tint of red that
could only be seen when the sun shone directly on the floor.
After the furniture was removed to a consignment store, the
house sat empty and slowly began to deteriorate. Rumors
began to spread about the house being haunted with some St.
Clair residents claiming that a light would sometimes turn on
upstairs in Tilly's bedroom. While no one could confirm that
they had seen the light, the rumors spread enough for the
haunting to become folklore.

Five years after the Adler murders, the rumors had soft-
ened and the mystery of who killed them was left unsolved.
Sheriff Haydon hated driving by the home as it conjured up
terrible scenes of the heinous murder and he would often
avoid driving by the farm.

Years later, a coal miner had a few too many and began
breaking furniture in his own apartment before striking his
girlfriend with a firearm. A domestic violence call came into
the office sending two deputies and Sheriff Haydon speeding
down Peach Tree Mountain Road in their cruisers with lights
flashing and sirens wailing. Their route took them past the
Adler farm. Sheriff Haydon was on and off the CB radio and
focusing on driving at high speeds while following two other
cruisers, not thinking about where he was at the time. The

house crept up on him like a mugger coming out of the shadows. On the second floor of the Adler Farmhouse, he saw the light in the bedroom window.

The seconds slowed into what seemed like minutes as he looked back at the window to ensure he saw the light in the bedroom. As his cruiser sped by he took an even longer look, his head turning as he drove, eventually looking out the back window.

"Did anyone else see the light on in the Adler house?" he asked into the handset of his CB Radio with widened eyes and a hurried voice.

"Negative."

"Me either, Sheriff."

Chapter 2

1988 Washington D.C.

Robert Wood, 59, was never without a lit cigarette between his fingers; even when he visited his mother in the nursing home, he would ask the nurses to bring her outside as he wasn't allowed to smoke indoors. On the day he asked the young reporter to come to his office, he had just lit one cigarette with another that was about to burn out.

Her desk was one of twenty crowded around the center of the newsroom.

"Calvert!"

Jessica sprang up from her desk and grabbed a notepad and a pencil. She hurried through the sea of desks with ringing phones, loud typewriters and reporters shuffling papers. Once inside, she closed the door behind her and took a seat as Mr. Wood crushed the end of a short cigarette into his over-flowing ashtray. He puffed casually on the one that was lit and looked over his notes.

"I have an assignment for you. Hope you don't scare too easily."

"I am up for any challenge"...the go-getter attitude of a

female reporter always made the back of his neck scrunch together, forcing him to shrug it off. The bright and cheery work
ethic in young women was common in his business and he
hated it. Even though Jessica Calvert had never belonged to a
sorority, Mr. Wood called her a *Shit Stain Sorority Girl* in his
head. While this silent moniker was currently aimed at Jessica,
it was a blanket category into which he placed all young, go-
getter female reporters.

"In St. Clair, Pennsylvania, there was a murder about five
years ago. A family was found in their house all stabbed to
death. The murder is unsolved," he explained while reaching
for a can of Diet Coke. He took a sip while Jessica scribbled
down notes. "People in the town believe the house is haunted.
I want a haunted house piece for the Sunday edition the last
week of October. The last two weeks of a presidential election
causes our paper to be chock full of political content and we
need a few pieces to break it up. That means your deadline is
in two weeks."

"Two weeks?" she said in a surprised tone, as her dead-
lines were normally a few days. Mr. Wood looked at her over
the top of his eyeglasses and counted on his fingers as he
spoke.

"You have to go there," one finger, "Interview the towns-
people," second finger, "And get some photos," third finger.
"Take one of the camera bags and get back here as soon as possible. Your deadline is in two weeks, but you should only be
staying a couple days. Three tops. Got it?"

"Got it. Where is St. Clair?"

"Four hours north."

"Quite a trip for a goose-chase piece."

"Sheriff called this one in. Said he also thinks the house is haunted. Interview him and get his take. A public official's opinion carries more weight on something like this."

"Better pack my Nancy Drew books for reference."

"You have the standard twenty dollar per diem and the accounting department will book your room. Take your own car and we'll pay mileage and don't forget receipts. Holy shit! If I have to hear from accounting one more time about a reporter not providing receipts, I'll have a coronary right here at my desk. No phone calls from accounting. I'm not kidding."

"Done."

"You wanted a break, here it is. Don't screw it up."

"I won't."

"Readers love this scary stuff. Don't embellish, but just write the piece with an eerie vibe," he said as he casually flung his hand in the air with a cigarette between his fingers.

Wasting little time, Jessica hurried home to pack. Comfortable clothes were placed inside a suitcase in neatly folded columns; toiletries were arranged meticulously in a red zippered tote with her notepad and tape recorder placed in a black-and-gray canvas messenger bag.

The drive up to St. Clair proved to be beautiful and calm-ing as the leaves spanned the autumn color palette and the un-mistakable scent of fall was in the air. Jessica rolled down her window to let some of the fresh air circulate inside her 1981 Honda Accord. Just shy of four hours later, she rolled into the small town of St. Clair and found the Mill Street Motel. The doors to all 50 rooms were facing the outside and in front of each door was a parking space. Parking at the main office, she hopped out of her car and went inside. Finding a thin, older woman at the front desk with big, red hair held up by bobby pins, Jessica asked for a room.

"Do you want a room that's smoking or non-smoking?"

"Oh, non-smoking. Please."

"Queen or twin beds?"

"Queen will work."

"No problem." the attendant said as she reached for a room key and a check-in form.

Jessica used her key to open Room 39 and set her things on the bed. Before using her folded brochure map of the town to find the Adler farm, she first headed over to the local diner for something to eat.

Jessica entered the Buckhorn Café after pushing the door open causing the top to ram into a bell above the frame. A pa-tron sitting at the lunch counter turned his head to see who had entered before going back to his cigarette over a plate of toast and runny eggs.

Her eyes quickly scanned the diner and focused on twelve

swivel stools with red vinyl seats arranged around the outside of the counter. She walked toward the far left side to avoid the smoke and tried to act as if she was local. Without any other patrons in the cafe, she thought that they might be closing and had just wandered in until a waitress came out from the kitchen holding a coffee pot in her left hand.

"Regular or Sanka, honey?" she asked as she blinked her eyes covered in blue eye shadow.

"No coffee for me please. An ice water will be fine. I must have missed the lunch crowd."

"You did. It was packed about an hour ago. Wanna hear the specials?"

"Actually, can I get a salad with ranch with a bunch of sliced cucumbers and carrots?"

"No problem. Want cheddar broccoli soup with that?" the waitress asked. Jessica was tempted, but thought it wouldn't be as healthy as she preferred.

"Could I get fruit instead?"

"Certainly," the waitress responded as she wrote the order on a ticket and set it on the cook's sill. After dishing out a scoop of ice from the icemaker and filling a tall glass of ice water from a nearby pitcher, she set it in front of her customer.

The smoker had extinguished his cigarette into his plate of eggs and left a ten-dollar bill on the counter before leaving. Deciding to strike up a conversation about the Adler family, Jessica took a sip of her ice water and thought of a question that wouldn't reveal herself as a reporter, but instead a curious customer.

"Have you heard anything about a haunted house in this area?"

"You mean the Adler Farm?"

"Yes. Is it well known around here?" she asked as the sound of a knife chopping on a cutting board could be heard back in the kitchen.

"Well, everyone around here knows it's haunted. They tried to sell the house for years, but no one will even think about it," she said as she popped a stick of chewing gum into her mouth. "Name's Gertie. What's yours?"

"Jessica."

"My friends call me Purty Gertie, but if I keep working here and eating all these damn cheeseburgers, I won't be so purty. I've already gained eight pounds," she placed her hands around her stomach and flattened her apron showing her pudgy stomach and spoke under her breath. "Oh, hell."

Jessica wanted to take the notepad out from her back pocket and take notes, but didn't want to reveal herself as a reporter just yet. Knowing that casual conversation always produced better results, she did her best to take mental notes. Steering the conversation away from weight gain, she slid the conversation back toward the topic of the Adler farm.

"Have you been to the Adler Farm?"

"I drive by there from time to time. You're a reporter aren't you?" she asked. Jessica was surprised and her eyes grew as big as quarters.

"Is it that obvious?"

"Sheriff said you were coming into town."

"Really?"

"You're supposed to interview him, I heard."

"I am. How did you know that?"

"Everyone here knows everyone's business. It's a small town. Plus my stupid brother is a deputy."

"Order up!" the cook in the back yelled as he placed a salad plate on the sill. Gertie grabbed the plate and set it in front of Jessica.

"Good to know. I forgot that was how small towns worked," Jessica said as she took a bite of her bland salad with what tasted like expired ranch dressing. Gertie leaned forward resting her elbows on the counter and spoke at a low volume.

"When I drive by the house at night I never see anything, but one time during the day I saw a priest outside on the front lawn."

"A priest?" she asked as she picked at the cucumbers and carrots.

"He's from here. He is with the Pottsville Catholic Church. I've seen him a few times, but I just call him Father," she leaned in and spoke at an even lower tone. "I don't much believe in the whole church thing."

"Where's Pottsville?"

"Up the road about ten minutes. That's where my brother lives. When people in St. Clair say that they're going into town, they mean Pottsville."

"I see. What was he doing?"

"My brother?"

"The priest in the front yard."

"Oh. He was reading out loud from a book. Weird right? No one else was there but I could see him move his mouth."

"The Bible?"

"Could be. I couldn't tell. I was just driving by."

"Maybe he was warding off spirits and ghosts or something."

"How's that?"

"You know, like *The Exorcist.*"

"Is that a movie?"

"You've never seen it? Where the priest reads The Bible to fend off demons?"

"No. Is it good?"

"It's very scary. I wonder if I should go talk to the priest before interviewing the sheriff?"

"Well, don't talk to my brother. He's an idiot with a gun. His name is Deputy Phillips."

"I'll steer clear."

"Sheriff once made him keep a single bullet in his pocket. Like Barney Fife from that TV show."

"So, this is a Mayberry kind of town?"

"The closest mall to us is in Harrisburg and it's like over an hour away. I wish we had a mall or even a strip mall. That would be something. At least Pottsville has a movie theater."

"At least you have a haunted house."

"Yeah, we got that going for us," she said with a smirk.

"So, if a priest is on a front lawn of the Adler Farm, that sounds like it could really be haunted."

"Could be."

A family of four walked into the diner prompting Gertie to pull menus, silverware and crayons. As she greeted the family and walked them to a booth, Jessica removed her notepad from her back pocket and began jotting down notes.

Chapter 3

The Sheriff's office was nine minutes from St. Clair and located in a small building close to the courthouse. The interior of the office had limited space and featured open-ceiling offices. While each office had a door and wooden walls, one could easily toss paper wads over the walls and watch it land on the occupant's desk through the large, pane glass windows. Often when there were few people around and the sheriff was out, paper wad wars would commence between the deputies using old phone book pages. Direct hits cost the victim twenty-five cents.

Sheriff Haydon had the biggest office in the building, but it was still cramped and left a lot to be desired for a man who kept the county in line. His bushy white eyebrows and solid jaw gave him the stereotypical appearance of a county sheriff, but he refrained from wearing a cowboy hat. On his calendar for the next day was his interview with the reporter. The calendar was adhered to the wall next to his desk so whenever he looked up, he could see what was on the agenda for the day. After getting a cup of coffee, he sat in his solid wood swivel chair and looked up at the calendar and read the words *Jessica Calvert - Adler Article.* He recalled when Deputy Barnes had called it in on the CB radio. The crime was so heinous and disturbing that the murder scene had been permanently burned into his memory.

Mr. and Mrs. Adler were murdered downstairs in their home with what appeared to be a serrated saw normally used for cutting small trees and limbs. The jagged edges shredded the flesh around the neck of Mr. Adler gushing at least a quart of blood that pulsed from his jugular vein. The attacker continued to use the tool to puncture the left eye of Mrs. Adler and break her eye socket. The serrated saw entered her brain causing her to scream and her jaw to lock open. When the autopsy was performed, the coroner reset her jaw by breaking the condylar process. Mr. and Mrs. Adler had been murdered downstairs in the family room, but were found upstairs in their beds. The trail of blood from their dragged bodies looked as if a giant permanent marker with little ink left had made a red streak from the family room, up the stairs and into their bedroom.

The coroner listed in his report that the children were both murdered in the bathroom using the same tool. Each child had puncture wounds located slightly below their ears. The sharp end of the tool came to a stop deep inside their brain and both were dragged to their rooms and placed under their beds. Nothing in the house was stolen and no sign of forced entry was evident. The mystery of who wanted to murder the Adler family remained a mystery. Sheriff Haydon took another sip of his coffee and looked at a mountain of paperwork on his desk just as his phone rang.

Jessica drove into the parking lot of the St. Clair Catholic Church and easily found a parking space. The church was very small and looked more like a small post office than a place of worship. In D.C. the Catholic churches were designed using gothic architecture and appeared somber and medieval...a far cry from the quaint parish in Pottsville.

Hoping to find the priest who was seen standing on the front lawn of the Adler home, she entered through a wooden door on the side of the church and found herself standing in a small office with worn, green carpet. A TV could be heard in a room nearby—the sound of a football game, whistles chirping and the roar of a crowd. Then she heard the sound of someone walking in the next room. An old man with deep wrinkles around his eyes came into Jessica's view with his white clerical collar askew and the top button undone. He was holding a napkin and wiped his mouth as he spoke with what sounded like a tired, old motor in his throat.

"Hello," he said with a smile. His hair was very thin and silver in color.

"Hi. I'm sorry to bother you," Jessica started to say.

"Oh, no. You're not bothering me. I heard someone come in and I thought it was one of the staff," he replied as he put the napkin in his pocket and fixed his collar. "How can I be of service?"

"My name is Jessica Calvert and I am a reporter with *The Washington Post.*"

"How wonderful. What a wonderful newspaper."

"It is. I have only been with the paper for a short while."

"Well, come into my office. How may I help?" he offered with a simple gesture of holding out his thin arm as if to guide her inside his office. Accepting his invitation, she walked past him noticing the pronounced blue veins and wrinkles in his hand.

"Thank you," she said as she walked inside a carpeted room with a desk covered in papers. In front of the desk was a recliner and a console television that was tuned to a public broadcasting station. It wasn't what she expected, as it seemed more like a living room than an office. "Wow, this is nice."

"Well this isn't my clerical office. This is more of a home office as my living quarters are upstairs. But you are more than welcome here."

"Thank you," she said as she took a seat in the recliner.

"I'm sorry Jessica, I haven't yet offered my name," he spoke to her as he pulled his office chair out from around his desk and positioned it in front of the recliner and turned off the TV. "My name is Father Moretti."

"Very nice to meet you. Did I interrupt you while eating?"

"I just ate half of a sandwich. I tend to eat small portions throughout the day," he said with a smile. "Well, tell me, how can I help *The Washington Post*?"

"I am here doing a story on the tragedy that befell the

Adler Family years ago."

"Oh, dear. Couldn't *The Post* do a happier story?" he asked
as she removed her notepad and pen from her back pocket.

"Not these days. This is in regards to their house being
haunted," Jessica said with a grin thinking that Father Moretti
might smack his knee and laugh at how preposterous the focus
of the story was. Instead, he nodded and seemed to acknowl-
edge the claim.

"I understand."

"Well now I am a little creeped out."

"Why is that?"

"I expected you to laugh at the idea, but you seem to think
different," she replied. He sat back in his chair and crossed his
legs and arms. He looked off to the side in thought.

"I don't really believe in hauntings or ghosts. The Bible
does mention demons in scripture and Jesus healed men that
were possessed by demons, but I don't think they roam the
earth. It's possible for things on this earth to be affected by
demons, I suppose," he explained as Jessica feverishly took notes.

"I met a waitress over at the Buckhorn Café and she mentioned that she saw you on the Adlers' front lawn reading out
loud."

"She did? That's true. I was. Very observant of her," he
said as he nodded with a smile.

"May I ask why?"

"I prayed over the house and I sprinkled holy water on
the front porch. I asked God for peace and His mercy."

"Is this common to do at the scene of a murder?"

"I felt called by God to do so. It may be common. If at the very least, a prayer would certainly be warranted."

"What scripture did you read?"

"My. What questions," Father Morelli said with a smile. "I feel as if I am being interrogated," he said as he grinned.

"My apologies. I am just thorough."

"Where did you go to school?" he asked as he reached for a large black book with a leather cover.

"University of Pittsburgh. Grew up on Mt. Washington," Father Morelli looked down at his Bible and began turning pages with his veined fingers.

"Well, no doubt your education has made you an excellent reporter. Now, the scripture I read was from Romans," he said just before he read aloud. *For I am sure that neither death nor life, nor angels nor rulers, nor things present nor things to come, nor powers, nor height nor depth, nor anything else in all creation, will be able to separate us from the love of God in Christ Jesus our Lord."*

"That's nice."

"The Adler family were not devout Catholics, but they did attend church every so often, specially the annual spring picnic," he replied as he closed his Bible. Jessica asked a few more questions, taking notes and listened intently as Father Morelli spoke. Once she decided that she had gotten all she could, she thanked him for his time and he escorted her out to the parking lot.

Jessica drove back to the Mill Street Motel and parked her car in front of her room and immediately noticed a note taped to the door. She got out of her car and walked up to the door and read: *Message waiting for you at the office.*

In the lobby, she found a bald-headed man drinking a can of Pepsi with a green straw protruding out from the top. His feet were up on the desk and a baseball game was on a tiny black and white TV. Upon hearing her enter, he casually stood up and looked as if he was rudely interrupted.

"Calvert. Room 39. I had a note on my door concerning a message," she said. The man reached down and grabbed an envelope off the desk. He handed it to her and sat down, going back to his ballgame. Jessica opened the envelope as she walked out of the front door and pulled out an index card. On it were the words:

Call Mr. Robert Wood at 800-777-3456

Once in her motel room, she dialed the number expecting him to be at his desk even though it was late. Mr. Wood was rarely at home. His wife had left him long ago and there were rumors that he once had a dog. He had paid a kid in the neighborhood to look after the black lab, but when the kid left home after graduating college, the boy asked Mr. Wood if he could have the dog.

"Wood," he answered.

"Hey. This is Jessica. You called?"

"Good to go for your interview tomorrow?"

"Yes. In the morning at nine."

"You have the camera?"

"I do."

"You go by the house yet?"

"I just finished interviewing a priest who was seen on the lawn of the house reading aloud from The Bible. I haven't been to the house yet."

"He casting off demons or something?"

"Sort of. Not as creepy or exorcist sounding as I wanted."

"When you going to the house?"

"After meeting the Sheriff."

"Well, the reason I am calling is because in the editors meeting this evening, one of them brought up taking photos of the interior of the house with a thermal camera."

"What is that?"

"I don't really know. Apparently it can see ghosts."

"How can that be?"

"In the meeting they said to have someone take photos and hopefully the film will look weird enough to be creepy. We are really stretching for stories of interest that aren't political."

"Where do I get a camera like that?"

"You don't. Someone here is working on getting a photographer that knows about it. Not sure it will work or not."

"Well, either way I will take the photos of the house, inside and out."

"Look, let's be honest. You don't know a lot about cameras. I want you to take way more photos than a photographer would. Go ahead and expend all the film. If we are lucky, we'll get something printable."

"Thanks for the vote of confidence."

"I didn't hire you for your photography skills. See you in a couple days."

Chapter 4

Sheriff Haydon had straightened his office by moving and organizing files. He used an old cloth and dusted the lamp that sat on the corner of his desk and picked up the wayward paper wads that would accidentally land in his office while he was absent. Once things looked tidy, he acquired a bottle of spray cleaner from the janitorial closet and wiped things down, at the very least giving the office a pleasant, cleaner smell.

Due to the Schuylkill County budget, Sheriff Haydon was forced to pay minimum wage for both a receptionist and a dispatcher. After months of turnover and employees coming and going, he decided to seek out a receptionist who would also serve as a dispatcher. An employee doing two jobs meant he could pay double the minimum wage and actually keep an employee rather than have to keep training new ones.

Ruth Sawyer, 51, was a regular at the Little Brown Jug, a bar within walking distance of the Schuylkill County Sheriff's Office. Over the years she had gotten to know the deputies and even Sheriff Haydon on a first-name basis. One night at the Jug, after a few too many, Haydon rocked himself off his barstool and sidled up to Ruth. During their drunken conversation, he offered her the dual role position to which she accepted on the spot. The next day, she strolled in with a box containing picture frames, a fake Tiffany lamp, an array of coffee mugs and a jar of pens and pencils, ready to begin her new job. Sheriff Haydon was bewildered, as he didn't remember saying anything to her other than he was going to hire someone.

Eventually he gave in, thinking he could have said anything that night and proceeded to hire her, but every once in a while even after five years of her employment, he would think that there was a slight possibility that she pulled one over on him.

Jessica entered the sheriff's office and approached Ruth, the only secretary in Schuylkill County wearing a dispatcher's headset. Jessica looked pretty with her hair fixed into a bun and her makeup applied evenly.

"Hi. I'm Jessica Calvert from *The Washington Post* to interview Sheriff Haydon."

While speaking with Ruth, two deputies noticed the cute girl and strolled over to where she was standing, hoping she was a damsel in distress. Up until that point, the only sheriff's office she had ever seen was in Arlington County. Months ago, she had visited the office just outside of D.C. to get a quote for a story after a deputy who was involved in a shooting, was suspended with pay. She remembered that every officer in Arlington had clean pressed shirts as if they were dry cleaned after a single use. The edges of their collars were crisp and sharp. Each deputy was clean-shaven with hats that looked like weapons. Should an assailant corner them without a gun, a simple Frisbee toss to the criminal's head with their razor sharp hat would do the trick.

Jessica took a quick look at the deputies walking toward her with interest. Their collars were disheveled; their hats appeared to have suffered a tour of duty in a war zone and their facial hair seemed to have several days of growth.

The office building once stood resilient against a strong storm that tore part of the roof off. The gallons of water that rained into the building was the cause of the musty, moldy odor now wafting past Jessica's nose. While it was noticeable to her, the long time law enforcement personnel had gone nose-blind to the smell long ago.

Ruth turned to Deputy Phillips and asked him to escort Jessica to the sheriff's office. He was an overfed, small town boy with dirty blonde hair and was very timid as he asked her questions.

"You're from *The Washington Post*?"

"I am," she answered. As she walked beside him, she looked at his shirt pocket checking for the single bullet protruding from inside.

"This about the Adler Farm?"

"It is. You know anything about it?" she asked as she gave up trying to see if she could locate which pocket the bullet was in.

"Sheriff Haydon does. More than most people," he replied as he stopped at a doorway and raised his arm, guiding her into the sheriff's office.

"Thanks for the escort," she said as she walked past him. Introductions were made before Deputy Phillips promptly left. Sheriff Haydon sat back in his chair and tried his best to be comfortable.

"Can I get you something to drink?"

"I'm fine. Smells good in here."

"I cleaned it recently. I straightened it too. Didn't want you to think I am as big of a slob as my office looked."

"My desk is always a mess," she said as she pulled out her notebook and pen from her back pocket. "How familiar were you with the Adler family?"

"Very familiar. I knew them pretty well, but St. Clair and Pottsville are small towns and everyone knows everyone."

"Is it safe to enter the house?"

"I suppose. It's been locked for a long time. I guess you know it's haunted."

"Is that a fact? Can I quote you? Something like, Sheriff Haydon stated that the house in which the Adler family was murdered is indeed haunted."

"You're good."

"It's my job. So can I quote you?"

"You may."

"Why do you believe it to be haunted?"

"Have you heard about the light that turns on and off?"

"I have. Why does that make it haunted?"

"No electricity. There's no one to pay the bill. Power was shut off a month after the murder," Haydon said as he crossed his arms. As if a car hit her while crossing a street, Jessica felt the words as he spoke. The thought of the house not having electricity didn't occur to her.

She had thought it would have been a lamp simply malfunctioning, something that had a logical explanation and could be spun into a creepy part of her story. Instead, it was genuinely creepy and the idea of a house being haunted now seemed plausible."

"Can you tell me about those who've been in the house after the murder?"

"Years ago. Maybe two months after the murder, a few officers from this station and a few members of the community helped clean the house and move all the furniture out. Some of us cleaned the blood stains as best we could," he explained while Jessica took her time writing out his words in her notes. After a brief moment of silence, she looked back up from her notepad.

"It says that the address of the Adler family is in St. Clair, so is the St. Clair City Police involved as well?" During her question, Sheriff Haydon rolled his eyes and shook his head.

"The murder occurred in the county. Not the city. Years ago a car accident happened just inside the city limits. No big deal. Drunk driver ran into a guardrail. The driver was passed out. The city police officer put the man's car in gear and rolled it over the county line and called us."

"Sounds like another news story."

"It is. They think we're a bunch of rubes. They won't even play us in a softball game."

"Noted. Did anyone see anything out-of-the-ordinary?"

"Not at all, but the light turning on and off didn't start happening until six or seven months after the murder. No one will go near the house. Even Father Moretti prayed over their land. Holy water and all that," he said as he swiped his hand in the air and shook his head.

"Not a believer?"

"Not really. Hocus-pocus. But I guess if there are ghosts, there must be angels too."

"You ever see anything other than the light go on and off?"

"Nope. You mean like a ghost?"

"Yes, or anything else that would lead you to believe that the house would be haunted?"

"No. Just the light."

Chapter 5

Jessica had been given a single silver key to the front door to the Adler house. The sheriff had kept the keys to the Adler home in his top desk drawer and looked at them every time he slid the drawer open. They were shiny and still looked new as they hadn't been used since the lock had been changed years ago in 1983 on both the front and back door. After the interview, Sheriff Haydon offered to have Deputy Phillips escort her to the house, but thinking that if something were to happen, he wouldn't even have time to get the bullet out from his pocket and into his gun fast enough.

"Thanks, but I might not head over there right away. I have to call my editor and run an errand. I do appreciate the offer. I'll return the key when I'm done photographing the house," she offered her white lie with a smile, as no phone call was planned. No errand was needed. She thought she might go over to the house and begin taking photos and get it over with. She considered trying to take photos without ever stepping inside the house. *Maybe a lens pressed up to the window would suffice?*

Upon arriving, she saw a two-story farmhouse with a dead tree in the front yard. Instead of grass and a nice front lawn, the house sat on a plot of land void of grass or any kind of plant life. The ground was cracked from lack of rain causing her mind to drift to images of the American Dust Bowl. As she drove in the driveway and turned off the ignition, her memory recalled one of her high school history teachers standing in front of a classroom, explaining how The Dust Bowl was also known as the Dirty Thirties. Her eyes drifted toward the acreage behind the house where a barren wheat field spanned as far as her eyes could see.

She looked at the exterior of the house taking notice that the paint had begun to chip around the edges of the windows and the roof looked to be in need of repair. She exited her Honda Accord and she reached into her car from a standing position and hoisted the camera bag onto her shoulder and closed the door to her car. Looking around she took note of a tree line behind the house with a barn back in the distance with the doors closed. Crows cawed in the distance...the only sound to break the silence around the peaceful farm.

The next hour was spent taking photos of the exterior of the house. Capturing the Adler home from all angles, she imagined the kids running around the front porch, laughing and hollering out. Maybe the mother would have opened a screen door yelling out, *Dinner! Come inside, please!* After she spent a few rolls of film, she considered not even going inside. Maybe Deputy Phillips would have been good to have around as she walked around inside and took photos. She pulled out the silver key from her pocket and thought she could at least unlock it and open the door. After approaching the front steps, she looked around once again. No sounds. Complete silence. Not even the faint sound of a train and the crows had ceased cawing. She took a few steps up on the front porch and inserted the key and could hear the smooth tumblers racking over and she turned the key. The deadbolt unlocked with a snap. After removing the key, she opened the door open and remained out on the front porch.

"Hello?" she said, hoping no one would answer. A musty odor mixed with what smelled like metal singed her nose, prompting her to cover it with her hand. "Ugh," she uttered as she looked around inside while still standing on the front porch. Brown stains could be seen on the wood stairs and flooring in front of her. She then realized she was looking at a trail of blood that appeared to have been cleaned, or at least a vain attempt to do so.

Having had enough, she decided to close the door and return at a later time with an authority figure who had more than one bullet. After snapping the deadbolt in place with a smooth turn of the key, she placed it back in her pocket and turned around. A red 1984 Chevy Citation II pulled into the driveway just as Jessica stepped off the front porch. Once it parked behind her Accord, a young man opened the door and got out holding a large bag. James Extine, 33, kept his eyes on Jessica as he approached. She noticed he was thin, with neatly combed hair and a smile that was infectious.

"You must be Miss Calvert. Your boss is a difficult man. I could barely hear him between the puffs of smoke on the phone."

"I'm sorry, who are you?" she asked as he walked toward her.

"I'm James from Allentown. I work for a coal mining company and I photograph mines."

"Oh I see. You're here to photograph a few ghosts," Jessica said with a smile. James saw that she was pretty from afar, but close up she was easily an 8 out of 10. It was her smile that did him in.

"Well, I was told to take a bunch of photos with my thermal camera and send the negatives with you. Ghosts or no ghosts."

"I'm Jessica," she said as she reached out her hand.

"James Extine. Good to meet you," his eyes were close to a gray color, yet appeared warm and kind. Jessica decided to act like more of a reporter in front of James and whipped out her notepad and pen. She explained that she was just about to go inside and warned James about the bloodstains on the floor and the smell in the air. She unlocked the front door once again and allowed him to lead the way, making him the official buffer without his knowledge. As if he were entering a normal home under normal conditions, he walked right in and Jessica followed suit.

"Smells terrible," he said as he covered his nose.

"Awful," she added. Their conversations drifted toward *The Washington Post* and Jessica's job. Fascinated with the ability to write, he asked her questions about some of the past articles she had written. Most of their conversation took place on the first floor while James set up his camera and tripod. He snapped photos while asking Jessica questions about her job.

"What are your hours?"

"Kind of all over the place. I get up early and get to bed late a lot of the time. How about you?"

"Same. I take thermal photos of the interior of the mines to identify pockets suitable for blasting. It helps make a more productive mine," James continued to talk about the technology of a thermal camera as he gathered his equipment and headed upstairs. Without really thinking about it, they were both headed up to the second floor where the Adler family was murdered.

"So Jessica? No nickname? Do people call you Jess?"

"My friends call me Jess. You can call me Jessica," she said with a slight smile.

"Oh I see how it is," he replied, enjoying the banter.

At the top of the steps, the bloodstains were more noticeable. Bodies had been dragged from the top of the stairs and into three different rooms. The three trails of brown stains caused James to stop speaking. He walked along the biggest swath of blood which led him into the largest bedroom where the trail stopped. The room was barren. No dresser. No bed, just hardwood flooring and a light fixture in the ceiling.

"Wonder why the trail stops here?" he said as he spoke with his hands and looking around towards the floor.

"I think the bed was here?"

"I see."

"Why so much blood?" he asked.

"Their throats," she started to say until she heard a noise coming from one of the rooms. "Were cut," she continued as she looked behind her. She turned back to James. "Did you hear that?" she asked.

"No. What did you hear?"

"Sounded like someone sitting down in a chair. Creaking or something," she added. James walked from the large bedroom and out into the hall, looking down at the faded trail of blood.

"Hello? Anyone here?" he hollered as he started toward the two bedrooms. He took steps past Jessica thinking he might be impressing her with his bravery while inside the creepy feeling had turned into outright fear. He neared the bedroom on the left where the young boy was found and looked inside. A bloodstain on the floor, but nothing else. He turned his attention to the other bedroom. He could see a window as he got closer. Then more of the floor. Another bloodstain could be seen. Finally he looked into the room and saw nothing.

"I don't know," James said. "I don't think it was anything. Maybe just the house settling or something."

"So weird. I distinctly heard something."

"I'm gonna start in here," James said as he looked around the empty room of Tilly Adler. "I'll just grab the tripod." He walked out of Tilly's room and back into the bedroom where

Mr. and Mrs. Adler were murdered, grabbing his equipment. Jessica figured that she would look around for the lamp on the second floor thinking that maybe she could find out why it turned off and on for seemingly no reason. Neither Scott Adler's room nor Mr. and Mrs. Adler's room had a lamp as both were completely empty. Jessica walked into Tilly's room while James set up his tripod. Unable to find a lamp, she furrowed her brow in confusion.

"Weird. The residents of this town swear that a light can be seen coming from one of the rooms on the second floor. They say it is a lamp in the window. There is nothing on this floor."

"No furniture or even light bulbs in the fixtures for that matter. Look up," James said as he gestured with a flick of his head toward the ceiling. Jessica looked at the fixture. It was a socket for a bulb and nothing more. James began to take photos of the room, moving his tripod around to capture every angle.

His eyes rolled back and his mouth dropped wide open. The weight of his torso on top of his legs caused his legs to buckle and he fell to the ground with the strap of his camera still around his neck, pulling the tripod to the floor. When Jessica turned around she saw his unconscious body piled on the hardwood with the tripod on top of him.

Before she could speak, James was being tugged by something before being thrown through the window. Glass shattered and bones were snapped as his body broke through the frame before falling two stories and smacking the packed dirt below. Jessica ran for the door before feeling the paw of an animal grab her leg. The sinking feeling in her stomach was similar to the first drop on a rollercoaster as she was picked up and thrown through the window screaming. The sound of her screaming was quickly silenced as she landed on top of the dead body of James Extine.

Chapter 6

Eighty-Four Days Later - Schuylkill Medical Center

The Glasgow Coma Scale was created to assess the severity of a coma and to give a measurement of the patient's level of consciousness. Jessica had been given a GCS of 7, which prompted Schuylkill Medical Center to call in a specialist from Penn State to oversee her condition.

For nearly three months, she had remained unconscious while her father made weekend trips from his home in Pittsburgh to sit by her side. Bob Calvert, 59 was a machinist at Three Rivers Manufacturing Plant and lived and died each season the Pittsburgh Steelers were in contention. His diet consisted mainly of french fries and coleslaw that topped every sandwich he ate along with drinking ice cold Iron City Beer.

After driving four hours, Bob would read books out loud to her, mostly novels by John Irving, and he would often watch a ballgame on TV with the sound barely audible. He endured the bad times through her coma when her heart rate would decrease, prompting a cardiac unit to standby with a defibrillator. When her heart rate would rise after an injection, the staff would leave the room, pushing the cart out the door and Bob would be left alone sobbing at her bedside.

Shortly after Christmas, Bob left his car in the parking lot of the hospital and drove Jessica's Accord back to Pittsburgh. Thinking he would take a Greyhound bus back to Schuylkill Medical Center the following weekend, he drove along I-76 wondering how much a bus ticket would cost him. As he steered around a long curve, he felt a slight pull in the steering wheel followed by repeated rumbling. The passenger front tire had a flat and he was forced to pull over onto the shoulder of the interstate. While changing the tire, he broke down into tears as the traffic passed him at high speeds, thinking he could lose his only child.

For weeks, news outlets, the Schuylkill County sheriff's office and State Police asked Bob questions about his daughter. The official report expounded the incident as murder and attempted manslaughter. At the top of the report was a section filled out, noting that the murderer was still at large.

While law enforcement thought the assailant might have been a squatter who had lived in the house only to be surprised and use deadly force, the city of St. Clair thought different. The assault only furthered their belief that the house was haunted.

Bob Calvert was at work when the call came into the factory. He was working on a lathe when three administrative employees arrived on a golf cart.

"What?" Bob asked as he stepped back from the lathe and

spoke over the noise of surrounding machinery. His supervisor walked up to him and placed his hand on his shoulder and spoke loudly.

"Your daughter is awake!"

Bob sped along I-76 and unknowingly broke his personal record for the trip back to Schuylkill Medical Center. Upon his arrival, he found Jessica with a washcloth over her eyes while one of her doctors stood over her with a clipboard taking notes. He rushed to her side and spoke softly.

"Jessica! Can you hear me?"

"Hey, Dad," she said in a raspy and gritty voice. Bob took off his jacket and flung it onto the chair behind him and leaned over Jessica. He kissed her on her cheek as she started to cry, "I'm right here. I'm sorry I wasn't here when you woke up. I'm so sorry," he sobbed as he held onto her hand. He looked up at the doctor.

"What's wrong with her eyes?"

"Nothing. Her eyes are fine. She's just sensitive to light at the moment."

"Is she going to be okay?"

"Miss Calvert will have a long road of recovery ahead and we still have a lot of tests to run, but I think she can get through this," he explained. Bob felt his daughter's hand slip out from underneath. He looked down and watched as she put her hand on top of his and patted gently.

"I'll be okay, Dad," she said in a throaty, gravel voice.

The day Jessica woke was the beginning of a difficult road. Her physician created a schedule of medical tests which would require her to suffer through many injections and MRI scans. A few sessions were scheduled, where electrodes were adhered to her head to monitor her brain waves. In between nurses coming to her to draw blood and plasma, the state police visited Jessica with folders and photographs in hand.

The state investigators would sit at her bedside and ask questions about seeing anyone in the house and if she got a good look at who pushed her out of the window. The questions created more stress than she could handle prompting Bob to urgently request that the interviews cease.

When she wasn't being interviewed or watching her own blood be extracted from one of her veins, Jessica was in physical therapy. A nurse would hold her waist while she grabbed onto a wooden bar on either side of her and begin to take steps.

Once the medical tests were completed and she seemed to be on the right track to walking again, her doctor prescribed a strong painkiller and discharged her with a referral to a rehabilitation hospital in Pittsburgh. Moving Jessica back to Steel City, Bob took off work to help get his daughter to and from physical therapy. Having already used up his vacation and sick time while Jessica was in a coma, his bank account was quickly getting down to double digits.

While the rehabilitation was painful, the real damage came at night when she was asleep. The nightmares. The second she would begin screaming from the terror that unfolded during a nightmare, Bob would jump out of bed and run into her room to calm her down. Jessica would ultimately request that he bring her a glass of water and a Hydromorphone pill. Upon taking the drug, twenty minutes would have to pass before her eyelids would close like a garage door.

When spring arrived in late April, Jessica was only taking half of a Hydromorphone pill at night. Finally feeling a little better, she would walk in a nearby park with a cane enjoying the sun on her skin.

Jessica had been out of work for six months and her dream of being a notable journalist had been put on hold and each day that passed felt like a day lost. One day after coming home from the park, she had stopped by the mailbox before going back inside the house. Finding an envelope from *The Washington Post* in the stack, she sat at the kitchen table and opened the envelope that smelled of cigarettes. No doubt that Mr. Wood had written or at least handled it. She removed the letter from the envelope and immediately looked at the signature, Robert Wood. She looked at the top of the letter and read the typed words.

Jessica, I hope this letter finds you well. I have been asked to reach out to you concerning your accident. A man by the name of Henrik Frazier has a proposition for you which involves compensation and your expertise. Normally, I wouldn't even bother you with it but I would like to offer you a job and I think you could kill two birds with one stone. He would like to meet with you next Wednesday, April 19th at 1:00 p.m. I would offer to pay your hotel and airfare, but Mr. Frazier has already agreed to pick up the tab and I can save on my travel budget. Let me know if you are up for it. Lastly, I was going to put you up at the shitty Riverside Motel, but Frazier mentioned The Watergate Hotel. At least you'll be staying in luxury.

Even the linen paper Mr. Wood typed the letter on was yellowed and wreaked of cigarettes. With zero job prospects, and the promise of money and a stranger who needed her expertise, the words of Mr. Wood compelled her to accept the invitation.

Bob Calvert was a man who enjoyed watching TV while eating dinner. Sitting in his recliner with a TV tray full of food and a can of ice cold Iron City Beer was bliss. Since Jessica had been recovering under his roof, he had opted to eat at the kitchen table with her. To her surprise, when she informed her dad of the letter from *The Post* and her intention to pursue the invitation, the corners of his eyes filled with tears.

"Oh, Dad!" she said as she stood up and embraced him. "Don't cry."

"I'm so glad. I didn't want this to keep you down," he added as he continued to cry and hold onto his only child. Jessica smiled through the pain he caused her while hugging her with a fatherly embrace. Inside her body, her ribs radiated with pain and the left side of her leg felt weak as it throbbed.

Chapter 7

The trip back to D.C. was familiar, but the hotel was not. While working as a reporter, she had amassed many miles while driving around D.C. and had passed by the monstrous campus of the Watergate complex many times. After parking and checking into the hotel at the expense of the mysterious Mr. Frazier, she phoned her dad and assured him she had arrived safely. After hanging up with her father, she then placed another call to room service.

A fifteen-dollar Cobb salad and a glass of unsweetened tea was ordered and billed to the room. She sat on the comfortable bed with the room service tray in front of her while watching television. Jessica had forgotten about her tragic circumstances and simply ate and watched TV for the first time in a long time. The excitement of a new mysterious opportunity, or at the very least to hear a job offer from her old boss stirred up thrilling and intriguing thoughts. The excitement caused her to forget about the pain, which made her forget to take a pill before bed.

As she slept in the comfortable bed in her luxurious hotel room, she tossed between the soft sheets as she dreamed. She was standing barefoot on a hardwood floor in a very dark room. In front of her was a man facing away from her and sitting in an old, splintered chair. It was easy for her to discern his age as his hair was nearly white and his skin looked to be flaking and wrinkled from the sun. Just as she realized he was completely naked, her attention was drawn to a bed in the darkest corner of the room. It was a twin sized bed and covered with what appeared to be a child's colorful bedspread.

Jessica walked to the right side of the old man and saw he was staring at the bed and seemingly watching for something. She turned and looked at the bed, seeing something move underneath. The darkness enveloped the form moving under the bed, as it seemed to shift and come to a rest. Jessica moved closer and could see a girl covered in her own blood squirm in the small space between the bed and the floor. Jessica backed away and was now standing behind the old man once again.

From beneath the skin on the back of his neck, a worm chewed a small hole and began to exit the bloodless wound. The man sat still and didn't move as he was focused on the girl squirming underneath the bed. The worm crawled out of the hole, fell to the floor and wriggled. Her focus was on the insect twisting on the hardwood floor when she was suddenly startled as the old man got up from the chair and walked away. She could see that the man was wearing latex gloves just before he disappeared into the darkness.

While tossing in her bed and rolling over in a deep state

of sleep, her nightmares continued. Jessica entered her old apartment in D.C. wearing a winter coat and holding the mail. She looked down a hallway listening for movement. She knew she heard something. Someone was in her apartment. The sound of movement became apparent that it wasn't someone, rather something.

"Hello?" she called out down the hall.

She awoke in a panic and out of breath after experiencing the unusual dreams and turned her head, looking at the digital clock with red glowing numbers. 3:47 A.M.

It took her more than an hour to get back to sleep and when the hotel alarm clock went off, she opened her eyes and found them tired and stinging. After her shower, she looked at her naked body in the mirror and ran her fingers over the scars. Feeling her rib cage with a flattened palm, her face winced at the pain. Looking at the scarred version of herself, she wondered what lay ahead of her.

A guaranteed job offer and a meeting with a mysterious man who needed to speak with her. Excitement took over her thoughts and she proceeded to get dressed in the most expensive clothing she had bought after graduating college. A black pantsuit with a white shirt which made her look and feel professional.

She missed *The Washington Post*, the smell of an old building and the sound of her heels on the polished floor. Once the elevator doors opened, a few people gave her looks and even stared as she limped with her cane in hand. "Is that Jessica Calvert?"

she heard someone say under their breath. A coworker who used to work closely with Jessica called out her name.

"Calvert? Is that you?" Katherine Harkin, 33, was on her way to the elevators and stopped in her tracks as tears formed in her eyes. She covered her mouth and hurried toward Jess and embraced her. Others had stopped and stared at the two.

"Is that Jessica?" a reporter walking by said to another with a puzzled look on their face. Feeling the eyes of *The Washington Post* staff staring at her, she became self-conscious of the scar which ran down the left side of her cheek. People noticed, but didn't care. They all knew what she had been through and she had been the topic of conversation for months.

"Did you hear what happened to that Calvert girl?"

"She was nearly murdered."

Jessica walked into the newsroom where a round of applause erupted.

"Welcome back!"

"We missed you!"

Jessica smiled and held her cane behind her as she looked at everyone and mouthed the words *Thank You*. A man who could send every worker bee back to his or her hive with a single shout broke up the congratulatory applause.

"Calvert! Get in here!" yelled Mr. Wood—cigarette in hand—his harsh tone so very sharp and jagged. Jessica nodded in his direction. She gave everybody one last smile and an audible *Thank you* as she limped into Robert Wood's office. Once inside, she found him lighting another fresh cigarette with the one in his mouth.

"Don't sit. We're going in the conference room," he said as the cigarette bounced up and down with each spoken word. He grounded the lit end of his short Marlboro into his over-filled ashtray and walked toward her. He put his arm around her, something he rarely did to female staff members.

"Real quick. Fifty cent raise. No more traveling," he said as he walked toward the back of his office where a cracked door led to a conference room. "I have an opening in Environmental. You will support Henry Hackett. You know him? Just do what he says and write what he tells you to write. This covers mostly environmental politics. Job is yours if you want it. You start next week or should you take this guys offer," he said as he shrugged and motioned to the door in front of them, "then you start when this little project is over. Okay?"

"Okay. Thank you."

"You bet. You okay? Their little welcoming startle you?" he asked, but continued before she could answer. He spoke as he once again pointed toward the door in front of them. "Look, this is gonna be strange. I don't know how to prepare you for this, but you don't have to do it if you don't want to. Alright?"

"Now you got me worried."

"Oh stop, you're the toughest girl to ever be thrown out of a window by a ghost. We heard the story. Everyone's been talking about you," he said with a smile as if he was kidding.

His smile dissipated and then he asked in a lower tone of

voice, "is that really what happened? Forget it, I don't wanna know, I'm glad you're alive let's get this over with," he said as he pushed the door wide open.

Chapter 8

Jessica hobbled into the conference room and saw a thin, old man wearing a fine suit. He had a pencil thin, white mustache which matched his combed, white hair. Using a black cane, he stood up and reached out to shake her hand.

"Jessica, this is Henrik Frazier. Henrik, this is Jessica," Mr. Wood said as he sat down.

"Good to meet you, young lady. Looks like we have something in common," Henrik said as he jostled his cane up and down before gesturing to hers.

"Nice to meet you as well. I seem to have a hitch in my get-along," she said as she patted her leg. Once seated, Henrik started as he kept his right hand on his cane. Jessica sized him up they way she did when interviewing congressmen and senators. His suit was tailored. Expensive. His shoes were shined with a rag and a can of polish. He appeared to be in his seventies yet his eyes had vinegar in them.

"Miss Calvert, I am the co-owner of a mutual fund company called Hampton-Guarde and I retired some years ago. My interests since I was a young child have been centered around the paranormal and metaphysical phenomena and in my retirement, I have recently formed a small team of people whose interests parallel my own."

"I see."

"In 1977, I spent a good deal of money and time at the Collins House in Rock Hill, South Carolina. Are you familiar? The haunting in Rock Hill?"

"I am not."

"A family moved into a house where there was paranormal activity. The husband killed his family and there has been activity since. My intention in studying the Collins house was to prove conclusively that paranormal activity exists and I wanted concrete evidence. Now, to keep this story short, I was unable to collect any evidence despite my hired investigator and I having a few incredible encounters."

"Understood," Jessica said as she nodded, still not knowing what to think about Mr. Frazier.

"I was informed of your story by a gentleman on my team which consists of three people and myself. I have also invested heavily in some equipment that uses state-of-the-art technology to help us gather indisputable evidence that paranormal entities exist."

"I can't verify one way or the other after what I experienced."

"Well, I am certainly not asking you to," Henrik said as he sat forward and gestured his hand in a discarding motion as if he were trying to ease any concerns. "Not at all. About four months ago, I purchased the Adler Farm and all of its acreage. My team is set up outside the house and we have been monitoring it with our equipment," he reached his wrinkled hand inside his fine tailored coat. He pulled an infrared photo from his pocket and set it in front of Jessica.

"What's this?" Jessica asked. Henrik casually placed both hands on top of his cane as he spoke.

"The young man who was with you that day. Mr. Extine."

"Yes."

"He took this photo with his camera. A thermal imaging camera. Notice anything?" he asked. Jessica looked down at a black and white photo. It appeared to be a grainy image of a room which was mostly white. To the far right was a dark outline of a figure.

"It looks to be a room."

"Anything shot on thermal image film develops white for heat and dark for cold. Humans do not show up as dark outlines," he said as he looked back down at the photo in front of her. "That is an outline and it appears to be a young girl. See? Her hair?" he said as he pointed at the right side of the photo. His wiry, veined finger pointed to an outline of shoulder length hair.

"Sort of. I can sort of see it."

"See this behind her?" he asked as he again pointed to the right and above the girl.

"What's this?"

"We believe this to be something standing behind her. We don't know what."

"Why are you showing me this?" she asked in a polite and

inquisitive manner.

"I have a proposition for you. I would like for you to come meet my team. See our operation. I can assure you no harm will come to you. We are staying in very comfortable accommodations in trailers. Trailers similar to those of movie stars when they are on set. We will view the house from afar, never setting foot in or around the house and for your involvement, I will pay you a sum of five thousand dollars for one week of your time. Should my team find undeniable evidence of the existence of a paranormal entity, they will each receive a check in the amount of fifty thousand dollars. If during your stay with us, this event occurs, you will be included as part of the team and you will be paid the same amount."

"Isn't this proof right here?"

"It is," Henrik sighed as he sat back in his chair "but it will be debunked somehow. Dirt on the lens, a malfunctioning camera or something to that effect will be brought up and it becomes deniable."

"Thanks for your offer. I am not sure after what I experienced that I wish to return to that place."

"I do understand your concerns. May I ask what happened?" Henrik asked as he looked at her with eyes of a concerned grandfather. Jessica quickly recalled standing in the room, hearing James collapse on the floor. As she turned around, she saw the tugging of his pant leg and then his body thrown through the window. The sound was similar to an explosion as his torso, head and legs broke through the glass and wood frame.

Jessica remembered trying to run and feeling the paw of what felt like a bear with claws digging into her ribcage and breasts. She was picked up and flung through the now open window. Wind rushed through her hair, past her ears as she screamed hurling toward the body of James Extine. Warm blood trailed around her face and chest, as she lay unconscious on the ground. She gave this explanation to both Henrik and Mr. Wood while staring off in the distance, subconsciously rubbing the scar on her face with her fingertips.

"Is that it, Mr. Frazier?" Robert Wood asked as he now felt somewhat reponsible for Jessica's tragedy. He then thought that the girl deserved at least a dollar raise, not fifty-cents.

"It is."

"Jessica, does any of what Mr. Frazier has said appeal to you?"

"I don't know. Why do you need me? What can I possibly offer your team?"

"I have a scientist on the team along with a priest and a man who knows quite a bit about technology. I feel that having a journalist on staff to help record the story of what we are doing would be beneficial to our cause. Plus, Mr. Wood has agreed that what you write might be printed in *The Post*," Henrik said. Jessica turned to her boss.

"If you have anything worth printing, you know I will print it. No guarantees though. Either way, you still get paid."

"Exactly. You are there just in case we succeed on some

level and your presence as a witness and a journalist will help our cause," Henrik added. Jessica sat quietly, pondering the offer. She then looked at Henrik and shifted slightly in her seat as she spoke.

"Mr. Frazier, my father took off a lot of time from work to stay with me after the incident and what he lost in pay amounted to about ten thousand dollars. Up the amount to ten, and I will gladly be a part of your team for a week," she said as if negotiating was in her DNA. Mr. Wood turned his head toward Jessica with a smile that immediately vanished, replaced by an expression that communicated *Where did that come from?* Without hesitation, Mr. Frazier replied,

"Ten is agreeable, if I could extend the week to a full two weeks, should it be needed."

"Jessica, your job will be waiting for you when you return. Two weeks is fine by me. No hurry at this point." Mr. Wood said as he got up and pushed his chair in. He now thought different of offering her a dollar an hour raise thinking she might come back with a dollar fifty.

A girl he sent on an assignment almost died and spent several months in a coma, how could he say no? His budget was already stretched thin enough, although maybe an office with a door could be arranged. Henrik turned his head from Mr. Wood and back to Jessica. As he spoke, his white mustache moved and shifted.

"Agreed?"

"Agreed." Jessica replied with a nod.

The day after meeting with Mr. Frazier, Jessica once again drove into the small, sleepy town of St. Clair. Now sporting a new hairstyle, she had it cut to chin length with most of it tucked behind her ears. Next to the folded brochure map in the passenger seat was her old messenger bag. On the right bottom corner there was a large, noticeable blood stain. She had considered buying a new one, but her superstitions prevailed as she now considered it lucky.

Inside the messenger bag was a fresh notepad, box of BIC pens and a manila folder. The story of the Adler Farm was continuing and her notes from the interview with the sheriff could perhaps be used in the story which was never published. Perhaps she would uncover something else that would garner enough material for a feature in the paper.

She drove past the Buckhorn Café recalling the conversation with Gertie. After glancing at the map in the passenger seat, she turned onto a two-lane road and saw the Adler house in the distance and could see that something was noticeably different.

She slowed her Accord and took a deep breath as she approached a now illuminated Adler house covered in thin, opaque plastic sheeting, covering the roof and windows. Each step leading up to the front porch was covered and even the door was wrapped in plastic. Gasoline powered tower lamps were spread out in the yard and lit up the exterior of the home to an almost blinding illumination.

She could see three white trailers parked single file on the far right side of the house. As she pulled into the driveway, she inched toward the trailers and put her car in park. She leaned to the left and looked at the house, eyeing the window from which she and James had been thrown.

The window appeared to have been knocked out and the plastic sheeting stopped around the window, not even coming close to the edges. Most of the right side of the house was free of the plastic sheeting as if whoever tacked it up to the house was too afraid to get near the window. A gas-powered lamp was humming with power and the light was aimed directly into the open space. Beneath the mangled window was a hydraulic lift, retracted to the ground with no operator in sight.

"You made it!" a muffled voice said from outside her vehicle. Mr. Frazier walked toward the left side of her Accord, cane in right hand. Jessica cut the engine and didn't move. She watched as he walked around to the driver's side while she rolled the window down halfway. Her facial expression caused him immediate concern. "Are you okay?"

"I don't know. It is kind of hitting me all of a sudden," Henrik took a step back and placed both hands on top of his cane.

"I understand. No rush. Also, we don't go into the house. We just study it from afar. We are all safe out here. My team is anxious to meet you," he said with a warm smile. She took a deep breath and placed her hand on the door latch and pulled it, releasing the door from the frame. Instead of helping her, Henrik took another step back and allowed her to get out on her own, giving her space. She set the end of her cane down on the ground and used it to get out of the driver's seat.

"Has there been any activity?"

"Very little. Everything is recorded on our cameras," he said as he stood next to her as she righted herself. He then guided her toward the first trailer that was closest to her vehicle. "This is the operations trailer. We all work out of here. Trailer two is the men's barracks and shower including restroom. Third trailer is the women's barracks, shower and restrooms."

"Is everyone here?"

"They are. We ordered cheeseburgers from the local diner here, so it might smell delicious inside. Are you hungry? I have an arrangement with the café. They could bring you something."

"I already ate. Thank you though."

Henrik opened the door and walked in first, holding the door for Jessica. The team stopped what they were doing and looked her way as she stepped inside. The trailer was dark except for desk lamps and the glow of video monitors. Four workstations were positioned against the right wall. The left wall looked to be one big workstation. Computer towers, monitors, audio components, an oscilloscope along with a workbench complete with tools, cables and a magnifying lamp.

Henrik gestured to the chunky man sitting in a folding chair before he spoke.

"Jessica I'd like you to meet Father Abbott," he said as a man of fifty years of age stood up to greet her. He wore an old t-shirt with a pocket rather than a black clerical button-up and white collar. The first thing she noticed was his haircut. Either he did it himself or a barber must have lost control during a brief earthquake.

"Nice to meet you, Jessica. I was so sorry to hear about the injuries you sustained here. You are very brave for coming back. Very commendable."

"Thank you. You're a priest?"

"I am. Currently on sabbatical. I am writing a book on discerning paranormal encounters."

"A book? How's it going?"

"Slow," he replied with a smile. Henrik moved Jessica to the next person on the team, a muscular black man, forty-five years old who wore a tight white t-shirt and gold necklace. He had a deep reverberating voice which filled the entire trailer when he spoke.

"This is Ray Turner. Retired marine and technology expert," Henrik said with pride. Ray stood up and gently shook her hand.

"Glad you're okay," Ray said.

"Thank you," she replied. After working in D.C. interviewing many retired military personnel, the questions came without thinking. "What division?"

"The 4th."

"New Orleans?"

"Yes ma'am."

"Battalion?"

"Intelligence support."

"May I ask your rank?"

"Sergeant major," he answered. It had been a long time since anyone had asked him his background with formal inquiry. For a brief moment, it felt as if he was back in the service. He watched as Jessica reached out her hand once again. This time she shook with force and looked him in the eye.

"It's an honor to meet you," she offered. She could have easily sounded insincere or even naive, but instead she had bravado. Turner immediately liked her.

"You're not just a girl with a journalism degree."

"My father was a marine. Third Division. Opened the Marine Compound at the Da Nang Air Base, Vietnam."

"I see. Good to know."

"Good to know I'm not just a degree or that my father served?"

"Both," he said with a smile. Henrik then moved on to the final team member.

"Jessica, meet Dr. Thornhill. She is helping with the science aspect of our research."

"You can call me Shelby." At thirty-eight years of age, her hair was already turning gray and she did little to her appearance to make her attractive to the opposite sex. Instead of getting married and having kids, she had made a life in academia taking a chair at the University of Texas in the physics department. After publishing a paper on dark matter and theoretical dimensions, a phone call with the promise of a balloon payment made her jump on a plane headed for Pennsylvania.

"Shelby, nice to meet you. Are we the only women in the group?"

"We are. The entire trailer to ourselves. Good thing too. I was getting a little freaked out being by myself at night."

After the initial introductions were made, a few questions were fired at Jessica. Mostly about working at *The Washington Post*. When the conversation drifted to Jessica's experience inside the house and coming out of a coma, the team drifted over to the monitors where the house was being videotaped. Ray sat at the video controls to the tape machine and manipulated a large circular knob to rewind a tape.

"This was recorded three days ago. We have five cameras set up at different points outside the house," Ray explained. The team huddled around the video monitors. Father Abbott moved from the left side to the right to get a better view while Ray played it at normal speed. "This is from camera three, stationed outside," he pointed to the first-floor window as he spoke. "Keep your eye on this window here and look toward the floor." The time at the top left hand corner of the video read 1:37 P.M. Jessica looked at the screen and squinted when she saw a large shape slowly move up and down. "Can you tell what that is?" Ray asked aloud. Jessica could see the shape was large and was lying on the floor. She could only see part of it as the window wasn't large enough to allow for a better view.

"We've already seen this. We know what it is so we won't answer," Henrik said.

"Is it something breathing?" Jessica asked.

"Yes," Dr. Thornhill answered.

"Looks like an animal of some kind."

"It is," Abbott replied. Still looking at the video, the shape seemed to squirm and breath faster. The squirming turned into jolting as if it was in pain. The breathing slowed and eventually stopped. The shape seemed to sink slowly out of view and it was gone.

"What was it?" Jessica asked. Ray rewound the video to where the large shape was jolting, seemingly in pain and froze the video. He pointed to the right side of the frame.

"That's its leg and that right there is a hoof with a horseshoe."

"A horse?"

"Yes."

"It's laying down on its side? Where did it go?"

"We don't know. We don't think it was real."

"It's on video. How did it get there?"

"It appeared into the frame the same way it left."

"Isn't this proof?" Jessica asked.

"It isn't," Henrik said. "We could show this video to someone and they would come up with a way that would explain how it could be faked."

"When was this?"

"The third day we were here. We set up the cameras and that was the first thing we caught," said Ray.

"What about the light in the upstairs bedroom?"

"Haven't seen it yet," replied Henrick.

The conversation slowly turned to personal experiences with possible encounters with paranormal entities. The team sat around the long folding table in the center of the trailer and gave first-hand accounts of objects moving on their own, oddities which later showed up in photographs and sounds they had heard at night.

When the superstar of the group explained her encounter with an entity, she explained meeting James Extine and the brief moment they had together before he was flung out of the window. She then spoke of the sinking feeling in her stomach as she was seemingly picked up and thrown through the broken window, landing on top of the dead body of James Extine. The realization of what Jessica had truly experienced caused a silence to fall over the table. Ray was the first to break the tension.

"I think we all need a drink."

"I second that," Henrik said with a smile.

Ray produced a bottle of bourbon from a nearby cabinet while Henrik brought out several glasses and set them in the center of the table. Jessica glanced around at the others in an attempt to gauge everyone's level of participation. With her head down and using her peripheral vision, she was surprised when Father Abbott reached for a glass, as did Dr. Thornhill. Being a recent addition to the team, Jessica felt the need to fit in and taking a glass seemed like a step in the right direction. Ray stood up and poured bourbon into everyone's glass while talking.

"Nobody drink yet. It's bad luck to drink before a toast."

Jessica's nerves resembled those of a young girl on a first date. A nervous smile nearly gave her away. Ray finished pouring the final drink and everyone stood up and leaned toward the center of the table and raised their glass.

"What should we toast?" asked Father Abbott.

"Here's to swimming with bow legged women," Ray said as he smiled. Everyone smiled at his suggestion, then Henrik took over.

"To discovery and safety for all involved."

After two hours of light conversation, eleven-thirty crept up on the team and Henrik called it a night. Dr. Thornhill guided a tipsy Jessica Calvert out of the operations trailer and into the women's trailer. At first she had thought that the alcohol and her mangled leg caused her to be off balance. After a few steps, she then thought it might be something else.

"How much did you drink? It couldn't have been that much?"

"Not a lot."

"And you're plastered? Are you on any medication?"

"Painkillers," Jessica responded.

"Oh. That'll do it," Thornhill said as she rolled her eyes

and tightened her hand around Jessica's tiny waist in an effort to support her as she limped.

"It feels so good. My whole body feels good."

"You're gonna have to monitor your alcohol intake. Mixing alcohol with pain medication can have adverse effects and not to mention it has addictive properties."

The accommodations in the women's trailer were nicer than the Mill Street Motel, but a mile away from the Watergate. Jessica collapsed on her bed and before Dr. Thornhill turned out the light, Jessica was asleep.

It was after 6 A.M. when Ray knocked on their trailer door holding a flashlight. He let himself in and stood in the kitchenette; his combat boots squeaked on the cheap linoleum.

"Calvert, Thornhill. Wake up," he said in a loud voice. Both sat up in bed and shielded their eyes from the flashlight.

"What's the deal, Ray!" Thornhill moaned.

"Cut it off! Holy shit that's bright!" Jessica yelled through the Hydromorphone cloud that was taking up most of the space in her brain.

"You better come and see this."

Chapter 9

Huddled around the monitors once again, Ray rewound the tape and pressed play. The video showed the right side of the house. To the left of the screen was the hydraulic lift halfway out of frame. On the right side, a boy wearing a t-shirt and shorts walked into the frame. He was chasing something that was running on the ground.

Father Abbott had enough of squinting and fished out his eyeglasses from his pocket and put them on. Dr. Thornhill moved closer to the monitor and watched as the boy bent down and picked up a cat by its back legs. As if he was tossing a basketball underhanded toward the side of the house, he flung the cat into the wood siding.

The faint sound of the cat's bones and skull hitting the side of the house could be heard through the speakers next to the monitors. They watched as the boy bent down and grabbed the cat's legs once again and tossed it up against the side of the house.

"And how long is he on camera?"

Ray turned to everyone behind him while the video continued to play. The boy threw the cat against the wall, the faint sound of each hit could be heard as he answered.

"Over an hour."

"What?" Henrik asked.

"Yeah, over an hour. Look," Ray said as he pointed at the time code on the screen. Ray turned a knob and the video played in high speed as he fast-forwarded. The boy picked up the cat and threw it against the wall over and over as Ray pointed out the time. Ten minutes. Twenty. Thirty. Over and over the boy threw the cat, each time the poor animal squirmed as it hit the ground. "At one hour and six minutes, the boy leaves the cat," Ray said as he now played the video at normal speed. "And he goes here," Ray said as the boy walked over to an opening in the cinderblock foundation and crawled through an opening, disappearing underneath the house. The sound of compressed breathing came from behind them, the sound a person makes when frightened. Ray and Henrik were the first to turn around, followed by Thornhill then Abbott. It was Jessica. She had tears in her eyes as she covered her mouth and seemingly tried not to scream.

"Jessica?" Henrik said.

"What's wrong?" Ray asked as he stood up. She let out a piercing scream as she turned and headed for the door. Ray reached out and grabbed her arm. He pulled her as she continued to scream. He wrapped his python arms around her. "Jessica, calm down. You're okay. You're fine. I got you. I got you."

"That's my neighbor! I know him! He lived in my neighborhood!" she shouted with eyes that bounced around from one team member to another.

"Shhhh….take it easy." Ray said in a comforting voice as she was trying to fight him off in vain. Dr. Thornhill filled a syringe with a sedative at her workstation.

"That's Thomas Cafferty! That's Thomas Cafferty!" she screamed while she tried to get away from Ray. She lost her footing and started to slide out of his arms. He went to the ground with her gently as she continued to scream a shrill, eardrum-penetrating scream.

"I need a vein! Hold her," Thornhill said as she kneeled down. Henrik took a few steps back, holding onto his cane for support with each step. Father Abbott stepped up and held her legs down while Ray used his torso to keep her still and his other hand held down her arms. Flicking the needle and slapping her arm with two fingers, the sedative was quickly injected causing her screaming to cease and her eyes to roll into the back of her head.

Dr. Thornhill and Ray carried Jessica to her bed in the trailer. Ray returned to the operations trailer immediately where Henrik was ready to give orders.

"Father Abbott, I need you to go to the library and start looking for information on Thomas Cafferty. Jessica was raised in Mt. Washington in Pittsburgh. See if you can find any newspapers that mention this young man," Henrik said just before he turned to Ray. "I need you to go to the state police and tell them you are looking for information on Thomas Cafferty. Both of you take the van. Hopefully one of you will get some info."

"Why are we thinking that she's right? It could be that the boy looked like her neighbor," said Ray. Henrik replied, this time lowering his voice.

"With what we have seen, the reason she is even here, we have to believe that there is a reason for this. A connection. A message. Mostly we need to verify that she is mistaken."

Jessica was standing in the backyard looking over the city of Pittsburgh. She could see PPG Palace among the buildings in the skyline. Most residents called it the Crystal Building. Her mother had died when she was eight as a result of an accident in the Fort Pitt Tunnel. While looking at the city skyline, something caught her eye. She turned her head and saw a little girl of eight years old playing with a small, plastic toy swimming pool and her dolls sitting in the water. A garden hose supplied a constant stream. Suddenly the back door opened. Jessica's father, appearing much younger and thinner hurried to the young girl and picked her up with force. Tears were in his eyes as he hurried back into the house with the girl in his arms.

"What's wrong, Daddy?"

"Something happened to Mommy," he said as the back door slammed behind him. Jessica began to cry, realizing she was the little girl. Then her mother opened the back gate and walked toward her with a grin. Her hair was brushed, hair-sprayed and styled. She wore a flowing, white night gown yet the most unsettling thing about her was the frozen grin that stretched across her face.

"Mom?" Jessica asked. Her mother was barefoot, the bottom of her feet scraped the grass while her grin became a smile, revealing bright green material in her mouth. Unable to make out what the material was, she took a step back in fear.

"What's wrong Mom?" she asked as her mother took another step toward her and put her hand on her daughter's shoulders. The bright green material could still be seen between her teeth. "What is in your…" she started to say as her mother slightly opened her mouth revealing a wad of bright green ribbon shoved inside. She looked down at her feet as water started to flood in around her ankles, quickly rising to her knees. Strands of bright green ribbon floated past them. Jessica watched as her mother reached her left hand up to her teeth, pulling on the nylon green ribbon. She kept her smile as she pulled as much as a yard of ribbon out of her mouth before Jessica woke. Just before 10 a.m., Dr. Thornhill was by her side and held her hand as her eyes sprang open.

"Take it easy. Don't move. You passed out. You're okay."

"I passed out?"

"You're okay."

"I was dreaming."

"You're okay. Just take it easy," Dr. Thornhill said and she continued to hold Jessica's hand. Moments after opening her eyes, she closed them and easily fell back asleep.

While Jessica was sleeping off the sedative, Father Abbott and Ray had returned from their errands. In his right hand, Abbott held a Xerox copy of a newspaper clipping from the *Philadelphia Inquirer*. The article described a murder in Pittsburgh on Mt. Washington in 1979. The article reported that a 17-year-old male brutally murdered his high school principal and committed suicide before police discovered him. The boy's name was Thomas Cafferty.

"Is that it?" Henrik asked as he sat down in a folding chair. Father Abbott nodded.

"No photo though. The article talked more about the life of the principal and his accomplishments than Thomas Cafferty. I asked for articles from the *Post-Gazette*, but they said I would have to fill out a formal request. It would take a few weeks."

"Did you fill out a request?"

"Yes. They have the number here. They will call when it comes in."

"Guess what I found?" Ray said as he leaned forward and set a few papers face down on the table.

"No telling," Henrik replied.

"Thomas Cafferty had a record of abusing animals. Got so bad he was even arrested and brought up on charges."

"You get a photo?"

"Sort of. They had to get it faxed to the station. There's two photos," Ray said as he laid two pieces of fax paper on the long table in front of Henrik. "They are in black and white and a little difficult to see clearly, but that's him." The first photo was a mugshot of a fifteen-year-old Thomas Cafferty from the chest up. The second was an eleven-year-old boy smiling next to what appeared to be his grandmother wearing gloves and holding a trowel in her right hand while standing among flowers in a garden. Ray sat down at the video controls and rewound the tape of the boy throwing the cat. He paused the video and turned around and grabbed the photo of Thomas standing next to his grandmother.

"Look at this. The shirt this boy has on in the video we recorded has thick stripes. Now look at the photo of him and granny here," Ray said as he pointed to the photo. "Same shirt."

The door opened and Jessica stepped inside with the aid of her cane followed by Dr. Thornhill. Jessica looked at Henrik, Ray and Father Abbott with the photos on the table and a paused video screen behind them.

"Well Calvert, you were right about Thomas Cafferty," said Ray. "You were right to freak out," he continued as he stood up and put his hands on his hips and looked at Henrik. "Look, at this point, if you don't, I will. She has a right to know."

"I know. Sit. Sit. You'll scare her," Henrik said as he motioned for Ray to sit back down. Ray ignored his command.

"Tell me what?"

"It wasn't my intention to keep this from you forever. Just a few days until you settled in," Henrik said with a slight grin which was generated from embarrassment.

"She ain't settled," Ray chuckled as he spoke. "Pretty far from settled."

"Jessica, please have a seat. Ray, be gentle, but please explain," asked Henrik. Ray continued to stand while Jessica sat down with a puzzled expression.

"First, do you remember me holding you down?"

"I do," Jessica said as she took a seat next to Dr. Thornhill.

"Are you okay?"

"A little sore."

"I'm sorry. I just wanted to keep you from hurting yourself."

"Thank you. I'm fine. I don't want anyone to think that I am fine mentally though. I am strongly considering leaving at this point," she said as she looked down on the table at the photo of Thomas Cafferty. "It doesn't make sense. I know that was him. I saw him do that when he was a boy. I witnessed him doing that. Several years later he killed the principal of our school. How could this kid show up here at this house doing what I saw him doing nearly twenty years ago?"

"I might be able to answer that, but first we will need Ray to explain something," Henrik offered.

"Right," Ray said as he removed his hands off his hips and clapped his hands before rubbing them together in thought. "Okay. Let's start with this," he said as he pulled out a flat piece of wood. It was rectangular in shape and as big as a cafeteria tray. He set it on the table so that Jessica could see it clearly.

There were letters and symbols and a YES and NO written with a black marker. "Do you know what this is?"

"A Ouija board?"

"Right. This is what people believe is a way to communicate with the dead, but it is flawed. It only moves with human interaction. Now, listen to this," Ray said as he reached his thick muscular arm toward a rack of equipment and pressed play on an audio component. A hissing and buzzing sound boomed around the inside of the trailer with the sound ramping up in pitch and changing in tone. "This is the sound inside the room where you were thrown out of," Ray said before pressing stop on the controls. He then pressed another button on a different piece of audio equipment. This time the sound was a slight hiss. "This is the rest of the house. Quiet. Nothing, but the room without the window is filled with an electromagnetic field," Ray said as he pushed a button and silenced the hissing noise. He ended his explanation before nodding over at Father Abbott.

"Since the early 1900s, there have been documented cases of electromagnetic fields being associated with paranormal activity," explained Father Abbott. He reached into a folder and removed a schematic. The drawing was on vellum and had wires and circuit boards connected to a Ouija board. "This was an idea created by a paranormal researcher in Germany. I gave this to Ray and he made one."

"Took me a few days, but I made this and inserted it through the window using the hydraulic lift outside. I used a pole to reach in and place this on the floor."

"You're going to tell me this worked?" Jessica said with an attitude of skepticism.

"It didn't at first. We didn't really expect it to, but figured it was worth a try. Then we got a letter," Ray said as he pushed the *Page Down* key on the computer. The computer monitor showed the letter J on the screen. "It was like this for a whole day. Nothing else and we figured that it was an error. Until the second day, we got two more letters," Ray said as he pressed the *Page Down* key once more. The screen now showed *JES*.

"You have to be kidding me," she said as she stood up.

"Now I know you're not going to like this," Ray said as he briefly looked at Henrik before hitting the *Page Down* key again. The screen showed her name repeated over and over.

Jes

Jes

Jes

Jes

Jes

Jes

Jes

Jes

Jes

Jes

Jess

Jess

Jess

Jess

Jess

Jess

Jess

Jess

Jess

"Thomas Cafferty is a manifestation. Since it affects you, this proves that the communication of your name through the device was intentional," Father Abbott said. Jessica shook her head and took a step back.

"I am sorry you are finding this out now, but I felt it was better to ease you into it rather than hit you with it up front," Henrik explained.

"I shouldn't have come back," Jessica said as she turned around. "Keep your money," she said as she opened the door and hobbled to the women's trailer, dragging her cane behind her. After shoving everything into her overnight bag, she hurried out and limped to her car. No one came out to stop her as she got in and sped off.

Jessica drove South toward I-78 and came upon an asphalt operation which caused all traffic to take a detour. Leaving was the best thing. She knew that evil was present in the house and now, for some reason, it knows her name. She drove past signs that directed her around the path of the detour down a country road with tall pine trees on both sides. Coming up on a curve, she noticed a large pond on the right with bright green ribbons tied around all of the trees on the left side.

Ahead in the road was a large white truck complete with a wood chipper surrounded by men in orange vests cutting down trees and feeding branches into the chipper. Jessica stopped her car a few hundred feet from the white truck. She got out and limped over to a tree with a bright green ribbon tied around the trunk. She pulled on it, feeling the thin nylon stretch between her fingers. A man in an orange vest, seeing a pretty girl with a cane looking at the trees, walked toward her with a smile.

"I hope you aren't from Greenpeace."

"What are these ribbons?"

"They mark the ones we are to cut down. Only trees with a ribbon."

"For what? Why are you cutting them down?"

"Sugar Mill Pond Housing Development."

The phone rang at the operations trailer and being closest to the phone, Ray answered.

"Hello?"

"I need someone to meet me. I need to talk," said Jessica.

"Absolutely. Where?"

Chapter 10

The bell above the door at the Buckhorn Café rang as Jessica entered and quickly took a seat at a nearby booth where she could see the parking lot through a big picture window. She looked at her watch as she nervously bounced her right leg. A plump waitress much older than Gertie held an orange handled coffee pot walked over to her with a cup and saucer.

"You look like you could use some caffeine."

"Uh, no coffee for me, thank you. Could I have an iced tea?"

"Of course."

After fifteen minutes, a van arrived in the parking lot. Henrik and Ray got out of the van first, followed by Thornhill and Father Abbott. From her seat, she could see that Father Abbott was carrying a large, thick book which had inserted papers protruding out from the edges. When they walked in, they easily found Jessica and sat down. Father Abbott brought over a chair and sat at the end of the booth.

"You okay?" Henrik asked.

"I think so."

"You having second thoughts about leaving?" Dr. Thornhill asked.

"No. Not really. I found something."

"You found something? On your way out of town?" Ray asked. Jessica began to explain her dream with her mother followed by leaving town and finding the trees. She then asked the group if it was coincidence or if it meant something. Father Abbott placed the book he was carrying on the table. It looked very old and the edges were worn and frayed. He opened it to a section with a few flips and looked at her as he spoke.

"You have heard of purgatory. Yes?"

"I have."

"Purgatory is widely accepted to be the starting point of the paranormal. It's not heaven and it isn't hell."

"I've heard it called the in-between."

"Correct."

"You think purgatory and the paranormal are related?"

"It is my belief that ghosts are souls that don't go to heaven or hell. They stay in purgatory that is either temporary or possibly eternity. In this instance, I believe that the young girl who was murdered is currently in purgatory and has been for years."

"Why?"

"Most of the activity has been centered around her room."

"So she threw me and James through a window?"

"Doubtful," he said as he held up a finger. He pointed to a page in his book as he turned it around so she could see. It was a photo of an oil painting showing humans and demons co-existing on a mountainous terrain. "This is a painting of

Purgatory by an artist named Luca Signorelli. In the early 1500s, he was commissioned by a Catholic Church in Cortona, Italy to take the words of a man who had died and come back to life after experiencing what he believed to be Purgatory. This is what Luca painted. At the time, this painting was considered demonic and evil and his name was removed from the work. The church denied ever commissioning such a painting—but today it stands as a representation of what the Vatican considers a possibly accurate portrayal of Purgatory. See here," Abbott said as he pointed to a depiction of a demon.

"So purgatory contains the dead, angels and demons?" Jessica asked. Abbott nodded. Jessica continued. "Do you believe the house contains demons and the soul of the child who was murdered?"

"Tilly. Tilly Adler. Yes, I do believe that she is among demons. I don't think she did that to you and I think if we all look at the evidence, we could all agree that she is trying to communicate with you," he said as he closed the book. Jessica looked at Henrik who wore an expression of worry and concern before he spoke.

"In all my years of exploring the paranormal, nothing has brought me closer to being able to provide the world with concrete proof. If you leave, I feel that this may be the end for me. I certainly am not getting any younger," he said as he tapped his cane on the floor.

"Since you left, we have all been talking about the fact that you seem to be the desired communicator for whatever is inside that house. We thought about putting a speaker in the room and letting you speak through a microphone. The activity has picked up since you came around, that's for sure."

"This has gotten too personal for me."

"Tell me what would it take to keep you on board our team?" Henrik asked is a desperate tone.

"I don't want to sleep next to the house. Not after what I have seen. I don't even want to be near the house. At all," Ray nodded his head.

"I understand. I would too. The only thing is, I don't have long enough cables to run from the house to the trailer for all the CCTV feeds and microphones and the wired Ouija board."

"Can you get longer cables?" asked Henrik.

"I can. Might take a few days."

"Will it be safer having the trailers moved further away?" Dr. Thornhill asked.

"It's safe now," Abbott said with a shrug.

"Moving the trailers is nothing more than an effort to ease Jessica's concerns and for her comfort," Henrik added.

"It'll help. Not sure I will ever be comfortable near that house though," Jessica explained.

"I do understand. Your presence is definitely a big help to us all and we'll do everything we can to keep you on board. In the meantime, why don't we all take a break and I'll treat us all to our own rooms at the motel. Just take it easy for a while and when the trailers are moved, we will resume."

"I'll move the trailers back toward the edge of the tree

line. We'll be just over a hundred yards away," Ray said. "But it will be costly,"

"Money. It's only dirty paper," Henrik said with a grin.

A salad and an unsweetened tea was delivered to her door. Jessica tried to keep her mind numb by watching television while nibbling on the cherry tomatoes and cucumbers in her salad. After a hot shower she changed into a long, white t-shirt and brushed her teeth before bed. After an hour of trying to go to sleep, she could feel her jangled nerves keeping her awake. The anxiety of having another nightmare made the thoughts spin around in her head like the thumping of a warped tire turning a corner. While lying in bed, she heard the squeal of brakes and the sound of an engine cutting off.

She jumped out of bed and peered through the curtains and saw Ray getting out of the white van. Wearing camouflage pants and a dark green t-shirt, he shut the door and flipped the keys around his finger as he whistled. Just as he stepped up on the curb, the door to room 17 opened and Jessica hurried out of her room toward him, her large white t-shirt flapped in the wind with each step.

"Jessica? The hell! It's one in the morning!"

"Ray, do you have that bottle of bourbon? The one from last night?"

"Sorry to say I don't. You lookin' for some hooch? Why

are you awake?"

"It helps me sleep. Do you have anything?"

"You realize you're wearing your jammies out here in the middle of the night begging for alcohol? Got damn. Here I thought you were a preachers daughter or something."

"I'm not a drunk I just have difficulty getting to sleep sometimes. You got any or not?" she asked with dazed eyes which were hurting for sleep. Ray flipped the keys in his hand as he nodded.

"I do. You know those little bottles they give you on airplanes?"

"You got one?"

"Courtesy of Delta Airlines. Hang tight."

"Thank God," she said under her breath as Ray unlocked his door and went inside. Jessica ran her hands through her hair as she thought about how many pills she had left in the bottle. Ray returned with a mini bottle of Georgetown Vodka. He stood in his doorway and tossed it to Jessica.

"Catch," he said. He watched as she used both hands to receive the bottle. Jessica looked up at Ray as she started to turn around.

"Thanks."

"You take it easy, Calvert," he said in a tone that resembled an older brother looking out for his little sister.

Back in her motel room, with vodka and Hydromorphone flowing, she got comfortable in her bed as she thought about her father and the ten thousand dollars coming from Henrik

Frazier. If anything kept her going, it was the money. Jessica had been carrying guilt with her that she was the cause of his financial distress, which was true but took solace in knowing that she was doing something about it.

The next morning, after a quick drive to the Pottsville Package Store, a mini bottle of off-brand, bottom shelf Tequila was purchased thinking she needed to take it easy on her alcohol intake and that her purchase would only be used if she were in dire need. As she placed the bottle into her purse, she felt a familiar feeling of comfort. Similar to the comforting feeling she felt knowing she could rely on a coworker or friend. After leaving the package store, she drove to Peach Tree Mountain Road and could see the Adler farm on the horizon.

True to Henrik's word, the trailers were moved back by the tree line. With great hesitation and uncertainty, she drove back onto the property wishing that Dr. Thornhill had opted out of sleeping on the farm, making a case for staying at the motel. But no such luck. Thinking she would bolt at the first sign of danger, she entered the women's trailer and set her things on her bunk.

The house was much further away from the trailers, which was more of a comfort and she hoped that the increased distance would help her focus. After rigging up the trailers, Ray had also added a speaker to the room. Using the hydraulic lift and a long wooden pole, he set a box speaker on the floor and ran the wire back to the trailer. Now sitting at the controls in the trailer with the team surrounding him, he set a small mic stand in front of Jessica and spoke to her as he fitted the microphone into the plastic grip cradle.

"What is the deal with you not drinking coffee?"

"Why?"

"I was thinking if you drank coffee, it would keep you going throughout the day. Then you're tired at night. You'd probably sleep better," Ray said and waited for a response. Without really paying any attention, neither Jessica nor Ray could feel the eyes of the team behind them as they held a con- versation.

"I don't know anything about it."

"Light roast has more caffeine less flavor, dark roast has more flavor less caffeine. You should drink the light and make sure to add cream and sugar for flavor," Ray explained. Dr. Thornhill looked at Father Abbott who returned the same con- fused look. Henrik crossed his arms.

"I don't know. Maybe," Jessica said.

"Can we perhaps save the chit-chat for later?" Henrik asked. Both Ray and Jessica turned slightly and quickly became aware they were holding them up. Ray looked at Jessica and spoke loudly so everyone could hear him as he explained.

"Ask a question. I will then type it into the computer. This will send a signal to the Ouija board inside the house. If I type *red* here on this keyboard, the planchette on the Ouija board inside the house will move to the letters on the board in order. Keep the questions short. We'll see if we get a response. I thought maybe if we had sound in the house, it might speed

up a response. Who knows?" said Ray with a shrug of his muscular shoulders. Jessica cleared her throat and leaned in toward
the mic.

"Hello?"

Ray typed in the word *hello* and waited. The team watched
the video monitors showing the outside of the house. Inside
the house, the sound of Jessica's voice could be heard while the
Ouija board mechanically moved to each letter of the word
hello. After twenty minutes of not getting a response, Ray
spoke up with an idea.

"Try asking a yes or no question. The board has a *YES* and
NO area. Makes for an easy answer," Ray explained. Jessica
thought of a question and leaned in.

"Tilly, are you there?" she asked before leaning away from
the microphone. Ray typed in the question, the Ouija board
moved inside the room, spelling out Jessica's inquiry. While
they waited for a response, Father Abbott took the opportunity to bring out his large, old book once more.

He opened it to a page of text which described an encounter with several apparitions in the 1700s in the city of
Istanbul. While everyone occasionally glanced at the screen
for a response, they listened to Father Abbott read the story
from his book.

"A man told the city government that seven people stood
quietly in his bedroom and seemed to be holding up the walls
by bracing the room with their hands and pushing with their
feet as if the room was going to collapse. All seven apparitions

were gone when he returned from getting help. The man frightened and terrified, told the story to the city government and while it was recorded on city record, no one knew what to do with the information. Days later an earthquake hit the city killing many people."

"Why wouldn't the ghosts just look at the man and say that there is an earthquake coming? Why be so creepy about it?" Jessica asked.

"We cannot fathom what it is like to communicate from another time and place. Purgatory is said to be void of both time and mass. So we are left to interpret the images and symbols and encounters."

"In all my research, the greatest thing to happen in communication with the paranormal happened the day we received the word *Jess* on the screen," Henrik said with a smile.

Their conversation continued with Dr. Thornhill interjecting her thoughts while Ray scanned the monitors and listened to the interior of the house through large, bulky headphones. It was Henrik who noticed it first. He was speaking with Father Abbott when something caught his eye. He turned his head and saw the word YES on the computer screen.

"Dear God," he said as he stood up. "This is it."

Ray took off his headphones and positioned himself in front of the computer. Jessica turned around in her chair and looked at the screen. Dr. Thornhill covered her mouth in disbelief and Father Abbott grabbed his notepad.

"Okay, what do we say now?" Ray asked.

"The ribbons. Ask about the ribbons. If she knows then we can confirm that she has been communicating with Jessica," Dr. Thornhill explained.

"Yeah, whenever you're ready," said Ray as he placed his hands on the keys to type. "Remember to keep it simple. Simple worked last time."

Jessica leaned toward the microphone and spoke.

"Do the green ribbons mean something?" she asked as Ray typed on the keyboard. Inside the room, the Ouija board moved and spelled out the question. The first question Jessica asked took fifteen minutes to respond. This time, it was more than forty minutes.

"Maybe ask a simpler yes or no question," said Henrik. Soon after a letter appeared on the screen.

W

"One letter?" Ray asked. He put on his headphones and could hear the Ouija board still moving in the room. "Wait wait. Another letter is coming," he shouted as he looked at the screen.

A

"W-A? This mean anything to anyone?" asked Father Abbott.

"Hang on. It's still moving," Ray said as he covered the headphones with his hands. He looked at the ground with large, round eyes as he concentrated on the sound in the room. He then looked up at the monitor and saw a third letter.

T

"W-A-T and it's still going. Still moving," shouted Ray with a smile as Dr. Thornhill sat down next to Jessica. The planchette stopped moving and Ray stood up. "It stopped. It's not moving." He looked at the screen. No more letters.

The next two hours, they conversed about the green ribbon and the meaning of W-A-T and even went so far as to call the tree service at ten o'clock at night. A confused foreman was roused out of bed to take the unusual phone call.

"Do the letters W-A-T mean anything to you?" Jessica asked on the phone.

"No. You say you're from where again?" the foreman asked. His voice was tired and understandably upset.

"Uh...a housing development. The bright green ribbons, the ones that mark the trees. Do the letters W-A-T mean anything to you."

"No. Why? What's this about?"

While talking on the phone, Father Abbott pointed at the computer screen. There were now two more letters. The team turned their heads.

ER

Dr. Thornhill read the letters out loud in succession. "W-A-T-E-R. Water."

"Thank you. You've been a big help," Jessica said to the foreman as she hung up the phone.

The team waited for more letters, but none came. Half went to sleep and the others stayed up trying to figure out what the letters meant. The next morning just after 10:00 A.M., they gathered to go over their findings. Dr. Thornhill and Ray were standing over a map.

"This is where you found the green ribbons. The detour. Right next to them is a pond."

"Right. The housing development is called Sugar Creek Pond or something."

"What if the ribbons were leading you to the pond?"

The conversation for the next hour was centered around the trees, the pond and the ribbons until Henrik ended it by giving orders.

"Let's take the van to the café, grab something to eat and head to the pond."

"What are we going to do there? Are we just going to wade around in the water? We don't have any gear." Dr. Thornhill added.

"I am sure there are fly fishermen in the area with waders," said Ray.

"Try the hardware store," Henrik suggested.

"I'll ask around," Ray said as he turned to Henrik. "Get me some egg whites and toast with a coffee. See you guys at the pond. Jess, can I take your car?"

"Of course."

Chapter 11

When Henrik's van arrived at the pond, Dr. Thornhill began taking photos of the trees, the green ribbons, and the water which was as smooth as glass. It was a natural body of water fed from underground streams that flowed from the Wolf Creek Reservoir. Fish and turtles swam and darted, but provided little pleasure for fisherman looking for something other than bluegill. The occasional boat filled with two retired coal miners and a stockpile of beer wasn't uncommon, but those who wanted more than catch-and-release would make the drive to Tuscarora Lake.

Spanning eight acres, Sugar Mill Pond was good for incubating mosquitoes and skipping rocks, but not much else. Henrik walked around the edge of the pond with his cane in hand while Jessica followed him with a limp. They could hear the tree service in the distance, feeding branches and limbs into the giant wood chipper while the aroma of fresh cut wood permeated the air. The water was murky like any other pond. Nothing unusual. Soon after their arrival, Ray drove up in Jessica's Accord. He parked, got out and removed a wetsuit from the trunk.

"On loan from the fire department," he said with a big grin.

"Why would they have a wetsuit?"

"It was donated to them. Supposedly they were going to go through water rescue training and nothing ever came of it. Seems like I might not fit in it though. I'll try," he said as he kicked off his field boots. While Ray attempted to squeeze into the suit, Father Abbott strolled around the edges while Dr. Thornhill continued to take photos.

Ring. Ring.

"Schuylkill County Sheriff's Department," Ruth answered with her finger over the hold button, ready to transfer the call. When the caller explained their situation, she quickly put the call on hold and waddled back toward the office of Sheriff Haydon. Interrupting a conversation with Deputy Phillips, she spoke quickly.

"There's a Jessica Calvert on line one. Apparently she found a car in a pond over by the Sugar Mill development," she said and promptly left. Sheriff Haydon squinted his eyes and hollered out.

"A car?"

By the time the sun was setting, a tow truck had rigged a series of cables to the submerged car. Jessica and Father Abbott watched as the tow truck pulled a rusted 1977 Ford LTD through the sludge of the pond and up onto the soggy embankment. Henrik watched from the other side of the tow truck shaking his head while Dr. Thornhill took more photos. Ray sat in the passenger seat with a towel now having a much different view on the paranormal. It wasn't an accident. A dead girl in purgatory led them here. He stroked the top of his nearly bald head in thought as the Sheriff began looking inside the car with a flashlight.

"Give me them gloves," he heard the sheriff say to Deputy Phillips. Ray watched as the two men looked inside and around the interior of the car unable to open the rusted doors. The sheriff bent his doughy frame at the waist and poked his head into the driver's side window and reached in with a gloved hand. "Oh, God!" Ray heard Sheriff Haydon say. Everyone who surrounded the scene looked at the sheriff as he walked away from the car and wiped his mouth with his sleeve. He looked at Deputy Phillips and exhaled as he spoke.

"Call the coroner."

Food in Styrofoam containers were delivered to the operations trailer while the team watched as Jessica kept the questions simple and Ray typed them into the keyboard. No matter what she asked or said, the Ouija board never moved in response.

"Who owned the car?"

"Who is in the car?"

"Is the car related to your death?

"Is the person inside the car a relative?"

Thinking a response might come at a later time, Henrik pushed everyone to drink his bourbon around the table.

"This is a big moment. We are in the process of forming proof of the existence of the paranormal."

"I feel like I should call The Vatican. They would be very interested to know what's going on here," Father Abbott said being the first to participate in the drink in front of him.

"They will in due time. No outsiders at this point. We're doing fine on our own, wouldn't you say?" Jessica eyed the glass of bourbon in front of her remembering the euphoric feeling that surged through her body like a rollercoaster. Unsure if she should join in, she remembered how good it felt and her curiosity of whether she could get to that place again intrigued her. She sipped her bourbon with the team until her legs and torso felt light, yet her head felt heavy.

She laughed at the jokes told by Ray, most of them with a military theme accompanied by a string of curse words. Once Jessica felt she had accomplished the level of inebriation she desired, she excused herself and limped out of the operations trailer and into the women's trailer.

Jessica had a smile on her face when she removed all of her clothes and popped a Hydromorphone before slipping in between her sheets. Bourbon and painkillers made everything go away.

When morning came, the screen was still blank. Everyone but Henrik found their way to the operations trailer for coffee and donuts delivered by the Buckhorn Café. Opting out of coffee and the donuts, Jessica began taking notes of the events that had happened over the past few days, trying not to leave anything out.

"What'cha writing there?" asked Dr. Thornhill as she nibbled on a donut.

"Notes for my story."

"For *The Post*?"

"Yep. I'm gonna need to interview everyone too. Expect either a visit from me or at the very least a phone call in the near future."

"Count me in."

"On second thought, a phone call is too impersonal. Maybe we could go out to eat sometime?"

"Sounds good to me. I'd like to get to know a reporter from *The Washington Post*. Might come in handy if I make a scientific breakthrough someday."

"And having a scientist in my back pocket as a source could be useful too."

"Absolutely," Thornhill said with a smile.

The phone rang a full ring before Ray picked it up. After a brief conversation, he hung up and looked at the team.

"That was the sheriff's office. So, who wants to tell him that a dead girl told us about the car in the water? Gonna need a volunteer."

Once Henrik took a shower, drank a cup of coffee and swallowed four ibuprofen, the team piled into the van and made their way to the Sheriff's office in Pottsville.

Sitting in the conference room, the Sheriff walked in holding a clear, plastic bag with a rusted metal tool inside. The team was seated around the table with fresh cups of coffee in front of them except for Jessica. Deputy Phillips, upon hearing that Jessica didn't like coffee, brought her a cup of instant hot chocolate.

"The car belonged to a man named Gordon D'Silva. Lived in Philadelphia," the sheriff said as he set the bag on the table and took a seat. "Anyone know him?" he asked while Jessica took notes. No one answered. "Well, it seems that an insurance adjuster who has seen his fair share of cars in water ascertains that the car had been there for six years," he explained as he looked at everyone seated around the table. He looked at the bag on the table and picked it up and held it up. "This metal tool with a wooden handle is normally used for pruning trees. It has serrated teeth and is used to saw limbs," he set the bag back down, the pruning saw hit the table with a thunk. "The coroner gives it a 90% chance that this is the murder weapon of the Adler Family. State police are taking over this investigation and I will no longer have anything to do with it, but I do have to hand them a report so why don't one of you tell me how you found the car in the water," he pulled a pen out of his shirt pocket and clicked the top as Ruth brought him a folder. "Thank you Ruth," he said as he waited to write down a statement. "Don't be shy. Speak up."

"We received a message on a computer terminal," Dr. Thornhill said. The team watched as the sheriff wrote down the answer.

"Okay. So someone communicated through a computer to tell you that there was a car in a body of water? Who was it?"

"We don't know," answered Henrik, taking the lead. He looked at his team with an expression which made it clear not to give too much information away.

"I'm sorry?"

"We don't know."

"What did the message say?"

"Water."

"Water. Okay and then what?"

"That's it."

"Nothing else?"

"No."

"You're telling me that someone sent you a message on a computer that read the word *water* and you go to one of a thousand ponds in this area and find this car?"

"Yes," Henrik answered with a smile as if he helped answer the question. Sheriff Haydon dropped his pen on the table and sat back in his chair.

"The Sugar Mill subdivision is in the city annex which means the St. Clair City police has to get a copy of this. If I put this nonsense in the report, they will think that I don't understand how to obtain pertinent information to a murder case and I can't have that! We cannot leave this room until I have something tangible to put in this report," he said with his hand over the folder, fingers spread out like a spider's legs. He gently smacked the folder as he looked at everyone.

Over the course of the next hour, the team told the sheriff a better version of the events but left out anything which sounded paranormal. While it still wasn't what the sheriff wanted, the team was excused and they drove back to the operations trailer hoping to find another response on the computer screen.

"Nothing," Ray said.

"Okay," Henrik started as he sat down. "We have new information and I would like to try to make contact again using Ray and Jessica." He turned to Jessica, "Specifically, I want you to ask questions about the car. If we were led there, there has to be a reason."

Ray jumped into the folding chair in front of the computer while Jessica sat in front of the microphone. The others remained behind them and looked at the monitors. "Start with the murder weapon." Henrik added. Jessica gathered her thoughts into short yes or no questions and then spoke.

"Is the saw the murder weapon?" she asked. Ray typed in the question. They waited five minutes and asked the question for the second time. Father Abbott and Dr. Thornhill talked in whispers behind them while Ray and Jessica sat quietly. Finally, a response appeared on the screen.

Yes

Ray pumped his fist and Henrik's eyes became glazed over. The team let out a sign of amazement and relief.

"Oh my God. This is irrefutable!" Dr. Thornhill said aloud. A light seemed to fill her eyes with a glow. She tossed her logbook and pen onto the table and covered her mouth.

"This is historical. Biblically historical," said Father Abbott. Henrik hung his head in relief, nearly coming to tears as Jessica continued.

"Is the man in the car the murderer?" she asked. The team sat still, not saying a word and on the edge of their seat. After five minutes Jessica prepared to ask the question again, but before she could speak the response came back.

No

"No? He isn't?" Ray said in disbelief as his voice jumped a full octave.

"Who is the man who murdered you?" Jessica asked into the microphone. She nodded at Ray who sat in shock and eventually typed in her question. They stared at the screen long enough to ask the question three more times over the next hour. One hour became two. Two became three. When midnight came around, Dr. Thornhill offered to take the night shift. While the rest of the team was exiting the operations trailer, Jessica felt a hand on her shoulder.

"You can sleep in here if you want," Dr. Thornhill offered. Terrified of sleeping by herself, she briefly considered the offer.

"Thanks. If I am unable to sleep, I might run back here

and take you up on it."

"Just bring your pillow and a blanket. Not much comfort in here."

Instead of attempting to sleep in a dimly lit room, the thought of a euphoric cocktail surging through her bloodstream sounded better. Being far away from the house seemed to help, but the fear was still there.

After thanking Dr. Thornhill for her offer, she left the operations trailer and hurried to her bedside. After downing the emergency mini bottle of tequila and a Hydromorphone, she slid off her khakis and socks before sliding between the sheets and turned out the light.

As the night wore on, activity in the operations trailer was minimal. Dr. Thornhill would often wake and look at the monitor and see nothing. No movement was seen on the video screens and all seemed quiet.

While everyone was sleeping, an odd occurrence happened. Something that the team had heard about, but never witnessed, nor caught it on videotape. Upstairs in Tilly's room, a light turned on. Five seconds later, the light turned off only to turn back on again. The light continued this pattern for some time unbeknownst to the team.

Just before dawn, the operations trailer door opened, startling Dr. Thornhill from her sleep. She opened her eyes and saw Father Abbott and Henrik helping Ray up the steps into the trailer. Ray was injured.

"What happened?" Abbott had much of Ray's weight

around his shoulders as he helped him inside while Henrik held the door open. Abbott strained as he answered Dr. Thornhill.

"He's bleeding. A lot."

"Looks to be puncture wounds," Henrik said. They helped Ray into a folding chair while Dr. Thornhill grabbed a flashlight off a workstation.

"You got any morphine?" Ray asked.

"That bad?" Thornhill replied as she clicked the flashlight on and looked at his leg. Multiple punctures. She started counting.

"I count sixteen. Four are pretty deep. What did you do?"

"Nothing! I woke up like this!"

"He was sitting up in bed cursing and pulling the sheets off of him," said Abbott. Dr. Thornhill opened the first aid kit and opened a brown bottle of antiseptic along with removing packages of bandages.

"I need water," she said.

"How could this have happened?" Henrik asked as Father Abbott gave Thornhill a canteen of water.

"I didn't feel anything. The first thing I noticed was warm liquid. I thought I pissed the bed. Then I felt pain and began pulling sheets off of me," he explained. While rinsing the blood off with water, Dr. Thornhill stopped. She looked closer and then looked up at Ray.

"These look like bite marks."

"What? You saying I was bitten?" he said as he looked

down at his bleeding leg. Both Father Abbott and Henrik knelt down and looked for themselves.

"It does. Like a dog bite or," Father Abbott said as he stopped mid-sentence and stood up and looked at Thornhill.

"What?"

"It's not safe here anymore," Abbott said. "Nothing came in the trailer, you just woke up and you had these puncture wounds. We are far away from the house, supposedly far from the activity."

"You think we should move?" Henrik asked. Father Abbott stood up and crossed his arms. Deep in thought, he took his time as his looked down at the floor. When he raised his head, he looked directly at Henrik.

"I think we are onto something here and if we don't figure this out sooner than later, we may not survive this. We are slowly realizing the evil that lies in that house. It's like the boiling frog effect," Abbott explained.

"What's that?" Henrik asked. Dr. Thornhill jumped in.

"It's a sociology model which means we aren't perceiving the danger like we should. We need to make the decision now to go back to the motel. Don't let Jessica find out about this without knowing if we are moving back to the motel or not. We could lose her. She's already at her limit. This could push her over the edge."

"I rely on you all to give me this kind of information and your thought process, I thank you," Henrik said. "We will now take up residence in the motel at night. Also, I think we should be moving this faster than we have been so I'm sending Jessica to Philadelphia to find out who Gordon D'Silva was," he explained. He turned toward Ray. "At least it'll keep her mind off of what happened. We desperately need more info to proceed."

"I would like to look at the murder weapon and the car," Dr. Thornhill stated while wrapping Ray's leg.

"Do you think you can find anything even after the car and weapon were submerged for six years?" Henrik asked.

"Doubt it, but it wouldn't hurt to look."

"Fine. Everyone pack their things and let's get to the motel."

"Dr. Thornhill, would you please wake Jessica? Have her come to my trailer so that I may give her some cash for expenses."

"You gonna tell her?" Ray asked.

"Tell her what?"

"About this?" he asked as he pointed to his leg.

"Of course."

Chapter 12

Jessica arrived in Philadelphia at 7:06 P.M. and found a Ramada Inn before going to the police department to fill out a records request on Gordon D'Silva. A records request was her favorite source of finding info on a person of interest. When the record came back with no arrests, she circled his address on the report and drove over to 1131 Laveer Street. With a knock on the door a woman in a nightgown answered with rollers in her hair.

"Yeah?" she said with a voice that could crush gravel. Jessica asked a few questions and quickly discovered the woman purchased the house after Gordon was declared dead. Jessica thanked the woman who then attempted to sell her Mary Kay cosmetic products to which she politely declined and hurried off the front porch. After a lengthy trip downtown over the worst potholes Jessica had ever encountered in her entire life, she made it inside the County Recorders Office and requested a copy of the deed for 1131 Laveer Street.

Sitting in her car, she looked over a dot matrix printout of the deed. While eating a club sandwich, she read over the transactions and found a discrepancy.

I, Martin Peter Silva, father of deceased Gordon Peter D'Silva hereby release, remise, convey the property at 1131 Laveer Street to the following:

Jessica looked at the name *Silva* and noted the typo. The rest of the deed seemed in order and offered nothing else to go on. After filing everything in her blood-stained messenger bag, she headed back to the hotel, noticing a liquor store on the way. Thinking she could use some alcohol to mix with her painkillers, she pulled into a parking space. Bars were welded in front of the windows and doors and she suddenly felt unsafe. Thinking she should just leave, the thought of the greatest feeling she ever had was just beyond the door and metal bars. Another car pulled up and two men exited a filthy 1972 Chevelle while laughing and flicking cigarettes. Both were wearing Philadelphia Eagles jackets and walked like they were trying really hard to impress every female on every block in the city. Jessica decided against it and put her car in reverse and headed back to her hotel.

At 2:46 A.M., Jessica heard a noise in her room and opened her eyes. She sat up and heard the sound of a bare foot sliding on tile. She turned her head toward the bathroom and got out of bed. With enough light coming from the outer hallway and leaking into the room from under the door, she leaned to the left and peered around the wall. From where she stood, she could see both the door to the outer hallway and the entrance to the bathroom. Standing in silence, she could sense the presence of someone standing behind the bathroom door.

She remained quiet and stood very still and listened. The door moved a half-inch as if someone had bumped the door followed by another sound of a bare foot sliding across the tile floor. Jessica felt that if she spoke out loud or walked toward the door to leave the room, she would be killed.

She stared at the dark entryway to the bathroom and was certain she could hear someone breathing. She knew that someone was definitely behind the door and took a silent step toward the small table beside her bed and picked up the phone. She dialed zero and waited for the front desk to pick up.

"Hello, front desk," a friendly voice answered. Jessica spoke just above a whisper.

"I need help. Room 3366," she whispered.

"I'm sorry. I am having trouble hearing you. Could you speak up?"

"I need help. Room 3366."

"Hello? I'm sorry I cannot hear you?" the friendly voice replied. Jessica refused to speak up. She kept her eyes on the door.

"There. Is. Someone. In. My. Room. Please. Help." she said in clear and quiet words.

"Did you say there is someone in your room?" the friendly voice replied.

"Yes. Hurry."

"I'm so sorry about that, we must have double booked you," the friendly voice replied. "Let me see how I can help." the sound of typing on a computer keyboard commenced.

Jessica hung up. The door moved an inch and the sound of something brushing up against the door caused her to stop breathing. Her hands now shaking, she picked the phone up and dialed 911 and waited.

"Nine-Eleven. What is your emergency."

"Rape. Rape," whispered Jessica. "Room 3366 Ramada Inn. Rape. Rape." and she hung up the phone and continued to stare at the door. Almost ten minutes later of standing perfectly still, running could be heard in the hallway. Jessica then heard the sound of a key being inserted and turning the lock. A big flash of light came from the door as it was opened and the three policemen entered and found Jessica standing next to the small table near her bed. Wearing a t-shirt and underwear with tears streaming down her face, she sobbed in fear while covering her mouth.

"Ma'am. Are you alright?" an officer asked. He watched as she pointed toward the bathroom door. The last officer to enter the room turned on the bathroom light and walked in.

"Nothing here," the officer said. Jessica closed her eyes and leaned on the bed.

"Ma'am? Was someone in your room?" Jessica nodded her head Yes and continued to cry. "Can I get a description?" Jessica tried to stop crying as she thought about the overwhelming feeling of certain death if she had approached the bathroom.

"It was dark," was all she could say. The officers repeatedly assured her safety and asked questions to which she gave vague answers as to not sound crazy. Realizing she was still in her underwear, she grabbed a pair of jeans and walked with the officers down the hallway in an effort to calm down. Crying and using tissues to wipe her running nose and tears, Jessica spoke in a terrified, muffled voice.

"I need to get away from that room. I don't think I can sleep there tonight."

The officer's spoke in comforting tones to calm her down and stood by her side as she limped up and down the hallway, eventually coming back to her room. She packed her things with three officers standing by her side. Grabbing her suitcase and messenger bag, the officers escorted her out to her car.

Driving five miles north of Philadelphia, she found herself in Germantown. After happening upon a hotel named Chestnut Hill, she parked her car and hurried inside to the front counter where she found an elegant lobby and well dressed black woman.

"Welcome to the Chestn…" she began to say until she was rudely interrupted.

"Do you have rooms with mini bars?" Jessica asked ready to spin around and head back to her car thinking she wouldn't get a favorable response.

"We do," she replied keeping her composure. Jessica straightened and walked closer to the desk.

"Good. I'll take one."

After getting her luggage into her room, she sat down in front of a small refrigerator and opened the door. Grabbing a bottle of vodka, she took in a mouthful after popping a Hydromorphone. She swallowed, pausing briefly until taking another sip.

Grabbing a few hours of sleep before the alarm clock sounded. Her brain felt like the thick fog surrounding the Golden Gate and she found it difficult to get moving as she slowly put on her clothes. Thinking she should take up drinking coffee, she dismissed the thought and headed out to the parking lot. After finding a parking space at the library, it took her little time to locate and utilize a microfiche film roll which contained Gordon D'Silva's obituary.

Philadelphia, PA - Mr. Gordon Peter D'Silva, age 42 of Philadelphia, PA., a missing person of two years was declared deceased and entered into rest Wednesday, December 14th, 1985. Arrangements are under the direction of Bedo Funeral Home where services will be held at 11:00 AM Friday, December 16, 1985 with burial to follow in the Lost Spring Cemetery with military honors by the County Honor Guard. A native of Philadelphia, he was the son of Martin Peter Silva and Henrietta Silva and older brother Peter Silva.

Jessica noted that the name on the deed wasn't a typo at all. It seemed that Gordon had a *D* in his last name while his family members didn't. After making a few photocopies, she shoved the papers into a manila envelope and walked out of the library thinking she had found a small lead. Down the street, she saw a coffee shop which had the words *Sandwiches, Salads and Soup* in big lettering stenciled on the windows.

Craving a salad, she walked into The Liberty Diner and

sat down in a booth. After ordering a Cobb Salad and a glass of ice water, she pulled out her manila folder and looked over the photocopied documents once again. The obituary and news articles about his disappearance gave her nothing to go on. Upon looking over the deed once again and noting that his father had changed his name, yet Gordon had not, she saw a curious line she was unfamiliar with.

TL - filing #27049 transactions on property prohibited - Title 26/Subtitle F/Chapter 64/Subchapter C/Part II/6321

It was the words *transactions on property prohibited* that struck her. When the waitress served her the Cobb Salad, she closed the manila folder.

"Anything else?"

"Looks great, thanks. May I pay for this now? I am having to eat and run today."

"Of course," the waitress said as she reached into her apron for the check.

After scarfing down the salad and drinking half of her water, Jessica hurried to her car. As she opened her driver's side door, she saw a sign for a *Coldwell Banker Real Estate* office. Thinking it might save her a trip, she took a chance, crossed the street and went inside.

After explaining her needs to a receptionist wearing too much mascara, Jessica waited as the woman picked up the phone and summoned a tall man in a navy blue suit. Thick arms and chest carved from rock, he offered Jessica a smile worth the trip to Philadelphia. Feeling frumpy and out of his league, she overcompensated with a lively smile and a soft handshake. Hi, I'm Jessica Calvert from *The Washington Post*, she recited in her head before she spoke out loud, making sure in her sudden, nervous state to get her name right.

"Nice to meet you, Jessica. My name is Chad McCoy, how can I help?"

"Hi. I have a copy of a deed and while reading it, I came across this and I am not sure what it means," she said as she pointed to the line concerning the prohibitive transaction.

"Oh. Well, there is good news and bad news."

"What's the bad news?"

"I don't know what this means," he replied with a forced laugh as he handed the deed back to her.

"Ok. The good news?" she asked with a smile.

"I know someone who does," he said, again giving her a smile that made her ready to buy a home in Philadelphia. "Why don't you follow me? My boss will know what this is."

After walking through a maze of cubicles, she was escorted to an office with a thin man eating granola out of a glass bowl while sitting behind a desk.

"Mr. Dawson," Chad said as he knocked on the office door. Chad's smile was gone as he approached the thin man like a zookeeper trying to feed a grizzly bear.

"What is it?" Mr. Dawson replied, all business.

"This young lady has a quick question and I think you might have an answer for her." Jessica handed Mr. Dawson the deed and pointed to the *transactions on property prohibited.*

"I'm curious what that means" she said. Mr. Dawson took one look at the deed and began explaining it as he handed it back to Jessica.

"The letters TL stand for tax lien. The filing would explain the reason for the lien and what would need to be done to correct it. That is a federal lien and not a state lien so you would have to visit the Internal Revenue Service and give them the filing number," he said as he quickly went back to his bowl of granola. Jessica turned to Chad as he flashed a grin.

"See? I told ya. Jeremy here knows it all."

"Don't call me by my first name," Mr. Dawson said without looking up from his bowl of granola.

The next day Henrik and Father Abbott were looking at video footage from the night before while Dr. Thornhill tended to Ray's bandages. Sitting on the long table in the middle of the trailer, Ray kept himself propped up with his arms behind him, hands flat on the surface.

"How is it you know how to do all this stuff and you're not a doctor?" Ray asked.

"I am a doctor."

"You know what I mean."

"This is basic first aid. Cleaning a wound and bandaging."

"Injecting a sedative in a vein isn't first aid."

"Right but a paramedic can do it."

"You're a paramedic?"

"Was a paramedic."

"When was this?"

"In college. Helped pay some of my tuition. Worked weekends mostly."

The door to the trailer opened and Jessica walked in carrying a manila folder and closed the door behind her.

"I found something," she said with a proud grin. Henrik spun around in his chair and looked her in the eye.

"So did we."

Dr. Thornhill had spent a half-day looking at D'Silva's car and taking notes in her log book before deciding she would visit the sheriff's office. After walking in the front door of the station, Ruth had called up Deputy Phillips to answer her questions. He walked Dr. Thornhill back to his office thinking he might be able to help, however her questions weren't simple and he didn't feel qualified to answer them.

"I'm sorry, I just don't think I can be of any help to you."

"Well, how about taking a look at the pruning saw that was recovered from the submerged vehicle?"

"Could you come back tomorrow? Sheriff will be here then. He's out for a commissioner's meeting," Deputy Phillips said. His timid manner and awkward responses made her think that he was a bit of a push over.

"Well, what if you bring it out here and set it on the counter? I won't even touch it. Being an officer, I am sure you can arrange something like that," she said playing to his ego.

"I suppose if you promise not to touch it. I don't want to get in trouble."

"Cross my heart," she said as she made the motion of a cross on her chest. Deputy Phillips left and returned with the pruning saw in a plastic evidence bag.

"Okay, remember. No touching."

"I won't," she replied as she looked it over and made a few notes in her logbook. After a few moments, Deputy Phillips spoke up.

"It was the worst thing to happen around here. Ever. It's all people talk about."

"Still?"

"Especially around the anniversary. People have their theories as to who killed them."

"Nothing stuck, huh?"

"How do you mean?"

"None of their theories hold water?"

"No."

"You got one?"

"A theory? Sure. But it ain't mine. I just happen to agree with it."

"What's that?"

"The boy's name was Scott Adler. He was reported missing the same night they were murdered."

"Really?"

"Yep. Parents called us and reported him missing. He was supposed to be home after school around 3:00pm and was still missing by eight that night."

"Did you all go looking for him?"

"Well, around here it isn't uncommon for parents to call us when their child is missing."

"Why is that?"

"Small town. Nothing to do. Lot of kids mess around down by the creek or they play a stickball match in someone's backyard that goes on a little too long. Besides, a kid to go missing for several hours is nothing to get excited about. There hasn't been a child in this county go missing permanently in decades. They always turn up. No need to go crazy and scour the county with lights and sirens."

"So what happened?"

"We got a call back from Scott's parents about a half hour later saying he made it home."

"So what's the theory?"

"Some people say they saw the Adler boy get into a car at his school. When he went missing, we didn't have much time to get the word out before we got a call saying he was okay. A lot of us believe whoever picked the boy up, was the one that killed the family."

"Is this public information?"

"Not really. We didn't even file a missing person's report or anything. I know we recorded a witness telling us about the car picking up the Adler boy though. The statement was taken after the murder."

Back at the operations trailer, Dr. Thornhill was explaining the conversation she had with the deputy. Giving a detailed account of what was said, Jessica hung on every word and soaked up the details as she took notes.

"Did you look at the statement?" Jessica asked.

"I did. The witness was a teacher at the school named William O'Keefe," she said as she looked at her logbook. "He was also an assistant coach for the school basketball team. He said the car was a blue Ford station wagon. No model. No license plate. Said he knew Scott Adler, but the car looked out of place. Stated that it was very muddy."

"Did you speak to Mr. O'Keefe?"

"Not yet. I had the library find a few photos of blue Ford station wagons," she said as she reached for a book at the end of the table and opened it to a page which was bookmarked showing several photos.

"Where does he live?"

"An apartment off the square. 6th street."

"Can I go with you?"

"I'm counting on it. I feel like I have used up all of my limited investigative reporting ability," Dr. Thornhill said with a grin. Henrik looked at Jessica and turned the conversation to her.

"What did you find out?" he asked. She immediately opened her manila folder and slid out a few photocopies of news articles. D'Silva's obituary, police report, deeds to property and a record showing the name change of the D'Silva family.

"No arrest record. I can get his military record, but it'll take weeks. At first the only thing I found was a name change. For some reason, his family dropped the D in their name changing it to Silva. Gordon never did.

"He probably couldn't change it," said Ray.

"Why is that?"

"Military. Males are unable to change their name while in the service."

"Makes sense. Then I saw something on the deed. See right here," she said as she pointed. "This means a lien was placed against his property and couldn't be sold at the time."

"Who placed the lien?"

"The IRS. Gordon D'Silva deposited $9,999.99 into a bank account. In cash."

"So?" Dr. Thornhill asked.

"It's a red flag to the IRS," Henrik interjected. "Federal law states that anyone who deposits $10,000 in cash into an account, the financial institution has to report it to the IRS."

"Right," Jessica said. "This is what I was told at the IRS office. Only they said anyone who tries to deposit just under that amount, is enough to be visited by an agent and questioned."

"What does this have to do with anything?" Ray asked.

"The date the deposit was made was the day before the murder of the Adler family." At this, the collective response of the team encompassed a whistle, and a few gasps. Jessica continued, "But, if we are to take what we have learned from an entity in an evil house seriously, we know that this man is not the murderer."

"With the information we have at hand, I suggest we try to make contact again," said Henrik with a nod.

Over the course of an hour, preparations were made, food was delivered from the Buckhorn Café and the team surrounded the monitors. Ray sat at the keyboard ready to type, Jessica sat in front of the microphone ready to speak. She cleared her throat and leaned in toward the microphone.

"Tilly are you there?"

Chapter 13

For two hours, Jessica and Ray attempted to communicate with various phrases that were either a Yes or No answer.

"Tilly, can you hear me?"

"Is the murderer still alive?"

"Did you know the murderer?"

In between asking questions into the microphone, the team took breaks and began looking over the information on the table in the middle of the room. They looked over the deed and discussed a possible motive. While talking, they heard a loud rumbling sound similar to an earthquake, but felt no vibration. Looking at the video monitors, they saw black dust bellow out of the opening of the crawlspace.

"What was that?" Henrik asked. The team watched as the black dust settled enough to see a light appear from underneath the house.

"Something is moving. See that?" Thornhill said as she pointed to the monitor. The light appeared to be a flashlight on a hard hat. A man crawled out of the hole and started walking toward the operations trailer.

"Who is that?" asked Jessica. As the man walked closer, they could tell the man was wearing a coal mining jumpsuit

and black boots just before he walked out of view of the camera. Then they heard a voice.

"Hello?" the man said. His voice was muffled through the
trailer door. Jessica rose to her feet, as did Ray who spoke up.

"Who's there?"

"We need some help. The mine suffered a collapse and
some of my men were hurt."

"Where were they hurt?"

"In the mine. Could you unlock the door?"

"What's your name?"

"Please. Unlock the door! They're gonna die!"

"Are you injured?" Ray asked. No response this time. He
moved closer to the door and looked at the knob.

"Don't open the door!" Father Abbott yelled in a whisper.
Ray gestured quietly that Father Abbott was crazy for thinking
he would.

"Please sir, I need help. We need help. My men are hurt
please unlock the door."

"What's your name?"

"My name is Ray Turner."

"Ray Turner?"

"Please unlock the door. My men need help. You're all
going to die," the man said. Ray turned and looked at those behind him. Father Abbott walked to the door with cautious
steps while Ray backed away.

"Son, can you knock once on the door? Knock only once.
Please."

"Sir, please let me come in. Please. We need help."

"What's your name?"

"My name is Gerald Abbott," the man said. Father Abbott turned and looked at Henrik.

"We are not opening that door."

"Can't we call the police?" Dr. Thornhill asked.

"And what do we tell them?" Henrik replied.

"There's an access panel in the floor. I can open it and look where the guy is standing," said Ray in a quiet voice. "If he leaves, we could make a run to the van."

"Forget it. Could be the same thing as opening the door." Father Abbott replied in a whisper.

"We should call the sheriff," said Henrik.

"What are you going to tell them?" Jessica asked.

"Exactly what is going on. There is an unidentified man standing outside the door and he is trying to get in."

"Try asking again. See if he's still there," Ray said as he whispered to Abbott. Father Abbott leaned toward the door.

"I can't open this door," he shouted through the walls of the trailer.

"Please sir, my men need help," he pleaded. The team watched as Father Abbott reached down and put his hand on the lock and turned it.

"Stop!" Henrik whispered. "What are you doing?" Father Abbott turned around and looked at the team.

"It was never locked," he explained as he stepped away from the door.

"Okay. Have a seat," Henrik said as he gestured to the table. Everyone followed his direction and watched as he sat down with the assistance of his cane.

"Father Abbott, do you have any idea of what that is outside?"

"I don't. Best guess is a projection. That man isn't real."

"What is a projection?"

"It's usually an auditory manifestation, but it can be visual. That thing out there could be an apparition or something in that house is causing that manifestation."

"An apparition? You mean a ghost?"

"It's speaking which implies vocal cords. I don't think it's a ghost. Manifestation or projection is probably a better word."

"I still think we should call the police." Henrik said as he looked around the table. "Anyone disagree?"

"I do," Ray said.

"Why?"

"I'm never been a big believer in all this spiritual stuff. Ghosts and manifestations, but that thing out there is real. A dead girl told us where to find a car. I am now a believer. If it can't get in without us opening the door, I say keep the doors locked and let's use this time to examine the house. Send more messages. Things are happening."

"I kind of agree. I feel like we're close to something," said Dr. Thornhill. Father Abbott reached his hand out and grabbed the phone and put it to his ear. After putting the phone back on the receiver, he looked at everyone.

"No one thought of checking to see if the phone still worked. It does," as soon as he stopped speaking the voice was heard at the door.

"I have many men who are dead. A lot of them are injured. We need help. Please open the door."

"Goddamn, that is creepy," Ray said as he made his body shiver. A brief silence followed until Henrik spoke up. The second he did, the team began to move about and get into position.

"I would like Jessica and Ray to try to make contact once again. Father Abbott and Dr. Thornhill, I ask that you both draw up a timeline of the events so far. I will assist. At 11:00 P.M. we will attempt to get some sleep with a few on watch. Tomorrow morning, we will make a phone call to the sheriff and abandon this trailer. I will make arrangements with Ray to extend our operations as far away as possible. I would also like to add more video cameras."

"Sounds good. What will we sleep on?"

"There are two air mattresses in the storage closet and I think there are few blankets. Sorry, no pillows. Make do by wadding up some clothing."

"We'll make it work," Dr. Thornhill said. Ray and Jessica took their seats and began asking Yes and No questions.

After three hours of no responses coming from their questions, Ray and Jessica ceased their efforts and attempted to find a place to sleep. Both Ray and Dr. Thornhill woke every so often and looked at the computer screen. Father Abbott

snored loud enough for Henrik to poke him with his cane. By
3:00 A.M. everyone was asleep and no activity was present on
the monitors.

The following morning, Henrik made the phone call to
the sheriff's office. Once coffee was made the team began to
wake by sitting up, rubbing their eyes and clearing their
throats. Jessica slowly became anxious as she thought about
what happened the previous night. She took deep breaths in
an effort to calm herself down as Father Abbott grabbed an
empty coffee cup and walked over to the door and smacked the
mug against the thin frame.

"Hello?" he yelled out. Silence. The team turned and
watched the door waiting for an answer. Jessica continued to
take deep breaths as she nervously pulled at her bottom lip.
Now using his hands, he rapped his knuckles on the door. "Is
anyone there?" Silence.

"Anyone else as freaked out as I was last night?" Ray asked.

"I know I was. Still am," Dr. Thornhill said just as Jessica
spoke up.

"I can't stay here any longer. I'm done once we get out of
here. Sorry Henrik, but I'm not coming back." The team grew
silent. They all had been thinking the same thing. Most just
stared at the floor while Henrik nodded his head.

After a few rounds of coffee, a conversation about manifestations and projections ensued. While Dr. Thornhill sat at
the controls to review the tapes from last night, she started to
ask a question, but was interrupted by a sound that caused all

of them to jolt. Especially Jessica.

Knock. Knock.

"Who's there?" Ray shouted as he stood up.

"Sheriff Haydon and Deputy Phillips," Ray looked at the team behind him as he opened the door. Dr. Thornhill stayed seated at the controls and continued to review footage from the night before. Seeing nothing on the tapes, she increased the speed.

"Well, I appreciate the call, Mr. Frazier. Deputy Phillips and I are interested in what you have to say, especially since you were able to recover the vehicle of a suspect." Sheriff Haydon wore a curious expression as he spoke.

"Well, I do thank you for coming. Any trouble outside the trailer? Anything out of the ordinary?" Henrik asked.

"Well if you call a house wrapped in plastic sheeting out of the ordinary then yes." A weak chuckle emitted from Henrik's throat, the others on the team were still hanging on the words that everything outside seemed to be okay. While Henrik spoke, he glanced at the others with an expression that communicated to the team; *Don't say anything about the miner.* Dr. Thornhill spotted something on the monitor and stopped the tape.

"Well, what do you have?" Sheriff asked. Henrik began to spread out the documents just as Dr. Thornhill saw a figure near one of the cameras. She looked at the time on the video. 3:44 A.M.

"Here is a deed that was transferred after the disappearance of Gordon D'Silva," Henrik said as he pointed to the line concerning the tax lien. Dr. Thornhill watched the time on the tape as it rolled over to 3:45 A.M. just as a black man came into view of the camera. He was walking toward the house. Dr. Thornhill couldn't tell who it was exactly although she thought it looked like Ray. The man approached the front of the house and Dr. Thornhill watched as Ray limped up the steps of the house and went inside. It *was* Ray.

"Oh my God," she said as she stood up and covered her mouth. Her head turned and looked at Ray. "You went inside? You went in the house?" Henrik turned and looked at Dr. Thornhill as did everyone else. "Why did you go inside? Last night at 3:45 A.M. It's on the video."

"What? Last night?" Jessica asked. Ray was standing next to Father Abbott and didn't seem to be able to speak.

"Rewind that tape at once!" Henrik instructed. Ray grabbed Father Abbott around his neck with his python arm while he removed a large military knife from his cargo pants. Ray's face expressed severe hatred and anger showing his teeth like an animal.

"*Hic non receperunt ut et irrumabo loco isto,*" Ray's voice sounded deep and it scrawled like a table saw cutting into wood. Sheriff Haydon and Deputy Phillips drew their side arms and pointed them at Ray. Had someone looked at the monitor, they would have seen a faint light repeatedly flicking on and off in Tilly's room.

"What's he saying?" Henrik asked.

"Put the knife down now!" Deputy Phillips shouted, his

timid manner seemingly missing from his command.

"Cut him and I will shoot you down," Sheriff Haydon shouted.

"*Corpora intrinsecus! Corpora intrinsecus!*"

"What's he saying?" Dr. Thornhill shouted with tears in her eyes and fear in her voice. Father Abbott was gripping Ray's arm, trying to pull the knife away from his throat while listening to the Latin being spoken by Ray's grinding voice.

"Inside all your bodies. He's speaking Latin," Abbott said.

"*Hic regnat malum,*" Ray said in a raised voice as if ending a speech. He readied his hand.

"Don't do it or I will shoot!" Deputy Phillips shouted just as Ray's python arm swiftly moved, cutting the throat of Father Abbott, blood spewing out of his jugular followed by gunfire going off. Bullets ripped through Ray's body as he lunged forward at Henrik, knocking him to the ground. Ray's arm plunged the knife into the middle of Henrik's stomach. Blood gurgled and spewed from his wound as gunfire contin-ued while Dr. Thornhill plastered her body up against the wall of the trailer. Henrick screamed as blood gushed like a city fountain from his mouth before his eyes rolled up into his eye sockets. Jessica curled up in the fetal position in the corner covering her ears and shutting her eyes.

"Everyone stay still!" Sheriff Haydon shouted as he sur-veyed the trailer, pointing his gun wherever he looked. Dr. Thornhill looked down and saw Henrik's body and the blood pooling on the floor at her feet. She started screaming a shrill scream as if she was being torn apart.

"Let's get out of here," Sheriff Haydon yelled. He watched Dr. Thornhill start toward the door, eyes filled with terror and breathing as if she just completed a marathon. She started to fall, but he caught her just as he holstered his gun.

"I got you. Come on, I have you. I have you," he said as he wrapped his arm around her, helping her outside. Deputy Phillips bent down to help Jessica, taking notice she had urinated and soaked her pants. Grabbing her arms, he set her up while she still grabbed her legs with a grip he couldn't release.

"Come on, we have to get out of here," he said as she fell over, eyes wide open and beginning to hyperventilate. As he pulled her outside, just before the door closed, she could see once last glimpse of the computer screen. A single word, in green letters: farm

Chapter 14

Bob Calvert measured a piston with calipers and decided that
it needed a few more turns on the lathe. He clamped the piston
back into the vice and turned it while applying pressure with
a lever. Before the high pitch whine took over his hearing, a
man yelled out in Bob's direction. He turned his head and saw
that one of the foremen was trying to get his attention.

After being called into the administration office for a
phone call, he once again bolted out of the plant and ran for
his car. Even though they assured him she was fine and was
only suffering from an acute stress reaction, he still hurried
and abused the speed limit to Schuylkill Medical Center. When
he walked into the hospital room right at three hours later, he
hugged his daughter who was awake yet heavily medicated.

"I'm okay, Daddy. I'm okay."

"What happened? How did this happen?" he asked.
Jessica began to cry and couldn't explain. "I'm okay," she
replied. Her eyes looked different. When she looked at him, it
appeared she was staring instead of making normal eye contact. Jessica wasn't herself and he could easily tell.

A few hours after her father's arrival, she was evaluated
by two physicians and ultimately discharged from the hospital.

Bob drove his '87 Ford Taurus around to the lobby entrance while a nurse navigated Jessica's wheelchair and waited outside the revolving doors. While moving Jessica from the wheelchair to the car, a female reporter with a cameraman approached them asking questions.

"Are you one of the survivors of the haunted house in St. Clair?" the reporter asked as the cameraman moved around to get a better shot. Bob buckled Jessica's seatbelt and closed her door while the reporter followed him to the driver's side. "Sir, is this your daughter?" Bob ignored her and got in the driver's seat before closing his door and driving away.

"This can't be happening again," Bob said to himself as he made his way to the interstate. On the way back to Pittsburgh, Jessica sat in the passenger seat and stared out the window. Her father would ask questions and only get back single word responses. Once at the house, Jessica somberly explained that she was very tired and needed to go to bed early. She thanked her father for coming to get her before limping off to her old room without her cane. The first night's sleep began with another nightmare.

Walking along weeds, fallen trees and rocks, Jessica looked up and saw a boy of nine running as fast as he could. She was able to hear him breathing as he ran, stepping on branches and twigs which popped with every step. Then the boy fell and his arm got stuck in a hole. Jessica watched as the boy was being pulled downward as if something had grabbed his arm and was pulling him.

"Are you okay? Do you need help?" Jessica said, but the boy couldn't hear her. She watched as the boy's arm was pulled and came out of the socket, causing him to yell in pain. The boy's arm continued to be pulled until the bones around his shoulder snapped and broke. His yelling turned into screaming, as he was pulled further into the hole. Jessica winced as she watched the boy being pulled further inside the hole causing his rib cage to crack and collapse and his legs to fold as he was pulled deep inside. Jessica jolted awake screaming. Soaked in sweat and breathing in a panic, she tried to calm herself down.

For the first week, the nightmares came in force causing her to wake in a panic. While each nightmare was different, they contained a similar theme. Trees. Running. Sometimes the boy would appear and run for a short distance before tripping and falling to the ground.

Having had enough of not getting a good nights sleep, and having to wash her sweat stained sheets every day, she pulled a twenty-dollar bill free from her purse and slid it into the front pocket of her jeans. Locking the front door behind her as she left her father's house, she started down the sidewalk headed toward Ruxton Drug Store located three blocks away.

As she walked down the sidewalk, she thought about Ray and how he looked when he killed Father Abbott. He didn't look like himself. His face appeared to be that of another man, a man who was cruel and terrifying. Ray was tough and strong, but he had a gentle way about him.

She didn't attend Ray's or Father Abbott's funeral and Henrik's was held in New Hampshire on his estate...a private funeral. Dr. Thornhill had moved to Dallas, Texas and had yet to contact Jessica. Once inside the drug store, she picked up a bottle of Nyquil and headed back to her father's house.

Over the next week, Jessica would take a full dose of Nyquil in combination with her pills before going to sleep, which caused her to not dream at all. Then it seemed that her body was building a tolerance to Nyquil so she increased the dosage. Before the third week, she was up to two full doses before bed each night.

At dinner, Bob would often confide in Jessica how worried he was about her. For nearly a month she stayed on the couch during the day, blankly staring at the TV screen while shows blazed by without her ever really watching them. He suggested counseling to which she shrugged him off saying that she would be fine and needed time.

Once the Nyquil was deemed ineffective, Jessica scrounged around the kitchen unable to find anything that would help accelerate her pain medication.

After checking the last cabinet, she found half a bottle of Chimalhucan Tequila. After four shots coupled with her Hydromorphone, she felt the pleasant effects. Like slipping into a warm swimming pool, she dozed off to sleep and didn't wake until after her father had already left for work.

That night, a baseball game was on TV and in an effort to normalize life in his house with his daughter, Bob bought a 12-pack of Iron City Beer and ordered a pizza for delivery. Sitting on the couch together watching the Pirates play the Cubs, a knock on the door caused Bob to set his slice of pizza down and hurry to answer it while the commercial break was coming to an end. At the door was a man wearing a red hat and an unzipped jacket. In his right hand he was holding the handle of a dolly with seven stacked file boxes. Bob opened the door.

"Can I help you?"

"Yeah, I have a delivery for Jessica Calvert."

"Oh. Ok. Just a second," Bob said as he hurried back inside. "Jess? It's for you. A delivery of some sort?" he said as she got up and walked to the door. Wearing an old t-shirt without a bra and jeans with holes in the knees, she looked at the man holding the dolly.

"I'm Jessica Calvert."

"I have a delivery for you," he said as he handed her a yellow slip of carbon paper which was stapled to an envelope. The manifest was printed on a dot matrix printer and each line listed the box count, weight of the shipment and in a space marked *Note*, was a message to Jessica.

Miss Calvert, the law enforcement officials no longer have a need for these materials and they were returned to us. We assume that if you write an article on the events which transpired while on Mr. Frazier's *team, then you might require this research more than we do. Also, we have included the check in the agreed upon amount of $10,000 for your involvement in Mr. Frazier's project.*

Sincerely,

Henrik Frazier Holdings Group

Jessica looked up at the man holding the dolly.

"How many boxes are there?"

"Thirteen. Where would you like me to put them?" he asked. Jessica didn't know what to say as she was blindsided by the delivery.

"Uh, the kitchen please," she said as she got out of the way of the door. Her father watched as the man wheeled the boxes inside.

"What are these boxes?"

"It's the research from the operations trailer."

"Whose research?"

"I think it's mine and everyone else's who worked on the project," Jessica said as she watched the man set the boxes off the dolly and wheel past her, headed for six more. Bob walked back into the family room, displeased that anything which connected Jessica to the two worst experiences of her life were being wheeled inside his house.

Once the delivery was complete, the man in the red hat removed a clipboard off the back of the dolly and whipped out a pen from his shirt pocket.

"Sign here please," he said as he pointed to the bottom of

the manifest. After signing, the man thanked her and exited the house. Jessica turned around and looked at the 13 boxes stacked against the dining room wall. The light from the faux stained glass fixture gave each box a shadow which fell across the group of boxes and for some reason, Jessica felt as if they were looking back at her. The configuration appeared ominous, but she shook off the feeling and looked down at the yellow packing slip and pulled it free of the envelope. She removed the ten thousand dollar check and walked into the family room.

"Dad?" she said as she took a seat.

"I don't think I like this."

"The boxes?"

"Anything connected to that place should be far away from you. I don't think it is a good idea to have them here."

"I will make arrangements to get them shipped elsewhere," she said as she handed him the check. "Here, it's made out to you," she said as he looked at it.

"Ten grand! Where did you get this?"

"It is my compensation for being part of Mr. Frazier's team."

"It's made out to me!"

"It's yours. I remember you saying it was costing you about ten thousand from being off work when I was recovering. I wanted to make sure you got it back."

"Honey, this isn't necessary,"

"It's already done," she said with a slight smile. Bob felt as if Jessica was making a lot of progress and seemed to be more alert and able to think clearly. He had been speaking to her more and more with each passing day. While it seemed she was improving, it didn't last. The imagery of Ray slicing Father Abbott's throat would replay in her mind without warning and cause her to jolt and desperately try to think of anything else. At night, she continued to resort to Tequila and her pills before bed and as the weeks passed, her intake went from four shots to six.

The boxes stayed in the kitchen and had been untouched for weeks until one morning while taking two aspirin to combat the effect of a hangover caused by tequila, Jessica walked toward the back wall of the dining room. She looked at the unmarked boxes and wondered what would be inside.

In the same way one would quickly remove a Band-Aid, she picked up a random box and set it on the kitchen table and flipped the lid off the top. Inside she found a SCUBA diving mask that Ray wore when searching the pond, a bright green ribbon from the tree service and Dr. Thornhill's logbook. The majority of the interior of the box was unused, as if someone simply threw a few items into the box and put the lid on top.

She put the lid back on and thought a moment. *Was everything in the trailer boxed up and studied by law enforcement? What did they see? What material is in these boxes?* She put the random box back and removed another one and set it on the kitchen table. After removing the lid, she found Father Abbott's old book and a stack of paper clipped documents with the deed to Gordon's home on top. She then counted seven videotapes and nine audiotapes. She put the lid back on and put the box back among the others when she noticed a box with a black strap hanging out of the side.

Is that my messenger bag?

She pulled the box free from the stack and opened the lid. Inside was her gray, blood-stained messenger bag. She removed it and set it on the table. She looked at it thinking that at one time she considered it lucky, but now she wasn't so sure.

When her father came home, he found Jessica lying on the couch as usual watching whatever was on TV, not even paying attention. He stood over her and moved a strand of hair out of her face.

"You doing okay?"

"Uh huh," she somberly responded. After he changed clothes, he made dinner. The entire time he stirred the pasta sauce on the stove, he thought of how the haunted house in St. Clair had changed her life and if only she hadn't gotten that assignment. He looked back over at the couch as she watched *Wheel of Fortune* with a dazed expression.

After dinner was over, he tried talking to her again about counseling and was shut down almost immediately. Instead of arguing with her, he went to bed early, but not before telling her to hurry up and get the boxes out of the house.

Before going to bed, Jessica walked over to the back wall in the dining room and picked out a random box and moved it to the kitchen table. After she removed the lid, she found a stack of loose paper which had been used as a notepad. Both

Jessica and Dr. Thornhill would scratch down notes of occurrences, dates, times and names. She rifled through the stack and found notes on William O'Keefe.

She recalled that Dr. Thornhill had found out that he reported something to the sheriff's office, but couldn't remember what. She packed the box up and put the lid back on before putting it back among the others and turned out the dining room light. Once more, Jessica opened the cabinet and found the bottle of tequila, but discovered it only had enough for three, maybe four shots. Hoping the remaining liquid would help her sleep, she drank straight from the bottle before popping a Hydromorphone and headed to bed.

For the first time in weeks, Jessica had slipped into a nightmare and began to breathe deeper and deeper as she walked along weeds, fallen trees and rocks. She looked up and saw a boy of nine running as fast as he could. Then the boy fell and his arm got stuck in a hole. Jessica watched as the boy was being pulled downward and then felt something tugging on her arm. She looked down and saw Ray. His body on the ground with his torso being supported by one hand and his other hand grabbing her arm. He pulled her down to the ground where she screamed and curled up in the fetal position. Suddenly, she was now being dragged out of the operations trailer by Deputy Phillips as he bent down to help her.

"Come on, we have to get out of here," he said as her eyes were wide open and she began to hyperventilate. As he pulled her outside, just before the door closed, she could see one last glimpse of the computer screen on the desk. There was a single word in green letters: *farm*

Jessica sprang up in bed. She remembered. She saw the word on the screen and jumped out of bed, soaked with sweat. With damp hair and t-shirt, she left her room and turned the lights on to the dining room. She looked at the boxes and began pulling them off the stack against the wall and onto the table, looking through the contents. *Why did the screen say farm? What was the significance? It had to mean something.* The clock on the stove read 3:37 A.M. and Jessica was wide-awake.

Chapter 15

Bob woke to his alarm, rubbed his eyes and sat up in bed. Another glorious day at the plant was ahead of him. He stood up just as he heard a noise coming from the front of the house and he quickly put on a sweatshirt. Once in view of Jessica, he squinted from the light.

"What are you doing up so early?" he said as he came into view of the dining room table. Seven or eight boxes were opened with files, videotapes and photographs scattered on the table.

"I thought of something last night and I am trying to figure it out."

"What?" Bob asked as his eyes hadn't yet adjusted to the light.

"It all happened so fast when I was being pulled out of the operations trailer and I forgot there was something on the screen, a word, and it means something. I'm just not sure what," she answered. The scattered boxes and files looked to have taken a while to assemble and move around. It seemed she was organizing and grouping the items together.

"How long have you been up?"

"A few hours. I couldn't sleep. I will take a nap this afternoon."

"Is this for your article for *The Post*?"

"Yeah, when I go back I plan on writing about what happened," she explained, never looking up at him as she moved documents around. He didn't like that she seemed to have a sudden interest in the Adler Farm. He would rather she move on and focus on getting back to work.

"Call me if you need me to pick up anything on my way home."

At 8:00 A.M., Jessica grabbed her blood-stained messenger bag and tossed her pocketbook inside and threw her hair up into a bun before heading out the door. She walked down the sidewalk headed for Ruxton Drug and had to convince herself that she actually saw the word on the computer screen as she was dragged out of the trailer and not just in her dream.

Once inside the store, she found a wire rack full of maps. She pulled out a folded map for the state of Pennsylvania and grabbed a package of red pens and TAC Adhesive Putty. She walked to the other side of the store and found a section of shelves which were labeled *Sleep Aids*. After she picked up a box that made a bold promise - *Fall asleep fast and wake refreshed,* she grabbed a Coca-Cola from a self-serve fridge and headed to the cashier.

After walking back to the house, she began looking at the notes Dr. Thornhill had written in her logbook as she drank the Coca-Cola. The notes were neatly written and labeled. She flipped through several pages of notes which mentioned the horse they saw breathing on the first floor of the house. Notes that mentioned Thomas Cafferty, the boy who abused animals in Jessica's neighborhood, and finally she found what she was looking for.

In the logbook were notes handwritten by Dr. Thornhill along with a folded up copy of a police report. William O'Keefe. He was the coach at the elementary school where the Adler's youngest son attended school and played basketball. William O'Keefe's phone number was scrawled on the police report and was barely legible.

Ring. Ring.

"Hello?" a man answered.

"I'm looking to speak with Mr. William O'Keefe."

"This is Will."

"Hi, Will. My name is Jessica Calvert with *The Washington Post* and I am doing a story on the Adler Family murders. I have a police report in front of me that lists you as a witness to an incident regarding a blue Ford station wagon that picked up Scott Adler. Do you happen to remember speaking with the police about this matter?"

"Yes, I do. I even spoke to the police about it not too long ago when they found the car in the pond."

"You did? Was it the same car?"

"It seemed to be although it was missing a luggage rack. When Scott Adler was picked up, I remembered seeing a silver luggage rack on top and the car. The one that was recovered didn't have one."

"Did you see who was driving the blue Ford?"

"I didn't. It was one of those things where you don't really realize what you saw until after it happened."

"I see. Did Scott seem apprehensive about getting in the car?"

"All I could see is that he was talking to someone before he got in the car."

"Did you know that his parents called the Sheriff's office to report that Scott was missing?"

"I didn't. Not until after the murders. I had heard that Scott was reported missing, then he came home and then everyone was murdered."

"I'd like to ask you a few more questions if you don't mind. Do you have a minute or did I catch you at a bad time?"

"I'm fine. Please go ahead."

"Does the name Gordon D'Silva mean anything to you?"

"No."

"Do you by any chance own a farm?"

"Well, I don't now. I lived on a farm when I grew up. My parents' farm."

"When was this?"

"Uh, we sold it in the early seventies. We lived in New Hampshire."

"I see. Just curious. You don't currently own any land or a working farm or do you own any interest in a farm operation?"

"I wish. That would be nice."

"Do you work for a farming operation?"

"No, I am a math teacher and I coach basketball during the season."

"At least you get summers off."

"That would be nice! I work a full-time job over at Yeoman's Hardware and Supply from June to mid-August."

"I understand. Maybe my next article will be on the plight of underpaid school teachers."

"Please allow me to help with that article too."

"Absolutely. Well, that's all the questions I have and I can't thank you enough for your time."

"Glad to help. I am curious though, what's with the questions about farms?"

"Just following up on a lead and I am a little overzealous. I'm running this lead into the ground since it is all I have."

"I see. Well, good luck."

Jessica hung up the phone. It felt good to ask questions. She liked the way it felt to be working again. Even though he didn't provide any information, she easily got back into the rhythm of asking questions. She began making notes in Dr. Thornhill's logbook, updating information about William O'Keefe.

Jessica then unfolded the map of Pennsylvania and laid it across the table. She looked at St. Clair and thought about the word farm. Using a telephone book that could double as a door-stop, she flipped through the pages and found the listing for Carnegie Library of Pittsburgh and called the number.

"Hi. I am looking for a list of all the farms in a certain county, do you know where I might find that information?" Jessica asked. A girl who sounded around her age responded.

"The Cabinet for Agricultural Development puts out an updated list every October. You can also go to the local USDA office."

"Is the updated list available at that library?"

"It is. It's a reference book, so you can't check it out, but you can make copies of pages."

Jessica's Honda Accord was still in St. Clair, but getting to the library from her father's house wouldn't be difficult. Growing up as a teenager in the early 1980s, she was no stranger to public transportation. She walked a very familiar seven blocks from her father's house to the Monongahela Incline, a wooden rail car engineered to carry passengers up the side of Mt. Washington. The rail car was pulled up the side of the mountain by way of a thick, steel cable. The ride up and down was usually pleasant unless it was a Friday night when the rail car would often smell like urine and cheap regurgitated beer.

After a ride in the incline down Mt. Washington and taking the light railway into downtown, she boarded a bus to Oakland. Once in the library she found a helpful assistant with a very thin waist and big hair that had been formed with a half can of hairspray. After walking Jessica toward the back shelves where the reference section was located, Big Hair removed a large floppy book with a navy blue cover and gold lettering.

The assistant handed the book to Jessica and scratched her nose as she spoke.

"This is an annual publication of farms by county. If you're a student needing photocopies, students only pay three cents a page instead of a nickel."

"Thanks."

Once Big Hair walked back to her desk, Jessica photo-copied a few pages which listed every farm in Schuylkill County and slid the copies into her messenger bag.

Feeling tired from being up so early and needing energy to get back home, she considered drinking another Coco-Cola as she took the bus back downtown. While riding the bus, she sat next to a man who wore a Vietnam field jacket and cyclist shorts. He had been staring at a nun sitting across from him, causing her to close her eyes and begin mumbling a prayer. When the bus came to a stop, Jessica got up from her seat and exited the bus as the aroma of ground coffee briefly hit her in the face. Thinking she could probably get more caffeine in a cup of coffee than a Coke, she walked inside.

Immediately confused at what to order, she looked over the menu, which didn't make any sense to her. She stayed out of the way and pretended she was waiting for someone while she listened to what other customers ordered.

The aroma in the coffee shop smelled wonderful, but she still detested the taste. Remembering what Ray told her about coffee, light roast has more caffeine less flavor, dark roast has more flavor less caffeine. She got in line and finally ordered.

"Light roast with cream and sugar."

The coffee had cooled down enough by the time she got back on the light railway and she took a sip. Certainly the cream and sugar had taken the bitterness out of the coffee and the flavor wasn't half bad. She continued to drink it after she got into the Monongahela Incline car.

Since she hadn't ever been exposed to caffeine other than a Coca-Cola from time to time, the amount of caffeine in the coffee surged through her circulatory system. Once back at the house, she used the TAC Putty to adhere the map to the wall in the dining room and began calling the phone numbers of the farms listed on the photocopies. To save her time, she had come up with two questions that she would ask each farmer. If the farmer didn't know much about either, then she could quickly move on.

"Hi, Mr. Hagen my name is Jessica Calvert from *The Washington Post* and I am writing a story that you may be able to help with. Does the name Gordon D'Silva mean anything to you? No? How about the Adler Family?" she asked. The response came back that he knew of the tragedy that occurred, but nothing else. She was prepared for nearly every caller to explain their knowledge of the murders, but was committed to asking in case someone knew something that would reveal more of the incident. Undeterred by the first call, she continued.

"I'm looking to speak with the owner of Parker Farms," she said in a polite tone of voice and asked the same two questions and got similar responses, but this time a more elaborate explanation of the Adler Family murders. The Parkers knew the Adler Family and were extremely upset by what had happened and had even come to tears on the phone.

Jessica made several more phone calls while using the information in the photocopied list to make crude outlines of the farms on the map. She shaded in the farm that knew nothing of Gordon D'Silva or nothing more about the Adler murders. When her father came home, he found his daughter shading in plots of land on a large map of northeast Pennsylvania.

"Is that tacked to the wall?" he asked. He caused her to jump, as she didn't know he was standing behind her in the kitchen.

"You scared me. No, it's putty. Like elementary teachers use to put up posters."

"It doesn't leave marks?"

"No. I promise."

"What are you doing?"

"Research. I am questioning farms. It's all I have to go on at the moment," Bob took a step into the dining room and surveyed the map on the wall. Several areas were shaded. News articles were adhered to the wall along with a list of addresses. Instead of a dining room wall, it looked more like a police investigation. He looked down and saw an empty coffee cup.

"What's this?" he asked as he picked up the Styrofoam cup.

"I drank a cup of coffee today."

"Why?"

"I was sleepy and it helped me keep going. I needed a pick-me-up and I was willing to try anything."

"You hate coffee," he said as he set the cup down.

"It wasn't bad. Cream and sugar helped," she said as he took a few steps around the table. He put his hand on her shoulder and looked into her eyes.

"Look. You're acting strange. I know it has everything to do with what you experienced and I'm sorry it happened to you," he said. Tears started to form in the corner of his eyes. "I can't have anything else hurt my only daughter. I can't even think about it."

"I know."

"You came close. Twice. I just don't want this to lead to anything. Do you understand my concern?"

"I do," she said as she reached her arms around his blue work shirt. He wrapped his arms around her and hugged her tightly. After releasing her from his fatherly embrace, he leaned in and looked at the map once again.

"What do you have shaded in red here?"

"It's the farms I am calling. The lead I have is the word *farm*. It means something and I am trying to figure it out."

"I see. Well, I am going to order a pizza, drink a few beers and watch a game. You wanna join me?"

"Of course."

The pizza arrived and the game began. Jessica sat next to

her father on the couch and watched the entire game, but she mostly thought about the conversation she had with William O'Keefe. She replayed the conversation in her head thinking maybe she missed something, but concluded it to be a dead end. When the game was over, Bob walked back to his room while Jessica brewed a pot of coffee. She drank a few cups with cream and sugar as she looked at the wall in the dining room. The answer had to be somewhere.

She grabbed her blood-stained messenger bag and found her sleeping pills she had bought at the drug store. She popped two pills in her mouth and washed them down with a swig of coffee. At 1:46 A.M., she took a Hydromorphone and finally went to bed. Without any nightmares to wake her up, she slept until 9:30 A.M. and immediately brewed another pot of coffee. She stretched while the coffee maker gurgled and hissed and she took the phone list off the wall.

"Hi, Mr. Simmons my name is Jessica Calvert from *The Washington Post*," she started in and was surprised by the response to her first question. "Does the name Gordon D'Silva mean anything to you?"

"D'Silva or Silva?"

"Either. Does either mean anything to you?"

"Silva is the name of a Doctor at the mine. I used to work there."

"At the mine? The coal mine?" she asked as she feverishly took notes.

"Yes m'am. Locust Valley Coal Mine."

"Locust Valley," she repeated as she wrote down the name. "Would you happen to know if he is related to Gordon D'Silva?"

Chapter 16

Ring. Ring.

"Locust Valley."

"Hi, I'm trying to reach Dr. Silva."

"He's not in today."

"I don't see his home number in the phone book. Do you have that number?"

"Are you an employee? His patients usually don't get his home number and if it is an emergency, we recommend you go to the hospital."

"I understand. I will try and reach him tomorrow, but I was wondering if you could confirm the first name of Dr. Silva. Would it be Peter Silva?"

"It is."

"Oh. Great. Thanks, I'll just try calling tomorrow."

Jessica hung up the phone and updated her notes in the logbook. The excitement of getting closer and finding two pieces of a puzzle that fit together made her bounce in her chair. At the very least, she found a connection to why Gordon would even be in St. Clair. Knowing she would have to wait until tomorrow to reach Dr. Silva, she drank two cups of coffee and called the rest of the farms in Schuylkill County.

In between calls she created a timeline of events beginning with the horse on the first floor then Thomas Cafferty.
Next came the day they found the car in the pond and Ray getting bitten by something. She ended it with the coal miner
outside the trailer and the death of Ray, Henrik and Father
Abbott.

To Jessica, it was a feeling similar to leaving the house for
vacation and thinking that she forgot something. Something
was missing or incomplete. She couldn't shake it and it was
the word that made her feel as if she left something unfin-
ished. *Farm.* She looked over the timeline and tried to find a
possible connection. She then looked at the list of farms and
ran her finger down the column of last names. Silva wasn't on
the list nor D'Silva.

When her father came home, she was working at the dining room table. Carrying a large paper bag, he set it on the
counter and pulled out containers of Chinese food.

"Hey, I got Heng Wall. Fried dumplings, crab rangoon,
sweet and sour chicken and egg rolls," he said as he arranged
the containers on the counter. Jessica thanked her dad and
made a plate and went back to work at the table. While her father sat in front of the TV, she poured over all of the articles
she photocopied about Gordon D'Silva's death.

After taking a bite of crab rangoon, she read articles beginning with his disappearance, his death and then a recent
article when his car was found in the pond. Nothing seemed
to fit even though she felt she had every piece of the puzzle in

front of her. Hours after her father had gone to bed, Jessica conceded the night and hoped for more pieces to the puzzle after speaking with Dr. Silva.

Upon popping two sleeping pills, she got distracted as she thought about the Adler Farm. What if the word meant something about their farm? After digging around in the pile of material on the kitchen table, the pills began to take effect and she turned in for the night.

Forgetting to take a Hydromorphone cocktail, she went to bed only to find herself walking along weeds, fallen trees and rocks. She looked up and saw the same boy of nine running as fast as he could just before he fell and his arm got stuck in the hole. Trying to get away from the cracking sound of bones breaking, she turned around and ran in the opposite direction. Behind her as she ran, she could hear the boy screaming in pain. The sound grew more and more faint as she ran toward a small house with a tiny wooden front porch. She reached front door and opened it, finding herself inside her bedroom.

While Jessica was asleep and dreaming, she had gotten up out of bed. Sleepwalking didn't run in her family and she hadn't ever stood up while sleeping. With her eyes closed, she slowly walked toward the bathroom, her feet sliding across the carpet, not taking full steps. In her dream she heard something behind the bathroom door. Someone was in the bathroom. She could hear the faint scream of the boy in the woods being pulled into the hole, but kept her focus. The lights were out and the door moved a fraction of an inch.

As she was sleeping and walking toward the door, she stopped. The dream began to unfold as she knew someone or something was behind the door. The fear of death crept over her as she came to understand that whatever was behind the door was waiting for her. If she walked through the door, she would die.

While she dreamed, Jessica was standing in front of the bathroom door. Not moving, completely still. While the door didn't move in reality, in her dream the door moved again, only an inch and ever so slightly. She chose to run.

Just as she took off running, Jessica no longer walked as she slept. She ran exactly two feet before hitting her head on her bedroom door and woke up as she was falling to the ground. She looked up at the bathroom. It was dark. Something appeared to be behind the door, and now it wasn't a dream. The door moved slightly and she let out a terrifying scream.

Bob woke and jumped out of bed, running toward his daughter's room. Upon turning on the lights, he found her holding her head and still screaming.

"Honey! I'm here! I'm here! What's wrong?" He knelt down beside her and held her as she continued to look at the bathroom door.

"Let me up. Let me up!" she said as he moved back and stood up. She walked toward the door and kicked it against the back wall before reaching inside and flipping on the light switch.

"What is it? What happened?" he asked as he peered inside the bathroom.

"There was someone behind that door. I was walking. I was, sleepwalking," she answered as she held her head.

"Sleepwalking?"

"I think so."

Her father took her out to the dining room and sat her down, looking at the knot on her head.

"I don't think I can escape this!"

"Escape what?"

"I never had dreams like this until I set foot on that farm."

For the next hour, her father comforted her while she talked about returning the boxes stacked in the dining room. While her father agreed and was relieved at her decision, Jessica couldn't look at him, as it was a lie. The only thing on her mind now was moving to St. Clair.

Chapter 17

Jessica had called a former co-worker at *The Post* and asked if they had a spare room to rent out. Heather Vanderwheele was an education reporter and lived in a run down building which was only a twenty-minute walk to the office. When Jessica called, Heather had been thinking about having extra spending money and the only way to do that would be to get a second job or get a roommate. After nearly a half-hour of catching up, they agreed to terms that benefited both of them. Heather would have a roommate in two weeks.

PNC Bank was a short, fifteen-minute walk from her father's house, but it took Jessica with her injured leg, a full twenty-five minutes. After checking the balance of her bank account, she discovered she only had $1,034.72 in her account. A paltry sum considering she would need to stay at a motel for a substantial amount of time on top of paying rent before she ever saw a paycheck from *The Post*. After withdrawing eighty dollars in cash for expenses, she pocketed the money and limped back home while wondering how to maximize her funds.

Back at the house Jessica organized the thirteen boxes of scattered documents, books and objects, condensing the contents into seven boxes of categorized material. Bob took most of the day to pack the boxes and Jessica's luggage into his Taurus as if he were solving a puzzle, ensuring that every nook and cranny was optimally filled in the backseat and trunk.

They hit the road at 8:15 A.M. and traveled for four and a half hours. For much of the trip, Bob kept expressing pride that she was moving forward and mentioned he would re-subscribe to *The Post* so he wouldn't miss a single story. Feeling the weight of the guilt that came with her deceptive plan, she kept her responses to a minimum, saying she was tired from not sleeping well the night before. Once in Schuylkill County, Bob pulled into the parking lot of the Sheriff's Office where Jessica's car had been parked in the back lot as a courtesy. After speaking with a Deputy inside and obtaining her keys, she walked out and helped her dad move everything from his car to hers. Once the Accord was packed, she gave her dad a hug.

"Don't take candy from strangers," he said with a smile as he pulled five hundred dollars from his pocket.

"Don't drink so much. I worry about you."

"I won't," he replied as he palmed the cash into her hand. "If you need more, you call me. Understand?"

"Ugh. Dad!" she said while exhaling a deep sigh.

While she was thankful for the money, the thought of him funding her lie was difficult to bear. Bob took her keys from her other hand and unlocked the driver's side door.

"I don't want to hear it. You just be safe on the road. I

want to make sure it starts up." Bob reached into the car and turned the key, listening for any kinks in the engine as it turned over. "Like a kitten." They said their goodbyes before he hit the road back to Pittsburgh.

After getting into her Accord, Jessica drove straight to the Mill Street Motel and hurried inside the front office. An attendant came out from a small room behind the counter wearing a green vest and glasses. He was a scrawny man with white hair and a scrawny voice to match.

"Can I help you?" he asked. Jessica could hear the sound of a game show coming from a TV in the back office.

"Hi, I need a room and I was wondering if I booked a room for seven days or more, could I get a discount? I might be able to pay in cash."

"I think we can make some kind of arrangement. Let me see what I can do," he said with a helpful and sincere smile. By 2:00 p.m., she finished moving everything from her car to her room and turned the air conditioner to the maximum cold setting. While she cooled off, she sat on the edge of the bed with her notepad on her lap and a BIC pen in her hand. Sweating from manual labor, she wiped her forehead and tucked loose strands of hair behind her ear. With her finger in the circular dial of a rotary phone, she dialed the number she had been waiting to call.

Ring. Ring.

"Hi, I'm trying to reach Dr. Silva."

"One moment please."

Click. Hum. Click.

"Dr. Silva's office," a female voice said.

"Hi, my name is Jessica Calvert and I am trying to reach Dr. Silva."

"Is your husband a patient?"

"No. I am with *The Washington Post.* I just have a few questions."

"Oh. Okay. Hang on please, I have to put you on hold." Jessica waited and made circles on her notepad wondering if the coal mine would somehow have a connection with the Adler murders. After drawing over twenty circles, a man's voice came on the line.

"Hello. This is Dr. Silva." His voice sounded old and tired.

"Hi Dr. Silva, my name is Jessica Calvert with *The Washington Post* and I was wondering if you could answer a few questions for a story I am working on."

"I suppose. I am very busy."

"I understand. I will try to be very brief. Are you the only physician at Locust Valley?"

"I am employed full-time by the company. I handle all medical care for the workers."

"Has there ever been a collapse at the mine?"

"There have been many over the years."

"How long have you worked there?"

"I have been here since '67."

"I see. And did you always practice under the last name Silva?" she asked. This time there was a pause and a slight hesitation in his voice.

"Is this about my brother?"

"Your brother? Gordon D'Silva?"

"My family changed our name except for Gordie. Are you doing a story on him? Is that what this is about?"

"Yes. It is part of the story. May I ask why you changed your names?"

"My father went through his whole life having to correct people on the spelling of his last name and we were tired of doing it also, so we changed the name before I went to medical school. Gordie didn't because he was in the military at the time."

"That's understandable. Were you shocked to hear that your brother's body had been found after all these years?"

"After our parents died, I distanced myself from my brother. He was never the same after Vietnam. The way he was acting in the months before he disappeared, I thought he had committed suicide. When he was found, I looked at it as a man was found, not my brother. As far as I am concerned, he died in Vietnam."

"I'm sorry to hear that. Did he visit you often? Is that why he was found in the pond in St. Clair?"

"He did visit me often. Usually to borrow money."

"Did you know that the day before the Adler murders he deposited just under ten thousand dollars into his personal account?"

"I didn't. Sounds like a lot of money for him."

"Did you ever give him money?"

"Sometimes. Maybe a hundred dollars or less each time."

"Did you know they recovered a murder weapon in his car?"

"I read that. Yes," he said, which ended in a long pause. In her early days as a reporter, she would have spoken during the pause, but since then she had learned to be quiet and to see if the interviewee said anything else. "I don't think he did it. He wasn't the kind of person to hurt anyone."

"I see. I just have a few more questions and I will let you…" she started to say before being interrupted.

"I'm sorry, but I have to go now, I am very busy as I have patients waiting on me."

"Is it okay if I come visit you later in the week?"

"Possibly. Give it a shot. No promises."

Upon hanging up the phone, Jessica tried to piece together the correlation between the coal mine, Dr. Silva, Gordon D'Silva and the Adler Family. With her mind racing, Jessica began flipping the lids off the file boxes and grabbing documents, photocopies and handwritten notes.

In an effort to create a timeline, she stood at the wall across from her bed and used TAC Adhesive and adhered the article written about the disappearance of Gordon D'Silva. Next, she tacked up a photocopied newspaper story about the murder of the Adler family. Jessica continued the timeline of events until she ended with the map of Schuylkill County.

As she stood at the foot of her bed and looked at the time-

line that spanned from one side of the wall to the other, she
repeatedly tapped her pen on the side of her cheek. Thinking
the mine was somehow important; she made a note where
Locust Valley Coal Mine was located by circling the location
on her map. Then the thought crossed her mind that she
would speak to Dr. Silva again and when she did, she wanted
to have more questions to ask him. Unable to write the questions as fast as she thought of them, she scribbled as quickly
as possible.

Did you know the Adler family?

Did your brother know the Adler family?

Was your brother acquainted with anyone else in St. Clair?

A small table in her motel room became her work desk.
She took out Dr. Thornhill's logbook and began writing out
some of the key words Dr. Silva had said in their conversation.

- *Handles all medical care for the workers.*

- *Gordon visited him often. Usually to borrow money.*

- *A hundred dollars or less each time.*

- *Doesn't think he murdered the Adler family. Wasn't that kind of*
person.

Jessica hung onto the belief that Gordon didn't murder
the Adler family. The responses which came from the Ouija
board had been accurate and if there was any doubt, Dr. Silva
explaining his brother wasn't the type of person to hurt anyone, solidified it for Jessica. She stood up and walked over to
the map on the wall and revisited the next set of questions for
Dr. Silva.

She looked at her watch and thought she might be able to get over to the mine right at 5 P.M. if she hurried. She jumped in her car and sped down the highway toward Locust Valley. As she approached the entrance, a man in a uniform stepped out of the guard booth and held up his hand up for her to stop. She rolled down her window as the guard spoke.

"Who are you here to see?"

"Dr. Silva."

"Was he expecting you?"

"Yes," she said as she pulled out her press badge. "I'm from *The Washington Post* and he said to come by and see if he was available."

"Sorry, he already left for the day."

"Oh. Well, I will try again."

"If you don't have an appointment, I can't let you through. Make sure you get him to put you on the list."

Instead of driving back to the motel, she drove to the sheriff's office and parked her car. While walking to the entrance, she heard someone shouting in her direction.

"Hey!" a man shouted in a shaky, unsure voice. She turned her head and saw Deputy Phillips headed to his truck with keys in his hand. "What are you doing back here?"

"I was looking for you."

"For me? What for?"

"I won't take long. I just have a few questions."

"Well, you wanna come inside?" he asked as he gestured toward the back entrance.

Deputy Phillips walked Jessica inside as they continued talking. The second she brought up the day of the shooting, he lowered his voice to a whisper.

"We had to leave a few things out of the report we filed with the state."

"Like what?"

"The weird stuff going on there. The ghosts and the guy being possessed," he said as he walked her into his office and closed the door.

"You left it out?"

"Sheriff said we would be tied up for months and we'd be subjected to psychiatric evaluations and it wouldn't go well. Have you seen the house recently?" Deputy Phillips asked as his voice returned to a normal pitch.

"No. I just got in town today."

"The trailers are now wrapped in plastic and there is crime scene tape everywhere."

"Sealed up?"

"Yeah. The family of that rich guy sold the property to the county. They are going to tear it all down, but they can't find anyone to do it. Everyone is scared to touch it," Deputy Phillips said as he looked out his office window, making sure no one was listening, as some conversations were known to travel beyond the open-ceiling offices.

"So what are you doing here?"

"I have a few questions."

"Shoot."

"Dr. Silva."

"The doctor at the mine?"

"Did you know he was related to Gordon D'Silva?"

"Yes. Although we didn't find this out until after the guy was found in his car in the pond."

"Is there an investigation going on?"

"Not really. The State Police are calling it a murder-suicide."

"He didn't murder the Adler family."

"How do you know that?" he asked.

"Long story. I don't have any proof though. You got anything else on this case?"

"I don't know. I can pull the file."

"Could you?"

"Hang on. I'm not supposed to do this so you're gonna owe me one," he said as he stood up and opened his office door. Jessica watched as he tried to appear casual as he walked toward the filing cabinets, yet he couldn't have looked more suspicious. With no one paying any attention to him, he opened a drawer while Jessica looked around his office and found a photo of Deputy Phillips holding a white cat as he stood next to a Christmas tree.

"I hope I don't get in trouble for this," he exhaled as he entered his office and plopped the file on his desk before opening it.

"I can at least make it worth your while. I'll give you a little side money if you like."

"Well, I guess I'd take a pack of cigarettes?"

"What?"

"I'd take a pack of cigarettes."

"You smoke?"

"I kind of have to. Part of the job."

"How's that?"

"Keeps me going. Keeps me awake."

"I just started drinking coffee, but I also take painkillers to help me sleep," she said as she reached into her messenger bag and pulled out her prescription pill bottle.

"Hydromorphone? Better keep that out of sight."

"Why?"

"People will steal them from you. Those go for about ten dollars a pill 'round here. We've got hundreds of 'em in an evidence locker labeled under the brand name Dilaudid. Big problem in these parts," he said as she put the bottle back in her bag.

"Good to know. Count me out for cigarettes though. Coffee is okay."

"Yeah, I drink coffee too. Stimulants help with the long hours," he said as he picked up a paper from the file. "I cannot be more serious. Don't tell anyone I let you see this. Got it? I mean no one."

"Okay."

"Say I promise. This could mean my job. Seriously."

"I, Jessica Calvert, promise not to say anything to anyone ever again as long as I live," she responded in a sarcastic manner. He read the notes to her as she looked at the photos of the car being pulled out of the pond. She saw herself in the photos as well as Ray and Henrik. As Deputy Phillips pulled back the corners of a few papers in the folder, he found one in particular and slid it out, laying it on top.

"Sheriff Haydon questioned Dr. Silva on the 8th and here are his notes," he said as he slid the paper over to Jessica. The notes were vague and didn't offer her anything new except for an answer to one of her questions. Looking at his notes, Jessica read a single line handwritten by Sheriff Haydon.

Does not know the Adler Family.

"I questioned Dr. Silva and he stated that his brother visited him often. Do you know if Gordon D'Silva visited anyone else or knew anyone here?"

"Yes. He did. Hang on. Let me find that. The guy that knew Gordon was questioned."

"Over in St. Clair?"

"Yeah, here it is. A man by the name of Clay Samson," Deputy Phillips said as he slid a single piece of paper toward Jessica that had been torn from a notepad. "He was a friend of Gordon D'Silva."

Jessica read the notes and found a few things of interest.

Long-time friend of G. D'Silva.

Vietnam together.

Was going to start a fly fishing guide business in the Poconos.

Doesn't think Gordon killed the family.

No comment on suicide.

"This is it?"

"It seems so. Deputy Matthews was sent to question him."

"This guy is a lead! He could have more information. Why wasn't he brought in and questioned?" she asked, getting excited.

"Keep your voice down," he said as he began gathering the papers together and sorting them. "I don't know. All of this was sent to the state police in a report. We didn't do much with this as we were told not to. It's out of our hands."

"Clay Samson," she repeated as she used her pen to take notes in her notepad. "You definitely earned a pack of cigarettes. I could use a coffee."

Moments later, Jessica followed Deputy Phillips' truck down North Center Street and parked in front of a convenience store. Once inside she bought a pack of Marlboro's and a to-go cup of weak coffee which was only tolerable after she added cream and sugar. Taking her purchases outside, she walked up to Deputy Phillips who was leaning on his truck.

"Thanks," he said as he took the pack from her and repeatedly smacked the end of the red and white package against his palm. Jessica nodded. "Please don't put any of this in the newspaper. They will know it was me," he said in a worried tone.

"Of course they will know it was you. I'm listing you as a source."

"Please don't kid about that," he said exhaling as he got into his red Chevy truck. She smiled as she sipped her coffee and stood on the sidewalk watching him light up a cigarette.

"You know those are bad for you, right?" Jessica hollered out.

"Aren't all stimulants bad for you?" Phillips replied with a grin and a cigarette dangling from his mouth.

As he drove away, Jessica turned around and walked to a payphone. She set her coffee on a small metal shelf near the phone and removed a few coins from her pocket. Looking at the phone book, she found the name Clay Samson and called the number.

"Hello?" a woman answered.

"Hi. I'm looking to speak with Clay Samson."

"Try the Wolf Reed Tavern," she replied just before she coughed and hung up. After looking up the number, she inserted more coins and punched in the numbers.

"Wolf Tavern," a man answered with music playing in the background.

"I'm trying to reach Clay Samson."

"Yeah, he's serving customers at the moment. Can you hang on?"

"Actually I was going to swing by. Just wanted to make sure he was there."

"He works 'til eleven tonight."

"Okay. Thanks!"

Having to stop at a few gas stations to ask for directions, she finally found Wolf Reed Tavern and parked her car. Once inside, she scanned the tables and found that all were taken.

Only a few stools at the bar were open. The jukebox near the only pool table in the bar blared hits from the '70s and the fog of cigarette smoke burned her eyes. As she sat on a stool between two men wearing blue jumpsuits and covered in black dust, the bartender approached her and yelled over the music.

"Whaddya have?"

"Two shots of Chimalhucan Tequila."

"We don't have Chimal, but we have Patron."

"That's fine," she said not really knowing if it was fine. Since she only drank to help fall asleep, she wondered if it was a good move. When the bartender came back with her shots, she asked about Clay.

"I'm looking for Clay Samson."

"I'm Clay," he replied, wondering what a young pretty girl wanted with him. She looked out of place as most of the customers came from the mine after their shift.

"I was wondering if I could ask you a few questions."

"What about? Are you from the bank?"

"No. I have a few questions about Gordon D'Silva." Jessica said as she fidgeted with one of her shot glasses. Clay responded by raising his voice over the guitar solo on the juke box.

"You a police officer or something?" Jessica leaned forward trying to gain leverage over the loud music and hollered out a response.

"No. A reporter,"

"I get a break in a half hour. If you want to ask me ques-

tions, I will be out back for a smoke break. You're welcome to
join me."

"Okay. Thanks. I'll wait," she said. He nodded and walked
away to serve another customer. A large man with a beard and
a throaty, grumbling voice turned to her.

"You sure you wanna down that tequila? You look like a
buck ten. You'll be shitfaced after one of those," he said as he
smiled and held a cigarette between his fingers. Jessica picked
up a shot glass and downed one and then the other and looked
at the giant in the blue jumpsuit. He laughed and pointed to
her as he looked at Clay.

"Get her two more on me," he said as he turned back to
Jessica. "Holy shit. Well done. You want one?" he asked as he
chuckled and slung his pack of Marlboro's at her causing three
cigarettes to slide out making them easier to grab. Thinking it
would make her seem more likeable, she grabbed one and put
it to her lips. The giant flipped his Zippo and sparked a flame.
The first cigarette of her life was lit and she took it slow and
easy knowing she could cough at any second. Trying not to
give away that she was a rookie, she spoke to the giant as she
barely inhaled the smoke from the cigarette. He asked her what
newspaper she worked for and she asked questions about the
mine and if he knew Dr. Silva.

"I know who he is, but I haven't had to go see him.
Hopefully never will."

When it was time for a break, Clay Samson tapped the
bar as he walked out from behind it to get her attention. He

walked toward a door leading to a kitchen while Jessica excused herself and took her fading cigarette with her. She followed Clay through the kitchen and out the back door. Only then did she remember that there was no reason to think he couldn't have killed the entire Adler family. Feeling a buzz from the tequila and alertness from the nicotine, she felt good. A high feeling of inebriation and stimulation she hadn't ever experienced. The back of the Wolf Reed Tavern was all gravel and a few of the employees' cars were parked around a large green dumpster. A light on a telephone pole illuminated the area where they stood.

"Thanks for speaking with me."

"No problem. You doing a story on Gordie?" he asked as he watched her remove a small notepad and a pen from her back pocket.

"Well, sort of. He is part of it. How long were you friends?"

"We were in the same unit in Vietnam. I got hurt and was awarded the Purple Heart and he would come by the hospital to check on me. We were the only ones in our unit to be from Pennsylvania so we kind of held on to that."

"Did he come to St. Clair to see you often?" she asked as she put out her cigarette on the brick wall behind her and dropped it on the ground.

"He did. We were going to go into business together and he was working on getting his half of the money."

"What business?"

"We love to fish. Fly-fishing is something we talked about in Vietnam and we thought we would set up a fly-fishing guide business. You know, take these rich doctors and lawyers out to secret spots and we knew all the good spots. I been fishing up at the Poconos since I was a boy."

"So you were good friends. You have any thoughts on his suicide?" she asked. He flicked his cigarette and stood silent before he eventually crossed his arms. She hit a nerve.

"Many of us that came back from the war were prone to suicide. Even I thought about it from time to time. Now, I'm not saying that he wasn't exempt from it, or even that he never thought about it, but I just don't think he did it. We had plans. We were going to start a business and he didn't seem like he was even close to suicide," Clay answered as he took out a pack of cigarettes and casually handed one to Jessica and lit his, handing his lighter off to her. She lit hers, careful not to inhale too much and handed the lighter back. Unsure if she looked casual and comfortable holding and smoking a cigarette, she did her best to act like it while going back to her notes.

"So you think he was murdered?"

"I do."

"Do you think he murdered the Adler family?"

"Absolutely not and I want you to quote me on that." he said as he pointed at her and stood with his feet apart in an aggressive manner. "You hear? His best friend who knew him well says that he absolutely did not murder those people. No way."

"I'll make a note of that," she said as she scribbled down his words. "I'd like to ask you about money that Gordon deposited into an account that prompted a visit from the IRS. Do you know anything about that?"

"Yes. Gordie sold a portion of land he owned to his brother."

"Dr. Silva?"

"Yeah. He and Gordie were given like, I don't know, $200,000 after their parents died. His brother said he wanted to invest in land and someday Gordie could collect a half million, sort of like a retirement investment."

"When was this?"

"After Vietnam. His parents died and his older brother wouldn't let him have his half of the money thinking that Gordie would have just pissed it away, which he would have. I guess it was a good move because when it was time to make an investment in the business, he asked his brother for enough to get started. After bugging him for three or four months, finally he gave him the money. Ten grand."

"Hmm…," her pen scratched and scribbled while she thought about how Dr. Silva had lied to her about the money. "So, he finally caved in and gave him the money and he was ready to start the business with you?"

"Yep."

"And then what?"

"A few days later, Gordie went missing."

"Okay. And he was never found until the car was pulled

from the pond?"

"Yep."

"Right. Okay." she replied as she continued to take notes. She wrote down everything as he continued to speak.

"We were putting in ten thousand each. I had sold my motorcycle and my knife collection and got my money to-gether. That would buy us a boat and gear, but we also had plans to build a marina and a boathouse. If Gordon could have convinced his brother to sell his half of the farm, we would have been set.

Jessica stopped writing. Her cigarette dropped from her fingers. She slowly looked up at Clay.

"Farm?"

"Yeah. It was land that was fenced off and trees were planted," he said as he used hand gestures to depict rows of trees.

"Trees? A tree farm?"

"Yep."

"Holy shit, Clay. Where is it located?" she asked. Her shoulders, hands and arms stopped moving, frozen from shock. Clay shrugged his shoulders.

"I don't know. Not too far from here though," he said as he flicked his cigarette.

Chapter 18

Jessica could have kissed Clay, but he was old and scruffy and had been burned by decades of recreational drugs. The biggest lead yet, Jessica paid and tipped him a ten-dollar bill and left the bar before heading back to the motel. She flipped open the logbook as fast as she could and began writing down her notes in an organized and comprehensible format. As she sat at her makeshift desk, she began to feel the effects of fatigue. In the middle of copying her notes to the logbook, she jumped up and walked to the front office.

The counter where guests were helped was quiet and the attendant was absent. In the lobby was a potted plant, two empty chairs and two vending machines. One vending machine was for snacks, the other dispensed cigarettes. Jessica deposited quarters into a slot and pulled the knob for Marlboro's. As she reached down into the tray, the same attendant wearing the same green vest and glasses approached the counter

"Can I help you?" he asked. Jessica could hear the sound of a baseball game coming from an office behind the desk.

"Coffee. I need coffee."

Back at the room, Jessica lit up a Marlboro, inhaled two

lungs full and drank her cup of coffee as she began to fit new found pieces to the puzzle. The stimulants kept her awake and jittery until 2:17 A.M. when she felt fatigue take up residence in her body. After changing into a large t-shirt, she took out two Hydromorphone pills and set them on the nightstand. Pulling back the covers, she slid into bed and watched reruns of a TV show called *Three's Company*. Nearly an hour later, she opened her eyes to a darkened and silent room as the TV was now off. An unexplainable feeling crept over her that there were people in her room.

"There's a lot of blood. Hold still," said a deep and calm voice which sounded as if it came from across the room. Jessica's eyes widened and her muscles tightened. Only the light from the street lamps outside that shone through the small separation of the curtain gave off the only light in the room. She summoned every ounce of courage to slightly turn her head and look in the direction where the voice came from. In the darkness she could see the outline of a man standing in the corner of her room. He spoke again in a calm and quiet voice.

"The blood is seeping," Jessica's eyes slowly grew accustomed to the low light enabling her to see the outline of several men standing in a single file line. The light coming from the streetlights outside was enough to make out that the men were wearing under shirts and boxer shorts, yet it was too dark to make out their faces.

Without moving her head, Jessica looked out from the extreme corners of her eyes and could see that the men standing in line spanned from the corner of the room up to her bed. Unable to see how long the line extended, she once again summoned the courage to slightly turn her head and saw that the line extended to the bathroom door. The men in line seemed to talk to each other under their breath the way customers would while standing in line for a teller at a bank.

Paralyzed by fear, she couldn't move as the creeping feeling that something was about to happen swept over her. In a moment of panic, she flipped the covers off and ran for the door. She gripped the knob and suddenly awoke, still in her bed. While it was a dream, the panic in her chest and the sweat soaking her clothing and sheets was real. The TV was still on and laughter from a TV audience could be heard. Catching her breath, she got out of bed and put on a pair of jeans while wiping the sweat from her brow. After grabbing the key, she walked out of her room to calm down.

After the near sleepless night, Jessica downed three cups of coffee and eventually felt the caffeine doing its job. At 8:28 A.M., she sat in her Honda Accord in the parking lot of the county clerk's office waiting for it to open. While she waited, she sat in the driver's seat with Dr. Thornhill's logbook in her lap. She reviewed the notes until she saw an employee unlock the glass front door of the clerk's office. Jessica gathered her things and walked inside, immediately filling out a records request. The attendant looked at the form with a frown.

"I'm sorry, but we don't file our deeds by last name of ownership. We can pull deeds by Tax Parcel Number, Auditor's File Number or by Address."

"Oh. I don't know the address. How would I find out who owns a farm?"

"Well, here in the office we usually look through an annual record book, but it isn't always accurate. Did you check the annual publication? We have a copy here," the woman said as she turned around and pulled out the large floppy book with a navy blue cover and gold lettering.

"I did. I went through it and I didn't find the last name I was looking for."

"Well, maybe I can help. What kind of farm is it?"

"A tree farm."

"Oh! Well, it wouldn't be in here," she said as she closed the floppy book and put it away. Jessica furrowed her brow thinking she had been wasting her time. She watched as the woman reached down toward the bottom of a shelf and removed a similar floppy book, but with a green cover. "A property like that would be listed in the forestry landowners record. Tree farms are registered under wildlife and forestry. Here, let's take a look."

"No wonder I couldn't find it."

"Now, which farm are you looking for? Is it this owner's name on the form here?" she asked as she picked up Jessica request.

"It is."

"Okay. Silva," she said out loud as she turned the pages and followed her finger down a list and easily found the name. "Here it is, first name Peter, 766 Cave Mill Road, Middleport, Pennsylvania, Schuylkill County. Now do you need the copy of the deed or…" she asked as she watched Jessica make quick notes in her notepad.

"Actually, this is all I need for right now. Thank you!"

"You're welcome! Glad to help, come back if you need anything else."

Jessica jumped into her car and unfolded a map, searching for Middleport, Pennsylvania and quickly drove toward Highway 209. Once on the highway, she steered the car while looking for Cave Mill Road.

"Cave Mill runs off Washington," she said to herself as she drove toward Middleport. Twenty-five minutes later she found Cave Mill Road, a scenic drive with trees on both sides with wildlife bounding and scurrying at the sound of Jessica's Honda winding around curves. The excitement of getting closer to finding a new puzzle piece made the speed of her car increase as she hurried around the corners. She sped past a metal gate that was blocking a dirt road and hit the brakes and came to a stop. She looked in her rearview mirror and saw no traffic behind her. She put the car in reverse and backed up to where she saw the gate.

An old, flimsy sign hung on the gate that read No *Trespassing Private Property/Hunters will be Prosecuted* but no mention of the address. She looked around, still no traffic. Thinking that she was probably in the right place, she pulled her car off the side of the road next to the gate, cut the engine off and got out of her car.

A dirt path could be seen beyond the gate and it disappeared deep into the forest. She locked her car and ducked in between the separations of the gate and walked along the path. The sound of critters scurrying could be heard around her as she took steps amongst the trees, but kept to the path. She was mindful of snakes and kept an eye out for movement that could cost her a bite. As she progressed into the forest, she thought that she might not be on the right property as nothing looked like a tree farm, instead trees were aimlessly scattered around the land.

She looked around and saw nothing, but could hear movement that didn't sound like a critter scurrying. The sounds were separated as if someone was taking strides. Walking. *Where was it coming from?* She turned around and saw movement between the limbs and trunks of the scattered trees. *Was it an animal? Was it a person approaching?*

She turned around and began jogging with a limp, ignoring the pain. She hurried up the path away from the noise coming from behind her. She picked up the pace and ran until she saw a clearing. Running toward open sky, she ran out into a row of trees. Hundreds of trees, planted in hundreds of rows.

"A tree farm," she said to herself as she slowed down and turned, looking behind her. No noise. Silence. Nothing was moving behind her. She walked quickly between the rows of trees which seemed to go on forever. Every ten rows she walked between, there seemed to be ten more rows ahead of her. Suddenly she felt a warmth come over her, an unexplainable feeling of knowing she was in the right place. The word farm on the screen in the operations trailer had led her here and she could feel she was exactly where she was supposed to be.

"This is it."

Now what am I supposed to do? She continued to walk among the rows of trees and quickly discovered she was lost. *Where did I enter?* She thought. She began an attempt to retrace her steps and head toward where she entered. When the sky began to grow dim, she began to jog. She jogged to where she thought she could find the path. As the sky grew darker, Jessica became more nervous. After fifty rows of trees, she found an unkempt section of weeds, fallen trees and rocks. Now to search for the path, she began to jog faster and felt the pain throb in her leg. With the rows of trees on her right and the forest to her left, she jogged and saw a blur out of her left eye. When she would turn her head, she would see nothing, but as she jogged she could see out of her peripheral vision, a boy running in the forest.

She found the path and stopped running and listened for movement. She couldn't hear anything. No noise other than birds calling out hundreds of yards away. As she hurried toward the gate, she saw her car. Upon slipping through the separations of the gate, she got into her car and sped away.

Chapter 19

On the way back to the Mill Street Motel, Jessica stopped at a liquor store and purchased four mini bottles of bottom shelf Vodka for ninety-nine cents each. After tossing them into her purse, she drove to the motel and parked in front of her door.

Once inside, she quickly entered her room and walked up to the map and raised her right hand placing her finger on Middleport, a borough in Schuylkill County. She traced along Cave Mill Road looking for where the tree farm was located. She then used a black marker to crudely circle the boundaries of the farm. She stood back and looked at the map thinking she found the answer to the green letters on the screen. Knowing she had to go back and look around, she decided she shouldn't do it alone.

Ring. Ring.

"Schuylkill County Sheriff's Office."

"Deputy Phillips, please."

Click. Hum.

"Deputy Phillips"

"Hey. The article about you showing me the police report came out today."

"I hope you're kidding."

"Yep. Kidding. I don't want you to lose your job and not be able to buy kitty food," she said as she smiled. He turned in his chair and looked at the photo on his desk.

"That was my high school cat. He died."

"What is a high school cat?"

"I had it all through high-school," he replied. A smirk appeared on her face.

"Well, I am calling you because I need some help. Would you be willing to accompany me to a farm tomorrow to make sure I'm safe?"

"You need me to bring my gun?"

"Yes, and the bullet in your front shirt pocket," she said. A long pause followed before he spoke up.

"Gertie," he said as he propped his head up on his desk with his other hand and exhaled. "You spoke to my sister."

"I confess. She told me about the bullet in your shirt pocket."

"Yeah, well that never happened. She just likes to spread the rumor that I carry a bullet in my pocket like that guy in The Andy Griffith Show."

"That's what sisters are for. So will you help?"

"When?"

"Tomorrow."

"Oh. Can't. I promised my mom I would help her paint."

"Paint what?"

"The kitchen and her bedroom."

"You sound like a good son."

"She needs help and my sister refuses to paint."

"Well, I can't wait. I have to go tomorrow."

"Sorry. Wish I could help."

She mentioned his high school cat again, poking fun at him before hanging up, only to pick up the phone and begin dialing. She called her dad knowing he wasn't home yet and left a message on his answering machine.

Apartment is great, Dad.

Getting back into the swing of things.

Will call you again soon.

Love you.

Feeling the guilt about lying to him, she decided to block out the thought and head to the Buckhorn Café to get a cup of coffee to go. On the way, she pondered the importance of the farm. What was it that she needed to find? She then thought about the operations trailer and how she wished it was still available to her. She recalled sitting next to Ray as they tried to get a response.

"Explain ribbons," she said as Ray typed on the keyboard. Inside the room, the Ouija board moved, spelling out the question. The first question Jessica asked took fifteen minutes to respond. This time, it was more than forty minutes.

"Maybe we should only ask yes or no questions," said Henrik. Soon after a letter appeared on the screen.

Jessica parked her Honda, went inside and ordered a cup of coffee to go. After paying sixty cents, she got back in her car and felt the pull and urge for more nicotine in her system.

Reaching into her purse, she grabbed a cigarette and a lighter while steering the wheel with one hand and managing a curve in the road. After lighting up, she tossed the lighter into her purse and took a sip of her hot coffee.

When she got back to her room, she turned on the TV and sat at her little desk and reviewed her notes. A movie was on TV about a police detective in the 1970s who was searching for a missing woman. He was showing everyone in town a photo of her as a cigarette dangled from his mouth. Jessica would look at her notes and back up at the TV every so often.

At one point, she saw the detective use his lit cigarette to light another one, just as Mr. Wood would do when she was in his office. Once the new one was lit, he flicked the old cigarette into a storm drain. After working for sometime on the possible meaning of the farm, she decided she needed a break and another cup of coffee. As she headed toward the front office of the motel, she lit a new cigarette just as the detective did on TV. Once it was lit, she flicked the old one in between two parked cars and kept walking to the front office.

The counter where guests were helped was once again quiet and the attendant was still absent. She couldn't hear the baseball game this time, only the two vending machines which hummed with power.

"Hello?" Jessica hollered. The attendant finally came out wearing the same green vest and glasses.

"Can I help you?" he asked in his scrawny voice.

"Could I please get another cup of coffee?"

"You know this isn't something we offer other guests?" he said with a smile as he filled a cup in the office. "I just do it to help you out."

"Well, I can't thank you enough. I recently became a coffee drinker and I can't seem to get enough. This way you're saving me a trip."

"Glad I could help."

Once back in the motel room, she sat on the bed and tried to relax, thinking about the trip she would make the next day.

Ring. Ring.

"Hello?"

"It's me," said Deputy Phillips.

"Change your mind? Can you go?"

"Sorry. I can't, but I thought of something."

"What's that?"

"If you come by the station, I have something for you."

"It's not a gun is it?"

"Lord, no. It's a radio. If you need help for any reason, you can extend the antenna and call for help."

"Aww. You're worried about me?"

"I worry about everyone. Plus, you don't have a good track record in this town."

"Well, thank you. I will come by tomorrow. What time?"

"Be here at 2:00 P.M. I can't give it to you before then."

"Okay, see you tomorrow. Thanks!"

The detective movie was still on and once the credits finally rolled, she felt like she could run a marathon with the amount of stimulants surging through her veins. Her new-found energy caused her to stand at the foot of her bed and look at the timeline which spanned the room. If someone were to enter, they might think she had gone crazy. The amount of material on the wall was alarming, but she knew what she was doing. She felt calm, yet frustrated, feeling like she might have hit another dead end.

Opting for two Hydromorphone pills instead of one, she washed them down with a swig from a mini bottle of vodka followed by a hot shower. She got in bed and curled up between the covers and was asleep in minutes without a single nightmare. When she awoke the next morning, she was in the exact position she fell asleep in. Once she was coherent enough to sit up and look at the alarm clock, the time read 11:16 a.m. She quickly put on jeans, a t-shirt and threw her hair up in a ponytail and brushed her teeth.

The first item on her to-do-list meant she had to drive to Yeoman's Hardware and Supply. Being a thin brunette in a male dominated retail store meant she had more help than necessary. After explaining her need for a compass, a tall man with salt and pepper hair disappeared into the back of the store and returned with a green lensatic compass. It looked complicated as he opened it up. She could see it had a lens and a sight wire.

"Good for land based navigation," the man said with a smile as he handed it to her. "You can get real technical with it or you can just use it to get a bearing on your direction."

After a brief conversation about magnetic fields, she spent little time at the cash register before she was back in her Accord. Knowing that her funds were depleting, she could only hope she would have enough to cover rent once she arrived in Washington. Arriving in the parking lot of the County Clerk's Office, she entered the front door and approached the counter with a smile after she saw that the woman had recognized her from before.

"You're back? Find what you were looking for?"

"I did. Thanks to you. I was wondering where I might find plots and land surveys?"

"The County PVA's office or public works and sometimes the community development department or even the local planning office keeps copies of plots. Depends on what you're looking for. Is it the farm you are wanting the land survey for?"

"It is."

"Hmmm…the County PVA would have it. Let me call over there real quick to make sure."

After the phone call, Jessica was directed to an office across the street. A few minutes later, Jessica stood at the counter and waited until a man walked around the corner carrying three reams of copy paper. It appeared that he enjoyed many good cheeseburgers over the years and as a result of his large gut and bad back, he grunted when he set the copy paper on a nearby desk. After walking toward her with a charming smile and warmth in his eyes, he placed his hands on the counter and spoke.

"Can I help you?" He asked. His voice reverberated through the fat rolls which collared his neck.

Jessica explained what she was after and was given a request form. Upon filling it out, the clerk asked her for a ten-dollar fee for the copies, which she promptly paid in cash. The copy of the survey took forty minutes to materialize and was rolled up and secured with a rubber band.

Back in her car, she drove to the Sheriff's Office and parked her Accord. Standing outside of her car, she removed the rubber band from the survey and unrolled the paper, spreading it out on the hood near the windshield. She looked at the lines of the farm, and realized that it was much bigger than she thought. The gate where she had entered the farm looked to be on the south side and made her wonder if there was a main entrance. The back door to the sheriff's office opened and out walked Deputy Phillips carrying a gray brick with an antenna sticking out from the top. He held it up in his right hand as he spoke.

"Here, it's got fresh batteries."

"Thanks for doing this."

"If you find yourself in a situation and you need help, this will reach the Ruth, the dispatcher. Just make sure you extend the antenna all the way up. It's long. Like four feet." he said as he showed her the antenna and then pointed to the side of the radio. "You turn it on here and press the talk button here. Just bring it back tomorrow," he said with a big smile.

"Okay. Thanks. They won't be mad at you for letting me use this?"

"I don't know, but at least you have something."

"Thanks, Phillips."

"You know my first name is Carl, right?"

"Yeah, I like Phillips better."

"And my mom went through all the trouble to give me a first name," he said as he rolled his eyes. Jessica rolled up the survey map and opened the door to her car.

"I forgot to ask you, what was your high school cat's name?"

"Snickers."

Jessica laughed as she sat down in the driver's seat and closed the door. Almost unable to breathe from laughing, she waved her hand at him as if she was expressing an apology for her laughter. Phillips shook his head and turned before going back inside the station.

Moments later, she traveled along Highway 209 toward Middleport. Once on Cave Mill, she easily found the gate and parked her car. She had packed her messenger bag with peanut butter crackers, her brand new compass, a container of water, a lighter and a pack of cigarettes. Before heading between the rails of the gate, she unzipped her bag and shoved the gray, brick radio inside and zipped it back up. Grabbing the rolled up survey of the farm, she ducked and eased herself between the bars of the gate.

Chapter 20

Jessica walked down the path looking around her as she made her way to the clearing. Finally seeing the rows of trees, she took out her compass from her messenger bag and a notepad and pen from her back pocket. As she walked, Jessica noted her direction using the compass and marked off the rows of trees by making a tick mark and drawing a diagonal line across for every five trees she passed. Every so often, she would unroll the survey map and find where she was, making a small circle with a black marker.

As she walked, she looked around for anything that would draw her attention to what she should be looking for. Nothing but rows and rows of trees as far as her eyes could see until she saw something which looked out of place. A brown tree in the far distance appeared to have been cut down. She noted her place on the map and where she was in her notes, being careful not to lose track with her compass. She began to cut across in a different direction and noted every five rows she walked, making the ticks in her notes along with the direction. As she got closer, she could see it wasn't a tree, but a brown structure. She continued to get closer and closer until she identified it as a shed.

Noting where the shed was on the survey map, she put her marker away and rolled up the paper and stuck it inside a side pocket of her bag. Standing about thirty yards away, she looked around and saw nothing but rows of trees in every direction. Wishing she had brought along a camera, she walked toward it and stopped every ten yards, knowing that she didn't want to mistake the shed for the house of a psychotic man with a gun. With each step, she made noise with her feet by dragging them along dead leaves and sticks in case there was someone inside. She could see the door was closed and secured from the outside using a crude twisting of a rusted coat hanger through two eye screws. Jessica continued to look around and saw nothing, even though she started to feel like someone was watching her. Shrugging off the feeling, she carefully approached the shed and reached out, pushing the flimsy door. It moved freely up until the wire rusted coat hanger prevented it from swinging open.

Gathering courage to proceed, she took a deep breath and began untwisting the wire hanger. The door was now free and started to open on its own before stopping to a point where she could see inside. Old wooden shelves, spider webs and what looked like gardening equipment could be seen. Thinking it was safe, she opened the door and looked inside. Shovels, ground stakes and rolls of wire were aimlessly set on the wooden shelves along with garden trowels and various sizes of pruning shears.

Nearly twenty dirty canvas bags hung from nails hammered into the studs of the shed. A few commercial grade hoses were rolled and stacked in the right corner, covered in spider webs. When she first laid eyes on the shed, the feeling that another piece of the puzzle had been found caused excitement mixed with fear. Instead, it turned out to be nothing more than a landmark.

She looked up at the sky and noticed that it had started to get dark. Using her compass and her notes, she easily made it out of the rows of trees and back to her car. On the way home, she couldn't help but feel that she failed. She thought about the shed and wondered if someway it could be connected to the word farm, but quickly dismissed it. She knew that wasn't it. It had to be something else. Upset and frustrated, she reached into her purse and pulled out a cigarette and lit it after she rolled down her window. The smoke she inhaled seemed to calm her and keep her level. The feeling of the nicotine entering her bloodstream was intoxicating and invigorating. She drove toward St. Clair as she brushed her hair out of her face as the wind from the cracked window flung loose strands from her ponytail.

Once back at the hotel, she parked her car and chain lit another cigarette and flicked the used one on the pavement before going into her room. She set her messenger bag down and grabbed the logbook and began making notes of what she found at the farm even though it was obviously not a good result. She unrolled the survey map and tacked it to the wall at the end of the timeline. Knowing she missed something and needing more information she thought about the last resort she had available to her.

Ring. Ring.

"Hello?"

"Hey, Phillips."

"Uh. Are you alright?"

"Yeah. I need a favor though."

"What's that?"

"What time do you get off tomorrow?"

"I'm off. Why?"

"Are you painting again?"

"I don't know," he said. "My mom is kind of mad at me."

"Why?"

"I spilled a small paint can on her carpet. I don't think she wants me to come back," he said. Jessica laughed while covering her mouth.

"It's not funny."

"I know. It isn't. It's not funny. I'm sorry."

"She was really mad," he replied in complete seriousness, to which Jessica had to pull the phone away from her face and muffle her laughter. Finally, she came back on the phone.

"I tell you what. You help me and I will help you."

"How's that?"

"I'll help you paint if you help me with my little project."

"I don't know. My mom doesn't like strangers."

"Well, how about two packs of cigarettes?"

"What do you need me to do?"

"Drive me some where and wait in your truck. You don't even have to get out."

"Where?"

"In St. Clair."

"Yeah, but where? The Adler Farm?"

"Maybe."

"That means yes."

"Maybe."

"I don't know," he replied, sounding like he would back out.

"Look, your truck won't even have to be on the property. Just sit in your truck."

"And for that you buy me two packs of cigarettes?"

"Yep," she said. She waited on the phone until finally he answered.

"I'll think about it."

"That means yes. Tomorrow at 11 A.M. and I'll meet you at your office."

Jessica opened Dr. Thornhill's logbook and reviewed every note in the book thinking she may have missed something. Growing tired, she brushed her teeth and began turning out lights and turned on the TV. Upon opening her bottle of Hydromorphone, she discovered she only had a single pill left.

"How did that happen?" One Hydromorphone, a sleeping pill and swig from a mini bottle of Vodka later, Jessica passed out.

The next day, Jessica woke with a hangover and was forced to take her time getting out of bed. She drank water from the tap and took four aspirin. She flipped through the phonebook and found a physician's office and made a note on her town map where the office was located. She called the main line and spoke with a nurse.

"Hi, I am from out of town and I am low on a prescription. Would it be possible to see the doctor today?"

"I think so. Hang on and let me get the schedule."

"Thank you. The earlier the better," she added.

"Okay. I had a cancellation for nine-twenty this morning. If you can be here in fifteen minutes, you can have it."

Jessica took the appointment and ransacked her luggage for clothes and quickly brushed her teeth. After jumping into her car, she broke the law several times by speeding and slow rolling through stop signs. Once in the parking lot, she ran inside and hurried to the front desk.

"Hope I made it in time," Jessica said as she looked at her watch with a smile. After filling out the medical forms, she was called back where a nurse took her vitals before leaving the room. Moments later, the door swung open and an old man wearing large glasses and a white lab coat entered.

"Hello. I'm Doctor Harrison. I see you're here about a prescription for Hydromorphone."

"I am," Jessica said as she handed him her empty prescription bottle. He took it and looked it over as she explained her injuries, pain and what she had been through.

"I have heard of you. You've been mentioned in our little paper here, *The Pottsville Gazette.*"

"Oh! I wasn't aware."

"I knew the Adler family. I wasn't their physician, but I saw them at mass from time to time. They were infrequent visitors."

"So I have heard."

"This is dangerous stuff here," he said as he held up the empty pill bottle. How many pills do you take at a time?"

"One and only at night. Helps me not wake up due to pain," she explained with a very convincing and nonchalant manner.

"I see. Well, I can't prescribe you Hydromorphone. I have a lot of concerns about the drug, but I wouldn't hesitate to give you Percocet considering what you've been through. How does 30 pills for 30 days sound? Can't do any more than that, but it should get you through until you can see your doctor."

"That would be fine," she said as a thought occurred to her. "I do have some pain in the middle of the day, does the Percocet make me sleepy?"

"It does. It's a side effect."

"Do you have anything else that could help during the day?"

"Uh, well Vicodin is a different opioid and can actually make some people hyper."

"Is that something I could try? I do have a hard time during the day," she added. Telling a lie to seek a drug was something she never thought she would do in her lifetime. While some people who possessed a moral compass would have a hint of guilt or shame, neither showed up in Jessica's conscious.

"I'll tell you what. I prescribe you an additional 10 pills of Vicodin. See if it works for you and if it does, you can discuss with your doctor. That okay?"

After leaving the doctor's office with two prescriptions in hand, she got it filled two blocks away at the nearest pharmacy. The next stop on her list was the Pottsville Package Store. After searching the shelves she found a 750 ml. bottle of Chimalhucan Tequila.

Once seated in her car, she pulled the bottle of Tequila out from the brown paper bag and removed the bottle of Vicodin from her purse. After opening the safety cap, she looked over the white, chalky pill before popping it with a swig of tequila. After swallowing the pill, she took in another half mouthful before screwing the cap back on and slumped in her seat as if she had just completed a 10K race.

Once she felt a hint of energy, she turned the key over in her Accord and drove to Yeoman's Hardware and Supply. After waving off assistance from the overzealous employees, she spent time in the aisle labeled *Scaffolding*. After grabbing 150 feet of rope, a harness, a flashlight, a two-gallon gas can and a package of walkie-talkies, she took them to the front counter. Once the total was said aloud, she nervously pulled cash from her pocket thinking she might have to call her dad soon and ask for more.

Making a quick stop and filling up the gas can, she then drove to the sheriff's office and waited for Phillips to pull up in his truck. Upon getting out with rope and her messenger bag in her left hand, she used her right to place the two-gallon gas can in the bed of the truck and got inside.

"Geez. You going rock climbing?"

"Sort of."

"I'm rethinking this. Not sure if I want to get myself involved."

"Look, we will park on the other side of the tree line. We won't even be on the Adler property."

"What are you doing?"

"I need to see something," she said trying to be vague.

"What? What do you need to see?"

"The operations trailer."

"What? The outside? The whole thing is covered in plastic and sealed. It's got crime scene tape all over it."

"Well, let's go look," she said trying to sound like it was no big deal. Her exterior showed a casual approach while inside she was nervous and jittery. To make things smoother, she reached into her messenger bag and took out a pack of Marlboro's and slid out a cigarette. She handed it to him and lit one herself before handing him the lighter.

"Wait. You smoke?"

"You were right, they keep me awake and going."

"I thought you said they were bad for you?"

"I did say that," she replied as she handed him the lighter. "Now, please. Can we go?"

"I don't know. I'm not sure about this."

"I can't do this without you and this is important," she said making full eye contact.

"How can this be important?"

"I will tell you on the way. Can we just go?" she said while making a hand motion to move forward. Her voice became firm and commanding, causing the pushover side of Deputy Phillips to emerge. He reluctantly threw the truck in gear and headed out onto the street. True to her word, Jessica told him the story beginning with the Ouija board hooked up to the computer, then on to the day where he pulled her out of the trailer and she saw the word on the screen. Then she spoke about Clay Samson and then explained her two visits to the farm. Stuck and nowhere to go she pleaded her case for him to help her get inside the operations trailer.

"Okay, but I don't see me getting out of this truck."

"You don't need to," she said as she removed a package of walkie-talkies from her bag. As she put the batteries in, she continued. "I am going to be tethered to your truck with a rope and a harness. If something happens, I will tell you to pull me out and you simply drive in reverse."

"That's ridiculous. It's unsafe."

"Trust me, the real danger is going in there at all. Hopefully you won't have pull me out," she said as she pulled the harness out of the messenger bag and began adjusting the straps.

Phillips reached his hand toward the bag and picked up a pill bottle that had fallen onto the seat. He looked at the label.

"Vicodin? I thought you were taking Hydromorphone?"

"Not anymore. Vicodin for day and Percocet at night," she replied. Phillips placed the pills back into her bag.

"I have seen first hand what this shit does to people. Be careful with this stuff."

"Okay, Dad," she said with a smile that Phillips didn't reciprocate.

Once they got close to the house, Jessica instructed him to drive onto the vacant field next to the Adler farm. He pulled up next to the tree line which separated the two properties. Through the trees, they could see the trailers covered in plastic with yellow tape wrapped around each trailer.

"You know it is against the law to go in there?"

"You ever break any rule in your entire life?"

"Maybe when I was in school."

"Teacher's pet?"

"Not really," he replied as he watched her put on the harness and tighten the straps. "Where'd you get that?"

"Hardware store. This is for scaffolding work. Like painting on a scaffolding and preventing a fall," she explained as she grabbed her flashlight. "Hey, do you have a pocket knife?" Phillips leaned toward the right side and slid a pocketknife out of his front left pocket.

"Here, if you get caught, you didn't get this from me."

"Nice. You get that line from a movie?" she asked as she opened the door and stepped outside and held up the end of the rope. "I'm tying this to the front of your truck. If I yell reverse, give it all you got."

"You see those trees up ahead? If I do that you're gonna pinball off every tree on the way out?

"I'll try to make a straight line going toward the trailer," she said before closing the door.

"She is a certifiable nut," he said under his breath.

Jessica tied a strong knot to the front of his push bar, picked up the gas can and started walking between the trees in a straight line toward the operations trailer. Upon reaching the plastic, she set the two-gallon gas can down and used a knife to cut the plastic around the door. Reaching inside the plastic she tried the latch and found it was locked. After fishing her car keys from her pocket, she used the key she had been given long ago and unlocked the door before pulling on the latch.

Before going inside, Jessica picked up the two-gallon gas can and looked around as she walked outside of the trailer and found the generator. Being cautious of her surroundings, she poured two-gallons of fuel into the tank of the generator and pulled the ripcord. Nothing. After three minutes of pulling the cord over and over with small breaks in between, the fuel eventually made it up the hose, priming the carburetor. After twenty-two pulls on the cord, the generator started up.

Phillips chimed in through the walkie-talkie.

"Ugh. I thought I you were going to summon me if it didn't work."

"Shut it. I still might."

"Yeah, count me out."

After looking in Phillips' direction and making a snarky face, she turned and looked at the door to the trailer and paused. Convincing herself it was okay, Jessica opened the door just enough to step inside.

Chapter 21

Jessica placed her thumb on the button of her flashlight and slid it upward until it turned on. With the door cracked behind her, she looked around the dark trailer at empty shelves and an open space where the long table in the center of the room had been. Bloodstains were splattered on the floor, most of it belonging to Father Abbott.

The only equipment in the trailer was the computer, monitors and A/V racks. Once she found a light switch and flipped it up to the *on* position, the lights flickered on and relief set in as she clicked her flashlight off. At the computer terminal, she flipped the power switch to the side and heard a sharp *click* and *hum* of the cooling fans and hard drive. Now reaching behind the monitor, she reached behind it with a groan as she felt for the switch and turned it on, watching the screen ignite with a green flashing prompt.

Inside the house, unbeknownst to her, the Ouija board reset itself to the middle top position.

"Everything okay in there?" came a voice from her walkie-talkie. Jessica closed her eyes and clutched her chest, temporarily paralyzed by sheer fright. Forgetting to check in with Phillips, she took a deep breath and reached around her back

pocket and removed the walkie-talkie before pressing the talk button.

"Yes. I'm fine. Lights and computers are on. Hang tight. I'll update you as I go. So far no reason to pull me out."

"Truck is in reverse. Foot is on the brake."

"I'm looking around the room. Feels like I forgot to turn something on. Hang tight."

Jessica tried to remember what the trailer looked like before, as she knew something wasn't right. Something was missing. Looking around she saw that the rack of audio equipment wasn't on. After searching for a switch and having to pull the rope to increase the slack to her harness, she finally found a switch behind a mixer. *Click.* The light on the front lit up and a needle fluctuated before settling on the far left. She stood in front of the microphone and blew into it and watched the needle jump. Inside the house, the small speaker projected the sound of Jessica's breath in Tilly's room.

Deputy Phillips sat in his truck a nervous wreck, his leg bouncing up and down while he chewed a stick of chewing gum. Inside the trailer, Jessica had unfolded a metal chair and sat at the computer. Thinking that she should stick to yes or no questions, she typed on the keyboard: *Is there something I am supposed to find on the farm?* She then spoke the words into the microphone with a clear voice. She picked up the walkie-talkie and pushed the talk button. Inside the cab of the truck, Deputy Phillips was looking behind him at a car driving down the road. When her voice came through, he closed his eyes and clutched his chest.

"Message sent," said Jessica. After taking a deep breath, he answered.

"What now?"

"We wait."

For a full hour, they waited with no response, only having their walkie-talkies to pass the time.

"You see anything weird around the trailer?" she asked as she moved her tethered rope to the side.

"No."

"You hear anything? Roll your window down and listen," she asked as she placed both of her elbows on the table in front of her.

"Can't hear anything over the engine. I won't turn it off."

"Well, I feel like I am okay for now."

"What are you waiting for exactly?"

"A response."

"Geez. How long does it take?"

"It varies. Hang on, I am going to try again."

Jessica asked the same question into the microphone and typed it into the keyboard. The Ouija board began to move asking the question. Within a few seconds of the Ouija board coming to a stop, it began moving again and rested on the word Yes. Jessica saw the word come up on the computer. She immediately grabbed her walkie-talkie.

"I got a response. Hang on," she said with a smile.

"This is so weird."

After a few minutes she was unable to come up with a yes or no question which would help her to know what to do next, so she simply asked a question and hoped for a response.

"What do I do now?" she said into the microphone and typed it into the computer. She grabbed her walkie-talkie and spoke, "Second message sent."

"*Do we have to wait another hour?*"

"I don't know."

"*So do they speak back to you?*"

"Sort of. You know what a Ouija board is?"

"*You mean a board game?*"

"Yeah, but this isn't a board game."

"*I thought those were a joke?*"

"Me too until I saw this work."

"*I don't get it.*"

"Apparently they have been around since 1100 A.D. and they were first used in China."

"*How do you know that?*"

"One of the guys on the team told me."

"*The one I shot?*"

"Let's not talk about this right now. At least not while I am in here."

"*Oh. Right. Sorry.*"

Jessica sat in the folding chair forced to be uncomfortable as the metal strap adjusters of her harness pressed against her skin. She looked up at the computer screen as a response came through. She froze as she stared at the word which came with a punch and felt as if it took the wind out of her. Three letters caused her to feel frightened and that it would lead to something terrifying. She reached for the walkie-talkie.

"We got a response," she said as she stared at the word and took a deep breath. In three letters on the screen in green letters was the word *Dig*. Jessica stood up and walked out of the trailer and closed the door behind her before locking it. Phillips watched as she cut the engine off to the generator before walking through the trees. Every step she took, Jessica wound the rope around her arm.

What was there to dig up? She thought about the tools in the shed as she continued to wind the rope as she approached the passenger side of the truck. Once she opened the door, Phillips grabbed the coiled rope and slid it onto the seat.

"You okay?"

"Yeah. I'm fine."

"What was the response?"

"Dig."

"Dig? Dig what?"

"I don't know."

Once she closed the door, Phillips let off the brake and turned the truck around, driving onto Peach Tree Mountain Road. "I have nine days until I am supposed to be back in D.C so I better get this figured out pretty quick."

"How big is the farm?"

"Huge."

"You're supposed to just start digging?"

"I guess. This is kind of how this has worked so far. Vague words and the rest has been a team of us trying to figure this out. I mean, I got the farm part, but now I don't know where to begin unless..." she paused in thought before speaking aloud. "Maybe something to do with the tool shed, but I don't know," she said as she shook it off. "At least I have a piece of the puzzle, but this one seems pretty small."

"And creepy too. You don't find anything good underground."

"Creepy is an understatement."

Once they got back to the sheriff's office, Jessica transferred her gear back to her car and removed six dollars from her pocket and handed it to Phillips. "This'll buy two packs and cover fuel. I appreciate your help."

"Where you off to now?"

"Back to my room. I have work to do. I have to figure this out."

"You need some help?"

"No. Why?"

"I could bring you a cup of coffee," he said with a half smile. Jessica turned around and walked toward him as he sat behind the wheel.

"Look. You're a very nice guy, but I'm not interested. You need to know that up front," she said in an assertive tone in an attempt to make it quick. She watched as his expression fell from a half smile to a look of confusion. He took a moment before he responded.

"Are you talking about dating?"

"What else could you have meant? You're gonna tell me that bringing coffee to my motel room doesn't mean anything?"

"Well, I live with my mom and I am an underpaid law enforcement officer. I certainly don't expect to be dating anyone, but most of my friends have moved away and it's nice to be around different people. I didn't mean anything by it. Coffee is sixty cents, not a big deal," he said as he shifted his truck into drive and slowly took his foot off the brake.

"Nice back pedal," she replied in a smart aleck tone. He stopped his truck before speaking.

"I was just being nice and trying to help since it seems like you need it."

"Well, right now I don't need help," she said, still thinking that he was attempting to get close to her. He looked at her with a dejected stare. "What?"

"I think you might need more help than most people."

"How's that?"

"I mean most people that don't have a drug problem."

"The hell are you talking about?"

"I've seen your pills," he said as he broke eye contact with her. "And the booze."

"You don't know what you're talking about! You know how much pain I'm in? You know that I can't sleep without passing out?"

"Sorry I brought it up. It's not my place," he said as he

took his foot off the brake once again and let his truck slowly roll up to the road. "Thanks for the money, I guess," he said as he shook his head. Jessica's heart sank as he drove away.

"Fuuuuuuck," she said to herself as she turned and walked toward her car. After parking in front of her door at the motel, she brought her gear inside and began looking over the time line and most importantly, the survey map. Holding her head and feeling weak, chills began to form in her neck and chest. She lit up a cigarette and stared at the circle she made where the tool shed was located.

Why am I such an idiot sometimes?

Chapter 22

The next day, Jessica had woken up to yet another hangover, but this time her headache was so great that she vomited in the shower. She had already taken three aspirin, but the pills weren't in her system long enough to have an effect. After throwing up the aspirin, she drank a handful of water which collected in her cupped hands from underneath the faucet in the bathroom and downed another three pills. Feeling chills and achiness, she curled up on the bed and wrapped her arms around her stomach waiting for the pills to take effect. Tears flowed down her cheeks and onto the cheap comforter just before, she fell asleep.

Walking along weeds, fallen trees and rocks, Jessica looked up and saw the boy running as fast as he could. She could hear him breathing as he ran, stepping on branches and twigs which popped with every step. Then the boy fell and his arm got stuck in a hole. Jessica watched as the boy was being pulled downward just as she vomited. She bent over and continued to vomit and woke up to the feeling of needing to purge the contents of her stomach. She got up out of bed and ran to the bathroom, not making it in time. She covered her mouth as vomit spewed from her lips and through the spaces in between her fingers before making it to the toilet.

Once she cleaned herself up, she looked in the mirror as she breathed in deep, heavy breaths. Her eyes were bloodshot and her skin looked pale.

"Something's wrong," she said as she turned around and looked at the door to her room.

Once outside her motel room, she threw up again as she hobbled to her car, allowing strands of unwashed hair to become soaked. As she sat in the driver's seat, strands of vomit hair swept past her face while starting the engine. Driving at high speeds, she navigated her way to Pottsville and parked at Schuylkill Medical Center near the emergency room.

Inside were two admission nurses who worked the ER department and were chatting about the next potluck when one of the nurses looked up and saw a woman through the window hobbling toward the doors like a zombie. She had stringy hair and a heavily stained t-shirt and appeared to be near death.

"Brenda? Do you see this? It's that girl from the haunted house," she said as the other nurse turned and looked just as the automatic doors opened and the girl hobbled inside. Falling to her knees she shouted.

"Don't call my father. Call Deputy Phillips," and then fell backward onto her legs, hitting her head on the floor. The two nurses jumped up to help her.

Jessica opened her eyes and saw a drawn curtain and a chair with a man sitting in it with his head propped up. She couldn't see his face as he was sitting in the dark, but he was wearing a tan colored officers uniform. She closed her eyes and spoke.

"Phillips is that you?"

"Yeah, it's me."

"What happened?"

"Don't know. The doctor wouldn't tell me."

"Am I going to live?"

"Looks like it."

"Hey, Phillips."

"Yeah?"

"You still mad at me?"

"I wasn't mad at you, just a little upset is all."

"Hey Phillips," she said. He could tell she wasn't herself as the drugs caused her to slur her speech.

"Yes?"

"Sorry. Thanks for saving me."

"I didn't save you."

"Yes you did," she said as the medication coming through the IV took over. A few hours later, she woke up to a nurse standing over her and calling her name.

"Miss Calvert? Honey can you wake up for me? Miss

Calvert?" Jessica slowly opened her eyes and saw a nurse with brunette hair and several gray strands. "There you go, we need you to wake up. You've been asleep for quite a while now. The doctor is coming up to see you in about fifteen minutes. Want me to turn on the TV for you to keep you awake?"

"No. I'm fine." The bed was being raised by a crank at the end of the bed, forcing Jessica to sit up.

"Okay, I will be back to check on you in five minutes or so. Hang on for me. Don't go back to sleep."

Jessica rubbed her eyes and waited in silence. Finally, the doctor came in and stood over her while looking at her chart.

"Miss Calvert, I am Doctor Ward and I have received a toxicology report which shows you had a good amount of alcohol in your system along with nicotine, diphenhydramine and two separate opioids. Are you a recreational drug user?"

"No. I'm in pain. A lot of pain," she groaned trying to play up her reasoning for her prescriptions. "I also have a hard time sleeping."

"You have trouble sleeping?"

"Yes. I have severe nightmares and if I don't drink a little tequila, I wake up screaming."

"Miss Calvert, it is very dangerous to mix alcohol with opioids. Furthermore, it is dangerous to mix diphenhydramine with opioids. The sleeping pills are causing you to become dehydrated. Did you have a headache when you woke up?"

"Yes. Severe."

"I bet. Alcohol and diphenhydramine can cause you a lot

of problems. This isn't the first time I have seen you. I remember you when you were here for your first visit here after your fall from a two-story window and you were in a coma. I don't believe you were conscious when I tended to you, but I see here in your chart you were here a second time after experiencing a tragic event. Correct?"

"Correct."

"Your symptoms suggest that you may have post traumatic stress disorder and I think I might have something for you that could help," he explained.

"Anything would be appreciated. I don't like taking the pills and drinking alcohol, I would rather have a better option."

"I understand and I want you to know you're not alone. Many people who have experienced something traumatic resort to medication and alcohol so don't feel like you're the only one. The medication I am going to prescribe to you is called Nefazodone and it is classified as an anti-depressant, but we have had a lot of success with veterans who experience PTSD and take this drug. Okay?"

"What do I do? I mean, how many do I take?"

"One a day. That's it. But you have to lay off the alcohol. You can still take Vicodin or a Percocet as needed, but take it easy on those as well. Just no more alcohol."

"Okay. One a day," she repeated in a dazed state, her eyes closed and reopened in seemingly slow motion. "Can I get a refill of the Vicodin and Percocet?"

"I can do that, but I need to see you in one week, so I will have my staff get in touch. The nurse will get your information as she discharges you so be patient, and we will get you on your way. Okay? Just remember, no alcohol. Not a drop."

"I understand, thank you doctor."

Jessica was discharged two hours later and was wheeled out to the curb in a wheelchair where she stood up and walked toward her car. A man wearing scrubs began folding up the chair before going back inside.

"You be careful now," he said as a disheveled Jessica Calvert limped toward her Honda Accord.

Chapter 23

A knock on the motel door woke Jessica from a deep sleep. She sat up and looked at the clock on the end table - 1:33 P.M. She got dressed through another set of knocking before answering the door with the chain still connected to the wall. The sunlight blasted through the crack causing her to shield her eyes, unable to see who was on the other side of the door.

"Miss Calvert?" a voice said.

"Yes?"

"We are going to need a payment at the front office for you to continue your stay."

"Oh. Okay uh, can I just give you a credit card? I'm trying to manage my cash and I'm getting a little low."

"You may at the front office. Sometime today will be fine."

"Okay."

"Sorry to disturb you."

Jessica closed the door and held her head. After a long, hot shower she brushed her teeth and dried her hair, putting on the same old jeans and a t-shirt not covered in vomit, yet days overdue for the laundry. Reaching into her back pocket, she pulled out her only pack of cigarettes only to discover that they had been broken and crushed. Upon entering the front office, she set her credit card on the counter and put two dollars in quarters into the vending machine before pulling the knob and retrieving a fresh pack of Marlboro's.

"Let me just run this real quick," the attendant said with his scrawny voice. He placed the credit card into a contraption with carbon paper and racked a lever back and forth before handing her the card back. He quickly filled in some information and had her sign at the bottom.

Lighting up a brand new cigarette, Jessica walked out of the office and took her time getting to her room. Her first cigarette in twenty-four hours, the nicotine was warmly welcomed into her nervous system, the calmness spreading through her head, neck and chest.

Once back in her room, she looked over the papers, documents and maps on her wall. She walked over to the survey of the farm pinned to the wall and placed her finger over the small circle where the tool shed was located and thought of what to do next. Standing next to the survey map, the thought of ending her crusade crossed her mind. *Maybe I should hang it up?* Leaning forward until her head hit the wall. She closed her eyes tightly and took a deep breath.

What now?

What am I supposed to do?

She sat on the bed and picked up the phone and dialed the only number she could think of. Whenever she ran into a dead end on a story, she called the one guy who usually had the answers, even if he occasionally yelled at her.

"Damn, kid! I was worried about you," Mr. Wood said as a cigarette dangled from his mouth. "When are you coming back? I am still holding this job, but I don't think I can for long. You don't come back soon, you're gonna end up sweeping shit off the floor in the press room."

"People shit in the press room?" she asked in a dazed tone.

"When are you coming back?"

"How about next week?" she asked with a cigarette hanging out of the corner of her mouth. I am in St. Clair finishing up this story, but I am stuck and I need you to try and shake something loose for me."

"You gotta cut that one loose, kiddo."

"No way."

"What's the issue? Where are you at with it?"

"I am supposed to dig around a hundred acres of land to find something."

"A hundred acres? What are you supposed to find?"

"I don't know."

"Where exactly are you supposed to dig?"

"I don't know."

"You're on a road toward insanity."

"I'm stuck."

"Sounds like it. You might as well look for a black cat in a coal cellar."

"Cut the shit. I need help, please," she said with her head still pressed up against the wall. A long pause ensued before he spoke again.

"Calvert. You talk to me like that again, and I will have to consider proposing marriage."

"I'd turn you down. It's not the smoking that bothers me, but the long hours," she replied. Mr. Wood began laughing to the point of choking and coughing. Once he calmed down he came back on the line with a chuckle in his voice as he spoke.

"I don't know what happened to you, but I like it," he said as he took a swig of Diet Coke. "Okay, so if you have to find something underground, it was probably buried. That usually means heavy equipment. I would be checking heavy equip-ment rental companies. They usually deliver so try to find equipment that would have been delivered to that address.

"Okay. Will do. Anything else?"

"When speaking with the rental companies, use the word excavate, not dig or digging. That's all I got. Good luck, gotta go."

Click.

Taking the phone book out of the drawer beside her bed, she left her room and jumped into her car. Wasting little time, she headed toward Whayne Equipment and Rental. Upon en-tering the front office, she approached the rental counter and discovered two fat men in their late twenties standing behind the desk.

"Hi, I'm Todd." When he spoke, he ended his sentence with his mouth still open. His arms hung like fatty slabs of meat on hooks and his finger chubs looked like they would smell of body odor and beef jerky if they got too close to her face.

"I'm Heather," Jessica said—protecting her identity from Fat Todd—"and I'm looking for past rental records of equipment delivered to a farm on Cave Mill Road. Would you have any records which I could look at or you could check?"

"Do you want to rent some equipment?" Todd asked. The other fat man looked at Todd and thought he might not be in the running for a date with the pretty girl. Without waiting for a response, he interjected his greeting before she could answer.

"Hi! I'm Kevin," he said with a grin and a forced nod. He wasn't as fat as Todd, but the glaze over his eyes made him appear dumber.

"Is there a manager I could speak with?" she asked as she took a step back from the counter. Kevin turned and walked toward a side office and hollered out.

"Brad! There's a nice girl out here to see you."

Jessica looked over at the office and saw a man wearing a button up shirt and glasses. He carried himself like a manager instead of an animal raised deep in the Appalachian Mountains.

Once he approached, a decent and civil conversation ensued. She explained that she was from *The Washington Post* and wanted to know if they had ever delivered equipment to a farm on Cave Mill Road. After twenty minutes, the search through past records in old boxes turned up nothing of value. The only other equipment rental company nearby was in Pottsville.

Pulling into the parking lot of Yale Pennsylvania Rentals,

her head dropped as it appeared they only rented forklifts and lift trucks. Deciding she could at least give it a shot, she walked inside and met a thin man named Charlie Waddell. Gray hair, small waist and wearing a tight polo shirt, he adjusted his glasses as she spoke.

"What are you trying to find out exactly," he asked.

"I need to know if a farm on Cave Mill Road ever rented excavating equipment. I've already been to Whayne Rentals."

"Hmmm...well, we don't rent that kind of equipment, but let's say the farm did rent equipment and moved dirt on that farm, then what?"

"What do you mean?"

"Just curious what that would mean and what would that tell you?"

"If equipment was rented, I might know more about why a hole was dug or why earth was moved."

"Right. I see."

"I might need to dig a hole to uncover something."

"Sounds mysterious," he replied with a smile.

"It is kind of. It's part of a story I am working on, but it might not lead anywhere."

"How many acres?"

"I don't know, a hundred or more."

"Oh! Well, that's a needle in a haystack problem."

"It is."

"So, ultimately you need to find something underground. Right?"

"Yes."

"Then I might have an option for you," he said as he walked around the counter and began writing an address and a name on a piece of paper. "This might not work, but it is worth a try."

"At this point, I will try anything."

"About a year ago, a manufacturing plant in Sheppton was accused of burying scrap metal near an underground water source. It was contaminating the water so the county rented a machine from the coal mine."

"Locust Valley?"

"Yep. Locust Valley. This thing was on wheels, looked like a hand truck or a dolly. They brought it out to the farm and they could somehow see images underground."

"Without digging?"

"Yes," he replied. Jessica whipped out her notepad from her back pocket and began taking notes as he continued. "I don't know much about it, but there was a guy named Gary Figgis that brought it out to the site. It was loud and we had to cover our ears when it went off. Like an explosion."

"Gary Figgis. So, he is with Locust Valley?"

"Yeah. He goes to my church and I see him from time to time. I think he is an engineer out at the mine. Not sure though," he said as he handed her a piece of paper with Gary's name and address.

"So you were there that day?" she asked as she took the paper from him and shoved it into her back pocket.

"Yep. A TV station from Harrisburg wanted an aerial view as they looked for the burial site so they rented one of our lifts and the cameraman got shots from up high. I operated the lift since they didn't know how."

"Charlie, I can't thank you enough. You have been a big help."

"Always glad to help. If you need a lift for any reason, give me a call," he offered with a smile that implied he knew she wouldn't. She shook his hand and headed out of the office toward her car.

The last time Jessica visited Locust Valley, the guard insisted that she be placed on a list in order to enter. Stopping at a gas station and using the phone book, she called the main office.

Ring. Ring.

"Locust Valley."

"Gary Figgis please."

"One moment."

Click. Hum.

"Hello?"

"Mr. Figgis?"

"Yes."

"Hi, my name is Jessica from *The Washington Post*," she said before going into her quick explanation of Charlie Waddell mentioning him in conversation about the water contamination.

"Would you mind if I visited you for five minutes? I need to ask you a few questions."

"No problem. Come on by, my schedule is pretty light today."

"Okay. Great! Could you put me on the list so the guard will let me in?"

"Of course."

Twenty minutes later, she drove up to the entrance of Locust Valley where the same guard wearing the same uniform stepped out of the guard shack and held his hand up for her to stop. She rolled down her window as he spoke.

"You must be Jessica Calvert."

"I am."

"I just put you on the list. I will lift the gate, but I need you to drive slowly toward the parking lot until I give you the thumbs up. I need to record your license plate in my log book."

"No problem."

Driving slowly through the gate, she watched in her rearview mirror as he wrote down her plate number and gave her a thumbs up before she sped up toward an empty parking spot. Once inside, she waited for fifteen minutes in an uncomfortable wingback chair until Gary Figgis opened a door with a smile. Similar to Charlie Waddell, he was thin and tall, but was bald on top with a horseshoe shaped haircut.

"Miss Calvert?"

"Yes," she said as she stood up.

"Not everyday we get *The Washington Post* in Schuylkill County. Come on back, we can talk in my office," he invited as he held the door open for her.

Jessica was guided to a big office with a wooden desk, a drafting table in the corner and a big picture window which had a grand view of the coal mining operation.

"Nice office."

"It's the only perk I get," he said with a laugh. "Just have a seat in either chair. Can I get you some coffee?"

"Oh please. I would be so grateful."

"Cream? Sugar?"

"That would be wonderful."

"Ok. Hang on for me, be right back." After a full minute, Gary returned with a Styrofoam cup. After handing it to her, he sat in his chair. "So, how can I help?"

As she sipped from the cup, she explained the need to find something buried on a farm, leaving out the paranormal and the fact that it was Dr. Silva's land. Then she brought up Charlie Waddell's idea.

"I see. That machine is very expensive, but I will say it is hard to break as it is very durable and industrial so I don't have much of a concern lending it out, but I guess I would need some kind of guarantee that it would be safe in someone else's hands. No offense."

"Oh, none taken. I freely admit I know nothing about such a machine. What kind of guarantee would you need?"

"Well, keep in mind that it is my job should it go missing or if it were to be damaged in some way."

"Okay. Maybe a deposit of some kind?"

"I believe that our investment in that device is around

twenty thousand or so, but really I wouldn't be looking for a deposit. How about a second person's involvement?" he said.

"Okay. Would that be you in this case?"

"Not necessarily. How about the landowner or perhaps Charlie Waddell or someone from the PVA office?"

"I see," she said. While Gary was a nice man and very polite, she could tell that what he really meant was he preferred a man to help her operate the device. "I do have a friend who is a deputy with the Sheriff's office."

"That would be satisfactory, sure. Now, this device is fairly big, it looks like a dolly that you would move furniture with and it will require a bit of training. You would also need a truck to transport it. Do you think both could be here tomorrow morning?"

"I think so. What would the charge be to rent something like this?" she asked. Gary smirked and looked up into the left side of his brain as if he was thinking of something before he leaned forward an answered.

"Tell you what, you let me keep all the geographic data you get from the farm, we can forgo a fee. Technically, we don't even rent equipment out. We rarely use it so no one will notice its absence, but there is something you will need to pay for."

"Okay, what would that be."

"You might want to write this one down," he said. She readied her pen. "You will need to buy a box of 12-gauge ammunition, 1-ounce slugs. This machine works like a sonar and the boom the slugs provide is what makes this device work."

"Charlie mentioned it was loud."

"It sure is. So, I will see you tomorrow then?"

"9 A.M. okay?"

"Perfect," he replied. As he was escorting her out, she suddenly stopped and looked at him with a curious expression.

"Gary, do you happen to know Dr. Silva?"

"I do. He works on the other side of the mine, but I see him every so often." Jessica then lowered her voice.

"I spoke to him on the phone about a week ago and he seemed a little stiff and harsh, is that an accurate description of him?"

"Uh, I would say he's a very serious man. I haven't seen the harsh side of him, but certainly stiff. He's kind of a stick in the mud," he said in a low voice with a grin. Jessica grinned and nodded her head.

"Good. It's not just me then. Did his brother ever come by here?"

"I don't know. I guess I didn't know he had a brother."

"The guy in St. Clair that was found in his car in the pond? That's him."

"Wow. That was his brother? I didn't know."

Jessica left Locust Valley and drove toward the Sheriff's Office with her window cracked and smoked a cigarette. Once she pulled into the parking lot, she flicked her cigarette out of the window and cut the engine. She could see Phillips' truck parked in the back as she got out of her car. Taking a deep breath, she walked inside gathering the courage to suck up to her only friend in Schuylkill County, and the one she had managed to piss off.

Chapter 24

Upon seeing Jessica enter the office, Deputy Phillips walked toward her, seemingly glad to see her. He motioned to walk outside with him and she followed him without saying a word. He had put his hands in his pockets and quickly removed them and crossed his arms. He felt and looked awkward as he started to speak.

"Sorry about running off the other day," he started in. His apology sounded sincere, yet hurried as if he was nervous and ripping off a Band-Aid.

"It wasn't your fault."

"I don't know. I somehow got it in my head you were using me."

"Using you for what?"

"I don't know. I just wasn't thinking right."

"I came here to apologize to you. I'm the one who acted like an asshole. You didn't mean anything by it."

"I feel like I was at fault."

"All you did was offer to help. I blew it out of proportion. It's no excuse, but I wasn't feeling well then."

"Obviously. You ended up in the hospital."

"Did you come and see me?"

"I did. When they said you were going to be fine, I went back to work."

"Well, thanks for coming. It means a lot to me."

"Glad to," he replied. Jessica wanted to move on to the reason she was there, but it would seem like she was using him again. "You headed to the farm?" he asked.

"Not right now," she said as she watched him pull out a pack of cigarettes. He lit one and offered her one. "You have helped me out a lot and quite honestly, I really need your help tomorrow, but before I get into it," she explained as she took him up on his offer, pulling a cigarette from the pack. "I thought maybe we could go get Chinese food. I'm buying."

"I don't know," he replied as he lit her cigarette.

"Why?"

"Look. I'm not interested. You're a very nice girl, but you need to know that up front," he said with a smile.

"Funny. Makes me feel bad though. It does sound like an asshole thing to say now that I hear from the other side."

"Yeah, well Chinese sounds good. You wanna meet tonight?"

"What time are you off work?"

"Coupl'a hours."

"I'll swing by and pick you up."

Jessica drove back to her room and picked up the survey map and pulled a few documents off the wall. After driving back to Pottsville and picking up Phillips, she drove to the Chinese restaurant and parked near the door.

Crab Rangoon, fried dumplings, sweet and sour chicken and General Tso's chicken were ordered and brought out to their table. While sitting in the smoking section, Jessica had partially unrolled the map and showed Phillips how much area she would have to cover. Then came the explanation about the machine she would borrow from Locust Valley.

"When are you doing this?"

"9 A.M. tomorrow morning."

"I work tomorrow."

"Is there anyone else you know at your office that could help?"

"I don't know. Maybe."

The conversation drifted to where she should start and questions arose as to what radius the machine would cover and how exactly it would work. Nicotine, caffeine and food loaded with salt made for a spirited and lively dinner with ideas and theories. For dessert, Jessica suggested tequila and lime.

"What if there is buried treasure?" he asked as they both took a shot.

"I don't know. I can't see it being a valuable find," she replied with a smirk.

"You think it's bad?"

"Hope not. So far we have been led down a path of less savory situations."

A few shots later, Phillips cut himself off and vowed to be the designated driver. When the check came, Jessica used her credit card and apologized once again.

"Sorry for the comment a few days ago." She reached into her purse and grabbed her bottle of pills and took a Nefazodone.

"Forget it."

"It's hard to. I still feel bad about it. I honestly haven't had a friend in a while. It's been all work for me, but it's what I want. I love the newspaper industry. So does my boss. You should see him. He's a complete mess."

"You're not far off," he said nodding at her condition as she opened a fortune cookie.

"I tend to agree."

Jessica walked to her car getting in the passenger seat while Phillips took over the driver's seat. The Nefazodone mixed with tequila soaked her brain in a black cloud, causing her to wake up to the red display of a clock on her nightstand the next morning. Fully clothed and drooling on her pillow, Jessica had to stare into the haze of her hangover and squint to read the time on the alarm clock. 6:37 A.M. She sat up and found a note on the floor scribbled in pen that read: *I'm outside.* She looked up and saw the door to her room cracked open, letting in a thin strip of sunlight the width of a human hair. Standing up, she walked to the door and opened it, finding Phillips reading a newspaper off the hood of her Accord while drinking a cup of coffee, dressed in full uniform.

"The hell, man?" she said.

"Morning. Get ready. I have to get to work."

"You been here all night?"

"No. I went home and slept. Drove your car. Hope you don't mind."

"I don't mind," she replied as she closed the door and headed for the shower. Phillips went back to his newspaper.

Twenty minutes later, instead of jumping behind the wheel, she rode in the passenger seat and let two aspirin dissolve into her system. She propped up her elbow on the window and held her head up with her right hand.

"I'm gonna ride with you over to Locust Valley. We'll put the machine in the back of my truck and go to the farm. Now, I can't stay with you. You're gonna be out there all alone."

"Can you get me a radio just in case?"

"I think so. But, this is the best I can do. Sheriff is cutting me a little slack. I'm getting more and more from him since the day at the trailer."

"I appreciate your help. I do need you to act as if you will be with me all day. This guy doesn't think a girl can operate this machine all by herself."

At the sheriff's office, Jessica and Phillips switched her car for his truck and made it to Locust Valley by 9 A.M. After going through the rigorous security check, they parked the truck just as Gary Figgis was wheeling a dolly out of the front door and headed their way. A tan colored machine was anchored to the dolly and looked like filing cabinet with a handle as big as a water pump on top.

"Hey guys! Good morning." Gary said with a smile. Jessica

introduced them to each other before Gary started in with the crash course.

"I hope this is easy to operate," said Phillips.

"It is. Very easy. Let me explain," he replied as he gently tapped the machine. "Power button is here. This operates on a car battery, which is why this whole thing is on a dolly. It's pretty heavy. Now, I want you to see this compartment here." Gary opened a small door on the side that revealed ten 3.5 inch floppy discs. "You take one of these out and insert it here," he said as he pointed to a disc drive on top. "the light will turn green and then you put a slug in here, see?" he asked as he pointed to a slot which appeared similar to a chamber on a shotgun.

"What is this for?" asked Phillips. A long explanation ensued as to how the sound waves bounce off objects underground. "Is this like radar?"

"Not quite. This is technically sonar. Once you load the slug, pull this handle here. Just make sure you have it placed where you want to image the ground before you push this button here," he continued. While Philips listened to the explanation, Jessica used her notepad and wrote down his instructions word for word. Once the crash course was complete and Phillips acted as if he knew exactly what to do, he helped Gary load it into the back of his truck.

"How do I see the images?" Jessica asked.

"Well, you'll have to let me interpret them. I will take the images off the disc and either read them on my computer or print them out," he explained. A little disappointed, Jessica had been under the impression she would be able to see the images immediately.

"Okay. Um…," she started to say thinking of the amount of ground she would need to cover. "What kind of radius am I looking at here?"

"Great question. With each pull of the handle, you're going to get about a ten-foot radius and a depth of about ten, sometimes fifteen feet if you're lucky. If I were you I would bring a tape measure with me. When this light on the disc drive turns red," he pointed as he spoke, "you'll need to replace the disc. You'll get about three images per disc," he answered. Jessica felt defeated already.

"So I will be able to cover about three acres or so?"

"Yep. We like to say three football fields. Just bring me the discs and I will see what is underground. Of course you have to record your location for each pull of the trigger in case you'd like to unearth anything we see in the images. Just keep a list of each pull." Jessica thanked Gary and shook his hand, as did Phillips. Once on the road, she conveyed her frustration as she lit up a cigarette.

"This sucks. I feel like I'm just gonna be spinning my wheels for nothing out there."

"Why?"

"Three acres? There's like a hundred-plus acres out there!"

"This is better than digging a hole everywhere."

"I don't know. I feel like walking out on this now."

"You're not even going to try?"

"Of course I'll try. I can't go this far and not even go through with it at least once."

Phillips pulled into the parking lot of a sporting goods store and purchased a box of 12-gauge ammunition, 1-ounce slugs while Jessica waited in the truck. Thinking of how far she had come, she knew giving up was not an option. When Phillips returned, he questioned her about her gear as he started his truck and drove out of the parking lot.

"We're going to be driving by a gas station. Do you need drinks? Snacks?"

"I've got enough in my bag for now. I filled up my water container before I left the motel. When can you come pick me up?"

"I was going to come by on my lunch break? Say two hours from the time I drop you off. That work?"

"I don't know."

"Or you could just take my truck."

"That's nice of you. How would I get the dolly out of the back?"

"Good question. I could probably grab some scrap wood behind the station. You could make a ramp."

"That might work."

"By the way, you should get a backpack. That bag isn't suitable."

"It's stupid to say, but I feel like it is lucky. It isn't really, but somehow it gives me confidence."

"Is that a bloodstain?"

"It is."

"Is it yours?"

"I'm not sure," she said as she looked down at the corner of the canvass bag. Deciding not to press further, he turned into the parking lot of the station. Phillips put three flat pieces of plywood in the back and used bungee cords to strap them down. Putting his hands on his hips with a smile, he nodded as he spoke.

"You're all set!"

"Is the radio still a possibility?"

"Oh!" he said as he snapped his fingers. "The radio. Hang on,"

"Would you also happen to have a tape measure?"

"I think so," he said as he ran inside the station and returned with the radio and an old tape measure. "Here ya go! You can keep this for a few days since no one will be missing it."

"Thank you. This means a lot to me. You are a huge help."

"That's what I'm here for. To protect and serve," he said as he chuckled. He playfully saluted as she backed out of the parking lot and turned out onto the street before waving goodbye.

Chapter 25

Jessica found the gate on Cave Mill Road for the third time and parked on the side of the road. After arranging the plywood boards at the back of the truck, she eased the dolly down to the ground. Grabbing her messenger bag and locking the truck, she squeezed the dolly through a space between the gate and a post and barely made it through without scratching the sides of the machine.

Wheeling the dolly over uneven terrain proved to be very difficult, causing Jessica to expend more energy and drink more water as she finally made it through to the clearing amongst the rows of trees. While she hadn't thought much about it, she wondered on where she should start. *The very first row? The twentieth row? Near where I saw the boy running? The tool shed?*

She unrolled her survey map and looked over the land. Deciding that the best place to start would be near the tool shed, she rolled up the map and stuck it behind her back. Moving north, she wiped the sweat from her forehead while pulling the dolly behind her.

Upon arriving at the shed, she made a note of her location in her notepad and unzipped her bag, removing the box of slugs. Ready to get started, she inserted a slug into the chamber just like she was shown and turned on the machine. The sound of components whirring and humming commenced. She removed a floppy disc from the compartment, inserted it into the drive. More humming and whirring ensued.

As she reached for the handle, she looked around before pulling it down. Not knowing how loud it would be, she angled her head so that her ear met her shoulder and she pulled the lever down. *Clack. BOOM!* The sound rumbled under her feet and scared her instantaneously.

"Whoa!" she yelled as she took a step back. Dust from the impact floated in the air around her causing her to cough. She waved the air in front of her as she took a step toward the machine and looked it over. Leaning the dolly back on its wheels, she pushed it forward a few feet before parking it. While looking at the ground, she examined the hole the machine had made. The size of a golf ball marked where she pulled the lever. Removing the tape measure from her bag and her compass, she measured north ten feet and moved the dolly. After making the note of her location, she inserted another round and pulled the lever. *BOOM!*

The next hour and a half was spent rolling ten feet, pulling the lever and making notes. She wished she had purchased ear protection of some kind as her ears were ringing from the loud discharge of the slugs. After spending the final floppy disc, she packed up her messenger bag and began the

long trek back toward the gate. The sound of the dolly rolling
over the uneven ground was muffled by the ringing in her ears
as was the sound of the boy running to her left in the thick
cluster of weeds and broken branches.

She stopped rolling the dolly. Standing still, she kept her
eyes on the boy, but couldn't hear him breathing nor could she
hear the sound of his feet stepping on branches and twigs as
she normally did. The ringing in her ears grew louder as she
watched the boy as he fell and his arm got stuck in the hole.

She winced as she always did when the boy's arm was
pulled until his shoulder snapped and broke. She closed her
eyes, the ringing continued as she took deep breaths and tried
to hold herself together.

This isn't real. It's not real. This is in my head. It isn't real.

Slowly she opened her eyes and gripped the handle of the
dolly and looked in the direction of where the boy was last
seen. The ringing in her ears began to subside. It was over. She
pulled the dolly behind her and walked forward wondering if
Phillips had been with her, would he have seen the boy? She
thought back to the team in the operations trailer when the
coal miner crawled out of the crawl space and stood outside
the door.

*"We need some help. The mine suffered a collapse and some of my
men were hurt,"* the man said.

"Where were they hurt?" Father Abbott asked.

"In the mine. Could you unlock the door?" the man replied.

"What's your name?"

"Please. Unlock the door! They're gonna die!"

As Jessica pushed the dolly up the makeshift ramp and set it in the bed of the truck, she recalled Father Abbott standing at the door as he asked questions. Recalling the incident caused her to become unnerved making her hurry into the cab of the truck and turn the engine.

Jessica rolled into the parking lot at the sheriff's office and walked inside. From inside his office, Deputy Phillips stood up with a phone to his ear and held up his finger, signaling for her to wait. A few minutes later, he walked up front and opened the door to the outside, holding it for her as she walked through.

"You're done?"

"Yeah. I filled up the ten discs. Have you eaten?"

"No."

"Can you take your lunch break now?"

"I think so. Why?"

"I'll buy lunch and we can go over to see Mr. Figgis and drop them off."

"Why do I need to be there?"

"Because he thinks you helped me and if he doesn't find anything on the discs, I will need to use the machine again."

"Oh. Right. Okay, but I'll buy this time. Hope you like cheeseburgers."

"No pickle, no onion."

Gary Figgis was sitting in his office reviewing a blasting estimate when his phone buzzed. He grabbed the phone and placed it next to his ear.

"Mr. Figgis, there's a Deputy Phillips here to see you."

"Thanks, Shelly. I'll be up in a moment."

In the lobby, Phillips stood next to Jessica as he held all ten floppy discs. When the door opened, he greeted Mr. Figgis and handed them off.

"Great! You think you got about three football fields on here?"

"I think so," replied Jessica. "Do you know when you might have a chance to look at them?"

"Uh, probably today or tomorrow. Not sure."

"That would be great. Could you call me at this number when you do?" she asked as she handed him an old receipt from a gas station with her name and number written on the back.

"Of course. Will do. You want to hang onto the tomographer?"

"If I could. I would like to take it back out once more if you don't find anything."

"Another day won't hurt," he replied with a smile. "I will call you as soon as I can."

"Thanks!"

Phillips drove to a small walk-up burger joint with an illuminated sign which read *Flavor Isle*. Burgers, milkshakes, corn dogs and snow cones made up the limited menu. While sitting at a picnic table, Jessica thought about the boy running through the forest and briefly considered talking about what she saw. She even considered talking about the miner who had tried to get inside the operations trailer. Phillips tore into his burger with a vengeance and slurped up his milkshake, giving Jessica enough time to reconsider bringing up paranormal appearances which would make her seem strange and weird.

"Was it easy?" Phillips asked as he chewed his food.

"Yes. It was loud."

"I bet. You think he'll find anything on those discs?"

"I don't know. It felt like a needle in a haystack since I only got a small percentage of the entire landscape. I hate it that the screen just said *Dig*. That's it. How vague is that?"

"Dumb ghosts," he said as he laughed.

"What time you get off work tomorrow?"

"Late. I have to be in Harrisburg in the morning for training."

"Training for what?"

"New arrest procedures and something about warrants. I can't remember. We have to go every couple of months."

The conversation drifted to Jessica asking questions about the three people Phillips had arrested so far. Since his lunch hour usually consisted of him eating by himself, he reveled in their conversation, smiling more than not, happy to break up the monotony of his day.

Gary Figgis had looked over enough blast estimates to

make his head spin. Trying to get away from the misery of the dot matrix data, he left his office and fetched himself a coke from a vending machine and opted for mindless chit-chat in the break room before returning to his desk. As he sat down, he figured he could prolong his procrastination by looking at a few images on the floppy discs sitting near his computer. He popped a disc into the drive and typed in a prompt, causing a program to load. After selecting the first image, he could see representations of rocks and changes in the density of the soil. The next image was similar with nothing to see nor report. He switched out the disc for a second one and viewed all three images. Nothing.

Jessica had gotten back to her room and felt the pull of nicotine urging her for a few drags. She lit up a cigarette as she looked over the survey of the farm and quickly got frustrated thinking about the small percentage of land she had covered. She turned on the TV to a rerun of the show, China Beach. Just as she got interested in the story, the phone rang. Thinking it might be Gary Figgis, she quickly answered.

"Hello, this is Jessica."

"Hey Jessica, it's Gary. How ya doing?"

"Oh please tell me you have good news."

"The best I can do at this point is say, I might."

"That's better than nothing."

"I have gone through all of the discs and I even stayed late to check them all. I don't get to do this often and it's good experience for me. So, here is what I found."

"I appreciate you putting your effort into this by the way."

"Glad to help. So…," he said as he typed on his keyboard in front of him. She could hear the keys *clack* as he typed. "There was nothing in the ground in open space. Well, nothing other than rocks and variations in soil densities, but there was a recurring object found underneath two trees."

"Under a tree?"

"Under, yes. It is something that is definitely man made and it recurs twice on disc eight in two different samples, two different trees."

"What do you think it might be?"

"Well, it is small whatever it is and it may be nothing. It is inside the root structure of the tree so I can't say for sure. It could have been a rod or a stake that helped prop up the tree during the early stages of growth, but if that is the case, I cannot figure out how it would have made it's way underneath the tree."

"Right," she said as she took notes. "Disc eight you say?"

"Correct. Disc eight, second and third image," he said as she took notes. "Looks to be the tree on the right if you were facing south."

"Well, I suppose the best thing I could do at this point is excavate around the root structure, right?"

"Possibly. What would you be digging with?"

"Shovels?" Jessica replied with a shrug of her shoulders.

"Well, I don't know. From what I am looking at here, you

would be digging a hole about three to four feet deep. That's quite a big hole and then you're going to have to get around the root structure and these appear to be very mature trees. I just can't say it is going to be that simple."

"What should I use instead of shovels?"

"Consider renting heavy equipment."

"I don't think I can do that."

"I see. So in order for you to unearth the object, you're gonna have to use hand tools?"

"It seems so."

"You think this might be what you're looking for?"

"Who knows. It's a lead I am following. So far it doesn't sound promising, but I will give it a shot."

"Well, good luck. I hope you find what you're looking for. I have to say all the mystery surrounding this little venture has aroused my curiosity."

"At some point, I'll either tell you or you can read about it in *The Post.*"

"Looking forward to it."

Jessica hung up the phone and looked at her notes with the survey map in front of her. Using her notes as a guide, she used a pencil to circle the area where she pulled each trigger for disc eight. From the tone of Gary's voice, she could tell digging at the base of a tree wasn't going to be as easy as she thought.

Chapter 26

Jessica parked her car in front of the Piggly Wiggly and went inside where she grabbed a hand basket and quickly perused the aisles. Crackers. Raisins. Bottled soft drinks and four apples filled her basket. While she wanted brand name, better tasting food and beverages, she opted for the cheaper, less tastier knock-offs. With her cash supply running very low, making the first rent payment was possible, but it would definitely drain her account. Back on the road toward Middleport, with one hand on the steering wheel, she transferred her purchases from the paper bag to her messenger bag.

Once at the gate, she quickly threw the messenger bag around her shoulder and squeezed through the bars. After walking to the clearing and trekking the distance to the shed, she used her survey map and notes to find the location where she pulled the triggers for disc 8 while noting the golf ball sized holes every ten feet. Stopping at the location where Figgis mentioned, she looked at her notes to confirm her location.

Disc eight.

Second and third image.

Tree on the right if facing south.

She removed her green lensatic compass from her right front pocket and opened the sight line and the lens. The metal was cool to the touch and the dial was righting itself as the needle zeroed in on her direction. Disregarding the technical functions, Jessica saw that she was facing north instead of south. Looking to the left of where she was standing, she walked up to the trunk of the tree. Pocketing the compass, she placed her hand on the rough and jagged bark of the tree thinking that maybe this was where she was being led. Did the word "dig" mean I was to find this tree? What could be underneath?

She let her bag slide off her shoulder and grabbed the strap before setting it on the roots of the tree. Reaching into her back pocket, she removed a pack of cigarettes as she walked toward the tool shed. Once a cigarette was lit and hanging from her mouth, she opened the flimsy door of the shed. Deciding not to step foot inside, she reached her bony arm inside, removing a small and large shovel followed by a garden trowel with a red handle.

Wasting little time, she stood next to the tree and picked up the small shovel. She broke ground by placing her foot on the backside of the shovel and forced it into the packed dirt.

For most of the day, Deputy Phillips had been confined to a room in Harrisburg, PA listening to a variety of speakers at a godforsaken training seminar. Bored out of his mind, he pretended to take notes in the white binder sitting in front of him. Surrounded by other county and state law enforcement officers, he used his body to block his notes, which were really drawings of General Lee from the *Dukes of Hazard* TV show.

He looked up at the speaker every so often and went back to his notes hoping no one would see his artwork. When one speaker would end his speech, another officer would walk up to the front of the room and utilize the overhead projector. He looked at the clock and thought about Jessica digging a hole somewhere on the farm in Middleport.

"Let's break for lunch, shall we?" A voice said at the front of the room. Closing his white binder, Phillips stood up hoping for cheeseburgers or pizza.

Jessica had hit many roots while digging at an angle to get underneath the tree. She would jump up and down on the back of the spade cutting the root in half, but some roots were too thick and she would be forced to dig around them.

By noon, she had dug down a foot and a half. From the sides of the hole, snapped and broken roots jetted out toward the center with one thick root running horizontally on the left side. She set the trowel on the ground and reached for her messenger bag. Crackers, raisins and a few swigs of a warm Piggly-Wiggly brand Cola, she belched as she reached for her Vicodin. She popped a single pill with another drink of Cola and belched loud enough to startle a cluster of birds in the trees above her. After throwing the bottle back into her bag, she heard it hit another pill bottle. Reaching inside, she pulled out her prescription of Nefazodone. Looking it over and remembering how much it affected her with alcohol, she considered tossing them away. It wasn't the same as Vicodin or Percocet. It caused a very brief euphoric feeling followed by a black hole. Thinking she would throw them away, she tossed them back into her bag and took one more swig of Piggly Wiggly-Cola and grabbed the trowel. Another belch followed as she began carving and digging.

Finally seeing what looked to be the bottom of the tree, she found a few loose objects which were a light, brown color. As she dug out dirt and cut roots with the shears, she pulled up objects which appeared to be bone. Jessica briefly considered the thought that they might be human until it was readily apparent that the bones were too small. *Maybe it was a family pet?*

Several hours passed and Jessica had made real progress removing much of the dirt under the tree. The sun started to disappear over the tree line, creating long shadows around her. She had pulled out four bones which resembled the rib cage of a dog. Then she hit something hard and sharp. Metal. Using the garden trowel and a good twenty minutes of clearing moist dirt from around the metal, she finally rocked it back and forth, trying to free it from underneath the tree. Finally, she was able to pull it out and she set it on the ground.

It was a long tool that was rusted and had jagged edges. A feeling came over her that she couldn't explain as it felt like she had seen this tool before. It wasn't just similar, but exactly like the pruning saw she had seen before on the conference room table at the sheriff's office. Jessica carefully inspected the tool and saw brown fabric on the blade of the saw. The fabric didn't look like burlap or even close to what a landscaper might use. She returned to the hole and looked where she had excavated the tool. Inside the hole was another piece of fabric and more brown objects she could only assume were more bones.

She grabbed the fabric and began pulling it in an effort to free it from the soil, only to have it rip off in small pieces between her fingers. Carefully using the garden trowel, she cleared out the dirt around the fabric until a large piece was exposed. Using her hand, she grabbed the fabric in her balled up fist and wiggled it until it tore. Now in her hand was a large piece of the cloth and she immediately noticed something. Buttons.

Grabbing her container of water, she soaked the fabric and rubbed the cloth together in her hands. The sun had disappeared over the tree line and it was getting more difficult to see. Using small beams of sunlight which blasted between the branches and leaves, she held up the cloth above her head into a stray beam of light for a better look. She continued to clean off the cloth until she saw something. Holding the fabric up once again and using a beam of sunlight, she could see two eyes, a mouth and a cape. A figure had been painted on the cloth.

The sickening and frightful feeling came over Jessica as she held the fabric in her hands. The figure painted on the cloth was a cartoon superhero that looked to have come from a child's clothing.

"Holy shit," she said as she backed away from the hole. She grabbed her bag and removed the radio. Extending the antenna, she pressed the talk button and nervously spoke as fast as she could.

"Hello? Come in. Come in. Hello?"

Deputy Phillips had suffered through a sleepy afternoon after eating more than his fair share of Domino's Pizza. Once the training seminar ended, he drove back to Pottsville and arrived in the parking lot of the sheriff's office. Every cruiser was missing from the lot, making him think a fatal car accident had occurred or maybe a truck overturned on the highway. Upon walking inside, he hollered out to the dispatcher.

"Ruth? Where is everybody?" he asked. She got up from her desk and walked toward him with a concerned look. "What?" he asked as he returned the look of concern.

"That Jessica girl called in on your radio. She found something at a farm in Middleport."

"What? What'd she find?"

"The remains of a child."

Phillips quickly grabbed a handheld radio and ran out of

the office, jumping into his truck. He sped along the highway until he found Cave Mill Road. Using his radio, he made an in-quiry for directions and soon found an open gate and a dirt path. He drove his truck along the path to the clearing and headed toward the barrage of blinding blue and red lights while a heavy equipment truck flashed its yellow lights.

Phillips parked behind the law enforcement vehicles and got out. The sound of the diesel engine rumbling from the equipment truck drowned out the shouting at the dig site. As he took a few steps forward, he could see five trees lying on their side while state troopers wearing gloves removed objects from the holes where the trees had been.

Jessica was standing near Sheriff Haydon with a blanket around her shoulders. Just as Phillips approached her, she turned her head with tears streaming down her face. She turned around and embraced Phillips, sobbing into his tan col-ored shirt. The sound of the backhoe ripping up more trees shook Jessica, causing her to tremble and shiver.

Emotionally drained and physically exhausted, Jessica closed her eyes and tightened the blanket around her. Phillips opened up the passenger side of the sheriff's car and sat Jessica in the seat. He walked over to the sheriff who was watching the state police exhume the bones of deceased children.

"That Jessica girl is something else," Sheriff Haydon said.

"I know."

"When we arrived she was shaking like a leaf. We could barely get anything out of her. She could only point." Sheriff picked at his teeth with a toothpick while Phillips surveyed the scene.

"How many bodies did they find?"

"So far they found five."

"Five?" Phillips' eyebrows raised in shock, his eyes as big as quarters.

"One under each tree. If this is what I think it is, this is going to be huge."

"What do you think it is?"

"Eh. Too early to be throwing around theories," he uttered as he kicked at the dirt. "She said she used a piece of equipment that belongs to the mine."

"Yeah, it's still in the back of my truck." he said as he used his thumb to point to his truck over his shoulder. Lights suddenly came from behind them as two vans pulled into the clearing. Sheriff Haydon turned toward the vans and shielded his eyes.

"I know you're off the clock, but could you escort them over to the state police?"

"Who are they?"

"Coroners. It's gonna be a long night." Haydon said as a state trooper called him over to the base of a tree. "Make that six," he said as he hung his head and walked toward the uprooted tree. Deputy Phillips looked over at Jessica sitting in the passenger seat of the Sheriff's cruiser. She was staring at the backhoe as it uprooted another tree. Shoving his hands into his pockets, he made his way toward the coroners who were just exiting their white vans.

Chapter 27

Jessica woke in her bed at the motel room still wearing her sweat soaked, dirty clothes from the day before. After jumping into the shower and scrubbing shampoo into her hair, she heard a knock at the door. After rinsing off, her phone started ringing. Once out of the shower, the knocking continued, but the phone stopped ringing. After putting her hair up into a towel, she put on jeans and a t-shirt and opened the door with the chain still attached. A microphone was raised up as a reporter asked questions. A cameraman stood behind her while focusing the shot.

"Miss Calvert, could you tell us how you came about uncovering 22 bodies of abducted children on a farm in Middleport, Pennsylvania?"

"Twenty-two?"

"Yes. Twenty-two. Is this the first time of you hearing the number of children found at the Silva Tree Farm?"

"Oh, my God," Jessica said as she stared off into the distance and shut the door. Covering her mouth, she slid down to the ground with her back against the wall. Sitting on the grimy motel carpet, tears fell and rolled off her cheeks. The knocking subsided, but the ringing phone resumed.

Between the rings of the phone, she could hear mumbling and chatter outside her door. Leaning toward the curtains, she saw reporters hanging around her car. Gathering herself and taking deep breaths, she crawled over to the end table and waited for the phone to stop ringing before she picked it up. Upon getting Deputy Phillips on the phone, she spoke in a hurried tone.

"I need you to get me out of here."

"The motel?"

"Yes. Please hurry."

"Are you okay?"

"Yes, just hurry."

Jessica packed her things and took everything down off the wall. She placed her bags and boxes next to the door. Moments later, she heard sirens grow louder and louder and finally came to a halt. The slamming of a car door could be heard followed by knocking on her door.

"It's me."

Deputy Phillips first loaded her luggage and files and then escorted Jessica through a barrage of questions, which she declined to answer. Once in the cruiser, Phillips sped away.

"This is ridiculous," Jessica said looking back at the cluster of reporters. "Is that what I look like?"

"This is a big deal. Guess who called the sheriff's office? CBS News. Like, the national news. They were asking all these questions."

"One of the reporters said they found 22 bodies. That

can't be right can it?"

"They unearthed forty something trees so far. More than 20 of them had bodies of children under them. They're still uprooting trees," he explained.

Trying to speak, she could only utter sounds as tears formed in the corners of her eyes and fell to her cheeks. "Sheriff thinks it's part of a kidnapping ring from the 1970s. It happened in New York around Rochester and Syracuse. It's an unsolved case and the state police are trying to connect the bodies with the kids who went missing twenty years ago."

"What about Dr. Silva?" she asked as she nervously pulled at her bottom lip.

"He was questioned at the station," he replied as if it was simply routine.

"Then what?"

"They let him go."

"What? Why! He's a prime suspect!"

"He isn't. His brother is."

"Gordon D'Silva didn't do it!" she said, getting excited and angry at the same time.

"He was found with the murder weapon in his car. In fact it was the only murder weapon found on a suspect. All of the others were buried along with each child."

"Every child was buried with their murder weapon?"

"Yes," he replied as Jessica sunk in her seat, a wave of horror washed over her thoughts.

"Silva needs to be questioned again. Is there a transcript?"

"I don't know, but I am sure the sheriff has notes," he replied as Jessica turned around in her seat and rummaged through her things in the backseat. Finding her trespassing gear she used in the operations trailer, she turned to Phillips.

"Head over to Peach Mountain Road. I need to find something out."

"We going to the house?"

"Yep."

"You going to ask more questions?"

"Yep."

Moments later, Jessica tethered herself to the cruiser while Phillips keeps the car in reverse. Holding a walkie-talkie, he spoke to Jessica while he could still see her walking through the trees towards the trailer.

"Why do you think Gordon D'Silva isn't guilty of murdering the Adler Family?"

"I was told he didn't."

"By who?"

"Can I plead the 5th on this?"

"What? A ghost told you?"

"That's the second time you have used the word ghost and it makes me cringe."

"Sorry. Too scary?"

"No. Not scary. It's just wrong. When someone says ghost, I think of a translucent dead person floating around. This has nothing to do with ghosts."

"Then what is it?"

"I don't know. Paranormal I guess, but even that word doesn't quite fully describe it."

Jessica approached the generator outside of the trailer and pulled the ripcord four times before it roared alive. Once inside the trailer, Jessica booted up the computer and flipped several switches. The hum of cooling fans and the rattle of the hard drive carried on while she stared at the screen. Once the green prompt appeared, she typed in her question and repeated it into the microphone.

"Did Dr. Peter Silva murder the Adler Family?"

She picked up her walkie-talkie and pressed the button. "Question asked." Inside the house, the Ouija board moved to each letter and stopped.

Jessica felt a slight tug before being violently pulled backward off her feet. Her body slammed into the door behind her causing it to blast open. She flew out of the trailer coming down hard onto the ground. Phillips slammed the cruiser into reverse, driving fifteen yards before realizing the rope was no longer connected. Jessica screamed in pain and in fear as she was quickly dragged to the side of the trailer and toward the house.

Phillips flipped the gear shifter into drive and punched the accelerator. The back tires flipped up field dirt before gaining traction. He drove around the tree line and onto the Adler property. He sped toward the house and onto the front lawn as Jessica was being dragged toward the front steps. She screamed as she tried to free herself from the harness around her waist and torso.

Every few feet of being dragged, her body would roll over. While she tried to pull out a nylon strap from a metal buckle, her body would twist and roll her onto her stomach. With her knuckles now being scraped underneath her, she let go of the strap as the pain burned and throbbed. Now at the front porch steps, her body thumped on each step upward until she was on the wood planked porch.

Her body hit the front door with a thud causing it to open. Jessica continued to scream as Phillips jumped out of his cruiser and ran up the porch steps. The front door slammed shut before he could force himself inside. He could see her through the beveled glass being dragged upstairs unconscious. Her head banged on every step as she was being dragged to the second floor.

Chapter 28

Jessica opened her eyes and found herself in Tilly's room on the floor. The Ouija board was next to her and the speaker box was beneath the window. Next to the speaker box was a small table and a lamp. The light was on and the bulb began to increase in brightness. At first, it lit up the entire room before becoming so bright, Jessica shielded her eyes and could see a figure standing in the corner until the light grew to a brightness no amount of shielding could defend.

The light subsided and Jessica was looking down at a bathroom sink. Hands that belonged to a man were in the sink washing a pair of pants. She couldn't control where she looked as it seemed she inhabited a man's body.

She watched as he scrubbed the pants under running water. Her hands could feel the warmth of the water and the tiny bubbles from the soap around her knuckle. The movement felt like her own, yet she was not in control. She watched as the hands turned off the water and carried the now clean pants into a bedroom.

She was now standing on a blue colored landscaping tarp and there was blood at her feet. The man reached up to his face and took off his glasses and set them on a dresser before kneeling down. His vision now blurred, she watched as the man shook the pants and aired them out revealing that they belonged to a child. The man then spoke causing reverberating vocals inside her head as if she was talking with her fingers plugging up her ears.

"You got your pants dirty, but they're clean now," he said in a caring and compassionate tone. The man turned his head and the outline of a dead child could be seen naked on the blue tarp. He bent down and proceeded to put the pants on the boy's limp body. Jessica cried only noises, yet no tears formed in her view as the man finished his task.

Standing up, the man walked back to the bathroom and rinsed his hands followed by a brand new bar of soap. She watched through blurry eyes as the package was unwrapped and the hands tossed the wrapper. The man began scrubbing his hands, wrists and forearms with steaming hot water flowing from the tap. Soap and a rinse followed by more soap and hot water, scrubbing as if to remove his own skin. She watched as he took the bar of soap and threw it into the trashcan.

Upon turning off the water, he grabbed a thick, blue paper towel and dried off his hands. Looking briefly into the mirror, Jessica could see that it was a blurry image of Dr. Silva and he was naked. He turned away from the mirror and used his elbow to turn off the light switch.

The sound of a shovel breaking ground followed and she could see that Dr. Silva was now at the tree farm, digging a hole. After 4 feet, the tarp was dragged over and the body of the child was rolled into the hole along with a serrated prun-ing saw. Loose dirt from a pile of fresh soil was shoveled on top of the naked, lifeless body of the child until the boy's flesh could no longer be seen. Jessica watched as Dr. Silva's hand reached for a sapling. The small tree was held in place by one hand while the other swiped handfuls of dirt, covering the bottom of the sapling.

Jessica then felt heat on her skin followed by the whip-ping of the wind. Her hand was now grabbing something and the sound in her ears grew louder. A car engine. A window was down. She could see trees, a road and a family camp-ground. Tents were scattered about, and kids and parents were playing volleyball. Children chasing and tagging each other could be heard laughing and shouting.

The car was put into park. The sun felt warm on her skin. She watched as Dr. Silva walked to a dock with a fishing pole and a bucket. Two boys throwing hooked lines into the water turned and looked seemingly into Jessica's eyes. They were dressed alike, and one appeared to be younger than the other. Brothers perhaps. The voice inside her head resonated with each syllable spoken by Dr. Silva.

"You boys need some bait?"

"Yeah, do you have some?"

"I do. What are you guys using?"

"All we have is crank bait and minnow plugs."

"I've got a bucket of live earthworms if you're interested."

"You gonna share 'em with us?" one of the boys asked, his

eyes lighting up.

"Sure!"

A bright light pierced her eyes before it dimmed. Now she was standing in a kitchen where Gordon D'Silva was listening to his brother give him instructions. Dr. Silva was out of breath and in a hurry. When he spoke, he sounded nervous.

"What happened?" Dr. Silva asked.

"Just as I pulled into the driveway, he ran inside."

"The house? He ran inside the house?"

"I couldn't stop him."

"What'd you do?"

"Turned around and left."

Jessica watched as Dr. Silva grabbed his brother and screamed in his face. Then came fists thrown to Gordon's face as he fell to the ground followed by kicks to his stomach.

"I'm gonna tell! I'm gonna tell!" Gordon screamed. Dr. Silva bent down and spoke to a face that was smeared with blood. Mucus covered his bloody mouth in strands as he continued to scream out, "What do you do with these boys! What do you do! Who are..." the tree saw was plunged into the side of Gordon's neck and up into his brain, killing him instantly.

Another bright light followed by hands on the steering wheel and headlights shining on a dark road. The blue station wagon pulled into the Adler's gravel driveway. Jessica watched as Dr. Silva's hand grabbed the bloody tree saw and got out of his car. She could feel each step as he walked up the stairs and made three strides toward the front door. Finding the door unlocked, Dr. Silva opened the door and went inside.

Jessica felt something grab her leg and pull. Unsure of what was happening, she looked at the image of Dr. Silva walking up to a curious and confused Mr. Adler as she got farther and farther away until a bright light seemingly ignited and blinded her.

Now being dragged across a wood floor, she saw the Ouija board and the table with a lamp. A figure stood in the corner as a hand continued to drag her across the floor and to the top of the stairs. Now being lifted into the air and slung over the back of Deputy Phillips, she felt the pressure in her stomach with every step he took down the stairs and out the front door.

Half awake, she was put into the front seat of Phillips' truck and opened her eyes as he was driving down the road toward the hospital. A wave of pain began to throb over her head, rib cage and arms. The degree of pain was so great, she gripped the side of the passenger door and Phillips' arm and screamed with rage.

"What? What?" he said as she continued to scream while shutting her eyes. She broke out into tears and began to cry out loudly as she thought about the boys murdered at the hands of Dr. Silva. Phillips slowed the cruiser as Jessica knelt in her seat and leaned toward him, wrapping her arms around his neck and sobbing. Tears flowed off her cheek and onto his collarbone. He embraced her back as she screamed.

"He killed them! He abused and killed all those boys!" she yelled as her grip on his shirt felt so tight that he swore she ripped the fabric. Continuing to scream, he held her tightly and tried to calm and slow down his breathing as he recalled seeing her being pulled out of the trailer and dragged away with nothing on the other end.

While he had thought she might have been a little crazy when talking about her paranormal encounters, actually seeing it firsthand caused chills to pulse throughout his body. The guilt of taking her explanations lightly increased with every second she spent clinging to his shirt.

Bob Calvert sat in the large, cafeteria-style break room of the Three Rivers Manufacturing Plant after eating his lunch. The room featured ten vending machines and over twenty tables scattered about with televisions mounted in the corners of the room. After visiting one of the ten vending machines, he opened a package of Twinkies and sunk his teeth into the sponge cake. The television closest to him was turned to the local news.

Bob had glanced up a few times to see the weather report, but was more interested in the Pennsylvania Auto Guide in front of him as he flipped the pages of used trucks. After shoving more than half the Twinkie into his mouth, he glanced up casually at the TV as he flipped a page in the Auto Guide. Jessica's work photo taken at *The Washington Post* was displayed on screen. The screen then switched to heavy machinery digging up trees.

Bob stood up and ran over to the TV and turned it up as a reporter stood near the scene of a row of uprooted trees.

"So far 22 bodies of children have been recovered and are believed to be children abducted in the 1970s as part of the Syracuse-Rochester Kidnapping Ring. The discovery was made by 28-year-old Jessica Calvert on a tree farm owned by the brother of the alleged killer, Gordon D'Silva." Bob watched as the TV showed Jessica opening the door to the motel room and then closing it. "Attempts to speak with Miss Calvert were unsuccessful..." Bob turned around and ran out of the break room leaving an entire Twinkie on the table still in the torn cellophane wrapper.

Chapter 29

Jessica awoke in a strange bed with sheets and a comforter which reeked of cheap fabric softener. As she looked around the room, she saw posters on the wall of baseball and basketball players. Fearful that Phillips was lying next to her, she turned her head slowly revealing a void of tucked in sheets and the absence of a pillow.

Exhaling and thankful she didn't do anything stupid, she slid into her jeans and walked barefoot down a hallway. As she approached what appeared to be a living room, she found Phillips on a couch fast asleep. Just as she turned around and tiptoed back down the hallway, the phone rang.

Ring. Ring.

She heard Phillips jump up off the couch and scramble for the phone on the end table.

"Hello?" he answered followed by a lengthy silence. "Yeah, I can do that. Is the sheriff in?" he asked. Jessica listened through her lightly throbbing headache. "When does he come in? Oh. Okay. Where? What's the room number? I will tell her," he replied making Jessica perk up and wonder if the conversation was about her. When Phillips ended the call, Jessica turned back around and walked into the living room as if she hadn't heard a thing.

"Hey, how did I get here?"

"Two of your pills and a few swigs of the booze in your luggage," he explained. Jessica furrowed her brow and crossed her arms.

"Sorry," she replied as she looked down at her bare feet. "And thanks. I appreciate it."

"I didn't know if you wanted to check into another motel. You weren't in any shape to be staying by yourself though. I just got a call from Ruth at the station. She said the sheriff is meeting with the state police and the FBI at 2 p.m. and he said if you could be there, that would be a lot of help."

"Are they going to question Dr. Silva again?"

"I don't know. That's all the info I have. If you want to find out, I suppose you're free to attend the meeting. Also, one more thing."

"What?"

"Your dad is in St. Clair looking for you."

Jessica arrived in the parking lot of the Mill Street Motel and parked near Room 12 and got out of her car. Not too far down from where she had been staying, she looked around for signs of reporters and cameramen. After knocking, she could hear someone hurrying to the door. Once it opened, she couldn't contain her guilt which showed itself in the tears that streamed down her cheeks. Bob reached his arms around his daughter and embraced her, coming to tears himself.

"You're my baby girl! You keep me so worried!"

"I'm so sorry dad!"

The phone call that woke Deputy Phillips included a request that he return the tomographer to Gary Figgis at Locust Valley. After a short drive, he arrived in the parking lot and removed the tomographer from the bed of his truck without the need for a makeshift ramp. Brute strength and a quick maneuver, the machine was back on the ground. Once in the lobby, Mr. Figgis appeared after a short wait.

"Deputy Phillips, good to see you again," he said as he reached out and took the handle of the tomographer.

"You as well."

"Is Miss. Calvert with you?" Gary asked as he pulled the dolly to his side and held it at an angle as he spoke.

"I'm sorry she isn't."

"Holy hell did she find something, huh? I've seen her on the news several different channels closing that motel door on that reporter."

"She's getting a lot of attention that's for sure."

"So weird too. The farm belongs to one of our doctors who works here at the mine."

"Dr. Silva, right?"

"Yeah. He's taking this very hard too," he replied as he turned slightly to head back to his office.

"I'm sure. Thanks for letting Miss Calvert borrow your equipment."

"Of course. Glad to help."

"Say, when you mentioned that Dr. Silva's taking it hard," he said with his body halfway turned to leave. Even though Jessica wasn't with him, he could feel the push of him needing to ask more questions. "How do you mean exactly?"

"Well, he was up for retirement next year, but it seems he doesn't have it in him to continue."

"He's leaving?"

"Gave his notice the day after Miss Calvert's discovery."

"Any idea where he's going?"

FBI Agent Warren J. Ford had recently sold his three bedroom house located minutes from the office in Harrisburg. Instead of making a safe purchase with four bedrooms for his growing family, he was making the mistake of listening to his wife.

"This one has five bedrooms and a basement. We'll have plenty of room to grow!"

"The mortgage payment will be more than what we're paying now."

"I'll get a job! Or we'll simply manage our money better."

With two kids in the fourth grade and the possibility of a third child in the near future, the prospect of a high mortgage payment scared him.

"This house has a pool! We don't need a pool. Who will clean it?" The conversations were mentally draining. Having to focus on work at the same time made it difficult to focus on buying a house and he knew that his wife would eventually get her way.

The most gruesome case he had ever been handed took place the day after a girl discovered the body of a child, which led to local law enforcement digging up another 21 bodies. As he looked through the file, he read where the suspect was found dead in a pond with a landscaping tool that had been identified as the murder weapon. Agent Ford's boss had sat him down in the conference room and explained that it seemed to be a case which simply needed to be officially closed and all that was left was paper work. Boxes of evidence, files and photographs were placed in his office, which he looked at and studied in between answering phone calls from his wife.

"We could have a pool service clean the pool. I looked into it and the expense isn't that bad if you factor in the chemicals you would have to buy anyway."

Warren's boss wasn't a detailed and thorough man as he was more off the cuff and loved to shoot from the hip. If he had reviewed the files, he would have mentioned to him that a girl who claimed to have contact with a paranormal entity led her to the discovery.

Having to deal with crazy people was part of the job and while a woman claiming to speak with ghosts was nothing new, it did have an impact on his report. Knowing he would have to speak with the young woman made him exhale as he plopped the file down on his desk and rolled his eyes. After scheduling a meeting with both the sheriff's office and the state police in Pottsville, PA he asked if it was a possibility to have Miss Jessica Calvert present.

Jessica took her father to the Buckhorn Café for lunch where they discussed her involvement of the discovery at the Silva Tree Farm. She explained how she used the machine and uncovered the first body. Her father winced during her explanation of exhuming the remains and found it difficult to eat the food on his plate. After she apologized for the third time for lying to him, he finally held up his hand and nodded his head.

"It's fine. I understand. This is something you had to do and I'm proud of you. No need to apologize anymore. What are you doing now? Are you writing the story for *The Post?*"

"I will write the story, but this isn't over yet. The police aren't looking at the right man."

"What do you mean?"

"It seems that they are putting all of this on a man who's deceased. He was the one found in the car in the pond. A landscaping tool believed to be the murder weapon was in his car that is believed to be connected to the family that was murdered here in St. Clair."

"And you think that the murderer is someone else?"

"I know who did it."

"Is this person here in St. Clair?"

"Yep," she replied. Bob's face fell to a look of distress.

"Now that worries me."

Their conversation continued down a path of worried father vs. overly-reassuring daughter. While trying to ease her father's concerns, she so badly wanted to pull out her pack of Marlboro's and light up, pulling the smoke deep into her lungs, feeling the nicotine pulse through her system. Exhaling with a crooked mouth sending the smoke up into the air and flicking the ashes into the ashtray beside her. Instead she downed a coca-cola and set the glass on the edge hoping for a refill.

"I have a meeting with the sheriff's office, the state police and," she said as she used her napkin to wipe the corner of her mouth, "The FBI."

"So you're just going to explain to them who this man is and that's it?"

"I'm going to try and get them to interview him one more time. See where that gets us."

Bob pushed his plate away from him and set his elbows on the table. He exhaled as he thought about everything she said.

"It's not like you to give up. It's not who you are. I should have expected something like this only more along the lines of politics, maybe uncovering another Watergate. Not a haunted house."

"It hasn't been easy. That's for sure."

"What time is this meeting?"

"In two hours."

Chapter 30

The meeting in the small conference room began with Warren
Ford, Sheriff Haydon and a state police officer named Jerry
Westerby. After asking Jessica to wait in a separate office,
Warren opened an FBI file on Gordon D'Silva. As he read from
the documents, Sheriff Haydon looked at the folder and how
neat and straight the documents were. The folder didn't have
frayed or bent corners and neither did Warren. His tie was angled and crisp. His hair was combed and appeared to be resist-
ant to wind.

He had met many FBI agents in his time in law enforcement. *They're all the same*, he thought. Warren began reading a
twenty-page report that started with information of the kidnapping ring in Syracuse and Rochester. He flipped pages with
a snap as he listed the dates of each child that was reported
missing including the location and the age of each victim.

Next, he read a section on the murder of the Adler Family,
beginning with the eye witness William O'Keefe when he saw
Scott Adler get into a blue station wagon who was never identified. He then read several lengthy paragraphs on the missing
person report which included a phone call that Scott Adler
had returned home. Warren then read the details of the mur-

der that spanned four pages. The next eight pages concerned the death of James Extine and the assault of Jessica Calvert followed by the purchase of the Adler property by a man named Henrik Frasier. The report included various details about the team assembled to investigate the house, which resulted in the deaths of three men.

Jessica sat out front of the station while the meeting was underway. Instead of showing up with a pack of cigarettes, t-shirt, jeans and a lighter, she had put on a pair of khakis and button up shirt. Opening her messenger bag, she placed her notes inside along with photocopied news articles, copies of documents and the large, folded survey map. While she waited, she looked at her watch and wondered if Phillips was on a call.

"Jessica!" came a loud booming voice from the back of the station. Standing up and looking over the reception area, she could see Sheriff Haydon waving her over. Once inside the room, she took a seat across from Agent Ford. Expecting a gypsy woman or someone resembling a palm reader, he was surprised by her petite figure and cute face. Confidence beamed from her mannerisms as she took a seat and removed her messenger bag from her shoulder while being introduced around the table. She quickly removed her notepad and pen from her back pocket, ready to jump into the meeting.

Warren Ford had expected to get an earful of ghosts and spirits that he could take back to the office and stand around the coffee machine telling his co-workers about the nut in St.

Clair. Instead, he slowly lost control of the meeting and for a while, Jessica was in charge.

"Mrs. Calvert, thank you for being here today. I am having some difficulty with a section of my report as to how you came to know the location of the buried children on the Silva Tree Farm. We are needing you to clarify this for us please."

Jessica began with the explanation of the technology residing in the operations trailer. She spoke highly of Sergeant Major Ray Turner and gave specific details of the Ouija board which was wired to the computer in the trailer. She then explained how they found the car in the pond followed by the death of Father Abbott, Ray Turner and Henrik Frazier. Next, she explained the rescue effort of Deputy Phillips as she was pulled from the trailer and spoke about the words she saw appear on the screen.

"How did the words appear on the screen? Who typed them?" he asked as he looked at his notes and continued writing her answers down. Her answers begged more questions from Agent Ford until she became frustrated with his tone and his skeptical attitude.

"Look, I can see where this is going, but I just can't let it. I can feel your skepticism crawling all over me."

"I cannot put spirits, ghosts or paranormal events in a report that will be seen by the director of the FBI," he said as he dropped his pen on his legal pad and sat back in his chair. He watched as Jessica stood up and walked out of the conference room and reached inside Phillips' office and grabbed his tape dispenser. She quickly walked back in the conference room like a fighter entering the ring.

The equivalent of shrugging a robe off her shoulders revealing her bright red boxing gloves and black trunks, she opened her messenger bag and removed all of the material she had placed on the wall in the motel room. After spreading everything out, she began to tape up the photocopies of the news articles, the copies of the deed to Gordon D'Silva's house, the notes from interviewing Clay Samson at Wolf Reed Tavern and ending with the survey map.

The timeline reached from behind Warren's seat and spanned the length of the wall. Sheriff Haydon and Trooper Westerby looked at each other as if they were third graders about to be given a math test by a furious teacher.

Before beginning with the entire timeline, she lit up a cigarette from her purse and tossed the lighter onto her notepad and began.

For twenty-five minutes, Jessica walked all three men through the timeline. She started with the news article of Gordon D'Silva's disappearance and continued with her notes on the first communication with the entity and how she found the ribbons which led to the car in the pond. By the time she was standing next to the survey map and pointing out her location of where she used shovels and a trowel to exhume the body of a child, each officer leaned forward on the edge of their seat paying close attention to every word.

The first two cigarettes had gone out and she had lit another while explaining being dragged out of the trailer and up into the second floor of the house where she was given a first person view of two murders which took place in the house of Dr. Peter Silva. Warren watched her mannerisms and noted that she was in control and her information was deeply rooted in well-researched information. When she finally sat down, Warren spoke first.

"Thank you for your explanation. I don't quite know what to say. I came in here needing a statement to your outrageous claims and I hoped I could put something in this report that didn't sound ludicrous. I didn't think I would come away from this meeting believing in your statement."

"I just appreciate you listening to me and hearing me out," she replied. Warren held up both of his hands in front of him as he continued.

"I'm not saying I believe all of it. It's a lot to take in."

"I understand," she replied with a half smile. Warren cleared his throat and stood up while looking at Sheriff Haydon. "You mind if I use the office across the hall? I need to use the phone."

As agent Ford left the room, Phillips poked his big head in the conference room and looked at Jessica.

"Yeah, I'm taking a break," Sheriff Haydon said. "Holy shit my head is spinning." Trooper Westerby followed him out of the room as Phillips sat down across the table from Jessica.

"How's it going?" he asked as he looked at the timeline taped up on the wall.

"Okay, I guess. I stole your tape dispenser."

"I might have to arrest you."

"Where have you been? I thought you would've already been here."

"I took the imaging machine back to Gary Figgis and then I had to serve a subpoena and two eviction notices."

"Sounds like fun."

"Not really. Day-to-day stuff. I did find something out while talking to Gary over at Locust Valley."

"What's that?" she asked. Phillips leaned forward with his elbows on the table and his fingers clasped.

"Dr. Silva retired."

"He did?"

"He's pulling up the tent poles and leaving town. He already has a for sale sign in his front yard. I drove by it on my way here."

"The FBI guy is calling his boss right now. Maybe he can pick him up before he leaves town and question him."

"Lot of boxes and movement in the back of the house. Hopefully he can move quickly."

"Wanna go outside?" she asked as she ashed out her cigarette. "These fluorescent lights are sucking the life out of me."

Soon after Agent Ford got off the phone, he sat in the conference room and waited for the others to return. Once they were seated, Warren began with the bad news.

"We won't be questioning him at this time. The evidence we have in front of us points to Gordon D'Silva and nothing gives us any reason to consider Dr. Silva."

"Even after everything I just said?"

"Yes," Warren said as he held up his hands in defense. "We have to have hard evidence, but I have been told that I am able to include your materials in the official report."

"What good does that do if he's still walking around out there?"

"It does a lot of good. It will be part of the record and if we obtain any evidence against Dr. Silva then we will reopen the case."

"Reopen? You mean you're closing it?"

"At this time, yes."

"Are you kidding me? What the hell man! I just sat here and told you!"

"It's not me. I have to do what I am told and right now this is what has to happen. I will say this, and this is off the record considering your profession," he said as he put his hand over her notes and fired off a look to show the level of seriousness. "Got it? Off the record."

"Yeah. Fine."

"I believe you," he said as he removed his hand and sat back in his chair. "If there is anyone who will be championing to get a second interview or uncover evidence that could put him away, it will be me. I promise."

"He's leaving."

"Who?"

"Deputy Phillips came in here and explained that Dr. Silva

retired and has already put his house up for sale."

"The FBI's jurisdiction is the entirety of the United States," he replied as he sat up in his chair and shifted his weight to a more comfortable position. Jessica was thinking of something, her eyes darted while her brow furrowed. Finally, she came back with an idea.

"What if I were to uncover evidence that he either killed the Adler Family or buried the children on his farm?" she asked. Warren started to grin, but restrained himself.

"I cannot condone you to do anything that would break any laws, nor put yourself in danger. If you were to somehow discover something that could contribute to the case, I ask you to do so without explanation as to how you came about such information. In fact, should you uncover something, please submit it anonymously."

The tide had turned in front of her eyes. While she was ready for a fight, it seemed that the looks coming from both Sheriff Haydon and Trooper Westerby supported the unspoken request from Agent Ford.

"If you do go looking for something, be careful. If you want to end it here, we understand," Sheriff Haydon said.

"You've done so much for the families of those children by bringing them closure."

"Closure isn't enough. I know the truth. This shit will haunt me for the rest of my life."

"The law says we have gone to the fullest extent. Should we pursue it any further and fail, legal repercussions could cost me and my boss our job and could make Dr. Silva very rich," Warren explained.

"Yeah, I get it."

"To make it easy on everyone, should you find something, turn it in anonymously."

Upon entering the conference room several hours ago, she had hoped that it would be settled. They would call Dr. Silva in for an interview, he would be interrogated and face the death penalty or even better, die in prison. Now she would be called upon once again, not by paranormal entities, rather three law enforcement officers.

Chapter 31

Agent Warren Ford entered his office building the following morning and stopped into an analyst's office to give him the name and address of Dr. Peter Silva. Shortly after lunch, he had Dr. Silva's social security number, birth certificate and a police record which showed a traffic ticket in Philadelphia and two others issued in Schuylkill County.

A copy of his medical license was attached to his college transcripts along with letters of recommendation from his professors. None of it would be of value to Jessica. He called her and explained that the record was perfectly clean with nothing to go on. She thanked him for his help and decided she would interview a few miners at Locust Valley and possibly scour the library and the county office for any available records which might give her a solid lead.

After jumping in the shower, she soaped up and rinsed off before wrapping a towel around her chest. Hearing the phone ring in the front room, she took a chance that Phillips wouldn't be coming home so soon and ran out to answer the phone.

"Phillips residence."

"It's me," Phillips said. "I just drove by Silva's house and he's still there loading boxes into a moving truck."

"By himself?"

"Yep. Also, the station got a call from the city about the Adler House. It's being demolished in two days. The demo crew went by the house and they have questions about the trailer."

"What about it?"

"They're going to junk it unless you want it."

"Me? Why me?"

"The Frazier family wants nothing to do with it."

"Me either."

"They asked specifically about the equipment in the trailer."

"What? They're asking if I want the equipment?"

"Yeah."

"No. I don't want any of it. It's not even mine."

"County lists you as a secondary owner," he said. A brief pause came between them before he had the gumption to ask. "Would it be okay if I took it?"

"The computer?"

"Yeah."

"I don't care. Go for it."

"You have to call and tell them you want it. Would you mind doing that? Tell them I will pick it up."

"No problem. Hey, did the crew go inside the house?"

"No. They're afraid to. They're bulldozing the entire thing to the ground and burning it with the fire department. It's become a big deal."

"Good. Move on. I would do the same."

Phillips gave Jessica the number and she called it soon after and explained she wanted the computer. She lit up a cigarette and thought about her next move. While thinking about the tree farm and the tool shed, she wondered if there might be something in the shed that could connect Dr. Silva to the murders. She closed her eyes and recalled opening the door to the shed.

Inside there were tools and she remembered the old wooden shelves, spider webs and what looked like gardening equipment leaning up against the wall. Shovels, ground stakes and rolls of wire were aimlessly set on the wooden shelves along with garden trowels and various sizes of pruning shears. She felt that her memory was fairly accurate and there was nothing in the shed that would help. The only feeling in her that was real and had any substance was the thought of Chinese food.

When Phillips came home, he found Jessica sitting on the floor in front of his coffee table ehivh he had bought at a garage sale. The table was covered in Chinese take out containers.

"Dinner's ready."

"Wow! You read my mind."

"You get the computer?"

"I did. It was crazy over there. A bunch of construction workers drawing straws to see who does what job. The closer to the house they work, the shorter the straw. They're freaking out."

"It's certainly warranted."

"I'm gonna change out of my uniform. Be back in a second."

After over eating and smoking a few cigarettes, Phillips ran down to his truck and carried the computer inside the living room.

"This thing is awesome."

"What are you going to do with it?"

"I want to get some computer games. It has a built in floppy drive."

"Do you know how to use it? That stuff is mystery to me."

"Yeah, I don't know much about it either. If I can't get it to work, I might sell it. I could pay my truck off," he said with a smile as he set it on the small kitchen table to the left of the living room. After plugging it in and flipping a switch, the screen flickered and words appeared in a single column:

BRING

SILVA

HERE

BRING

SILVA

HERE

BRING

SILVA

HERE

BRING

SILVA

HERE

BRING

SILVA

HERE

"The hell? Jess? Come here," he said as he stared at the monitor. She stood up and walked over and laid her eyes on the screen.

"Holy fucking shit."

Chapter 32

Jessica explained how the Ouija board worked and how the words appeared on the screen. While many of the words that appeared on the screen in the past were vague, the three on the screen were direct.

"Bring Silva to the house?"

"Then what?" Phillips asked.

"I don't know. Do we bring him to the trailer? The house? Upstairs or downstairs?"

"How do you get him there?"

"I don't know."

With stomachs full of Chinese food and Coca-Cola, the evening wore on them as they discussed options such as arresting Dr. Silva and taking him to the house. They imagined a scenario where they would tell him to walk upstairs after taking the handcuffs off of him while never giving him an explanation as to why.

"We could drug him in some way," Jessica said with a mischievous grin.

"You mean somehow get him to swallow a pill?"

"I was thinking chloroform."

"Doesn't work. You're thinking of what you have seen in

movies. Isoflurane is better. The second someone breathes it in, they're out like a light."

"How do you know that? What a creepy thing to know."

"We learned at the academy that a man would put it in a spray bottle and spray a mist of it in the face of female joggers and then put them in a van and drive away."

"Holy hell. Did they catch him?"

"Yeah. This was in Manhattan in Central Park. A couple decades ago."

"I don't think I could do your job and hear all the horrible shit that goes on in the world. Being a journalist is bad enough."

"The reason we were told about it, is because we have some in each county sheriff's office."

"What for?"

"Dogs. Horses. Livestock. Our supply comes from a veterinarian here in town."

"Why would a sheriff's office need to knock a dog out?"

"We are responsible for animal control in Schuylkill County."

"Oh."

"The house is being torn down the day after tomorrow and Dr. Silva is leaving. Whatever you need to do to lock this guy up, you better do it fast."

They spoke about other options late into the night. Finally, Jessica felt the effects of her full stomach and the long day she endured.

302   WHAT LIES INSIDE

"I'm turning in. You need anything from your room be-fore I go to sleep?"

"Nah. I'm good. Goodnight, Punky Brewster."

Jessica had fallen asleep without the aid of alcohol or medication, which might have caused her to wake due to a sound in the hallway. She sat up and saw that the door had been opened.

"Phillips?" she said as she peered down the hallway then something caught her eye. The door. It moved. The small space between the door and the wall appeared to move slightly as if someone was standing behind it. Instead of speaking his name, she called out for his help by yelling. "Phillips!" A man could be seen coming down the hallway walking toward the bedroom.

He was thinner than Phillips and had a long stride. Still dark and unable to see who it was, the man behind the door walked out from the shadow just as the thin man walked into the room. The man from behind the door was Phillips and he was holding a white cloth in his hand. He quickly placed the cloth over the mouth of the thin man who was wearing a lab coat and could only have been Dr. Silva. Jessica screamed and pushed herself back against the headboard as she woke up. Sweating. Gasping panicked breaths.

The scream woke Phillips on the couch and he jumped up and hurried down the hallway.

"Jessica?"

"Son of a..." she started to say as she caught her breath. "That was a bad one."

"Another nightmare? Did you take your medication?"

"No. Damn it. That was so real. It felt so real."

"What was it?"

She explained the nightmare and talked with her hands as she got out of bed and pulled a bottle of tequila out of her luggage and searched for her pills. She finished telling Phillips the story and sat on the corner of the bed and took a sip from the bottle. After an hour of trying to calm down, Phillips stood in the doorway.

"If you're okay, I'm gonna go lay back down."

"Yeah, I'm fine. Sorry,"

"No need to be sorry. If you need anything, just holler," he said as he strolled down the hallway. Jessica turned out the light on the nightstand and fell down on her pillow.

The next morning she woke to baseball and basketball players staring at her from the posters on the wall. After getting ready in the bathroom, she decided she better head to the county office and begin pulling records or even heading to the library and combing through old newspapers. After getting in her car, she considered the nightmares she had in months past.

Thinking the county courthouse may be a good place to start, she turned left and drove while thinking about the dream with her mother and the ribbons in her mouth. Even if she wanted to, she could never forget the boy who ran through the forest and was pulled into the hole.

While turning onto South Centre Street, Jessica recalled the men standing in line at the foot of her bed. They were waiting in line to see a man who was at the front. As she thought about the man who said,

"There's a lot of blood. Hold still"

She slowed her car as she thought of the boy in woods. He was a victim. The dream of her mother led her to the pond. The men standing in line waiting to see a doctor wasn't a nightmare, it was a clue. They were all clues. Seeing Phillips cover the mouth of Dr. Silva with a cloth was very clear and needed little interpretation. Jessica turned away from the direction of the county courthouse and sped toward the sheriff's office instead.

Deputy Phillips had been filling out reports on a wellness check and a traffic accident he serviced earlier that morning. As he completed the report of the wellness check, he put the papers in a file and glanced up before continuing with the traffic accident. The glimpse took a full two seconds to register that he saw the face of Jessica in the distance. He stood up and walked to the front of the station. She looked defeated like an athlete who had lost a big game.

"What's wrong?"

"Can we talk outside?" she asked. He followed her and listened as she explained the imagery in her dreams and nightmares. Once he agreed that she was definitely being communicated with, she laid out the nightmare that had played out the previous night and recalled something she said.

"Remember when I said that we could drug him in some way?"

"Yeah. You were joking."

"I was joking, but I have another feeling, a strong feeling that this is what I am supposed to do."

"Now we are talking outside of the law," he said in a tone that made it clear he wouldn't help her go through with something so severe. She had originally come to the station to ask him for the drug which would knock out Dr. Silva, but by his response; she knew not to even ask.

"I know."

"I can't help you."

"I know."

"Jessica..." he started to say. She put her hand up to her mouth as tears collected in the corners of her eyes.

"Don't say it," her voice quivered as she replied.

"I'm sorry. I think it's time to let this go. You even know what he looks like? He's an old man with gray hair and thin as a rail. He probably won't live much longer anyway.

"I've come too far," tears now pouring like rain, Phillips grabbed Jessica and embraced her. "I can't. I can't walk away."

"You've done so much."

"I have, but there's one more thing. I can't come all this way and not finish it," she said as she wriggled slightly and broke from his embrace, taking a step back. Phillips looked into her puffy, red eyes that were now full of anger and certainty. "I know you can't help. I'm not asking for it."

"You should think this through. It isn't even worth it. Don't," he said as she took several more steps backward toward her car.

"I have to." Jessica reached for her car door and opened the driver's side.

"Consider the alternative. You've done so well uncovering evidence and bringing things to light. Please think about what you are saying." He watched as she sat in the seat and closed the door. Feeling like he should help, he briefly considered abandoning the law enforcement profession altogether. As she drove away, he crossed his arms and looked down at the ground as he walked back inside the station.

Back at the apartment, Jessica cleaned out her belongings and packed her suitcase. Once in her car she used the phonebook she stole from her motel room and a folded map to find Pottsville Veterinary Care and Animal Hospital on Howard Avenue.

As she drove past her destination, she looked at the sign out front noting that they closed at 5:00 P.M. As she looked around, she found a gravel lot across the street and parked her car in the least conspicuous place. She looked around in the suitcase in the backseat, finding her bottle of tequila and set it in a cup holder between the seats.

Looking at her watch, she thought she might have at least two hours until she would commit the first breaking and entering crime of her life. After popping two blue pills and several generous swigs of tequila, she sat back in her seat and lit up a cigarette.

Chapter 33

Jessica grabbed a crowbar from her trunk and held it as discreetly as possible as she crossed the street and into the back parking lot of the building. A few caged barking dogs could be heard inside as she looked around for an entry point. After finding a door with a glass pane, she gripped the crow bar and shoved it into the glass. Once the glass was knocked out of the frame, she reached her hand inside and turned the deadbolt. The alarm began beeping the second she opened the door. Not knowing what to do, she ran down a hallway looking for a room that contained medicine.

On Tuesdays, Deputy Phillips took his cruiser home as he was on call. When he heard over the radio that a burglar alarm had gone off at Pottsville Veterinary Care and Animal Hospital, it didn't take much for him to put two and two together. He lit up the roof, punched the siren and turned around. At the scene of the break in, the city police were discussing how the alarm must have scared off the burglar. The veterinarian, a 39-year-old female, was called when the alarm went off and arrived at the scene along with several law enforcements officers. After a quick check of the building, she didn't seem to think anything was missing. Phillips thought that if the vet knew to count her vials of Isoflurane, she might find one or two missing.

Jessica had parked down the street from Dr. Silva's house and placed one of her socks in her pocket along with a single vial of Isoflurane. As she approached the driveway, she walked on the neighbor's lawn thinking that if he saw her, she would simply act as if she were visiting his neighbors.

A moving van was parked in the driveway and the garage door was open with boxes ready to set inside. Walking around the exterior of the house looking for movement, she hurried out of view as a car pulled into the driveway. Standing near a large bush, she watched as an old, thin man got out of his car. In his left hand was a brown paper bag. The man fit the description Phillips had given her. An old man with gray hair and thin as a rail.

She walked cautiously around the outside; keeping to the neighbor's property in case he looked at her. As she came into view of the back of the house, she saw the thin man through a big picture window which overlooked the backyard. Eating at the kitchen table all by himself, he was taking bites and chewing, looking off into the distance. Pulling the sock out of her pocket, she held the vial in her right hand and walked toward the garage.

Phillips had both the sirens and lights on as he sped toward St. Clair. The engine was being pushed to four thousand RPM's as he navigated Highway 61.

In the home of Dr. Silva, Jessica had opened the door to a

laundry room. Both the washer and dryer were missing. Thinking that if he should discover her, she would simply say that she was interested in buying the house and would play it off with a smile.

From the laundry room, she could see the kitchen and after a few quiet steps, she could see the kitchen table with Dr. Silva sitting with his back to her. Looking down at the vial she could see that she would have to unscrew the top. While keep-ing out of view, she unscrewed the cap and held it as she leaned forward to see Dr. Silva still sitting at the kitchen table.

From behind him, she saw his jawbone moving as he chewed each bite of the sandwich. Looking down at her feet, she could see a clear path to where he was sitting. She poured the contents of the vial into the sock, the fibers soaking up the clear liquid. Her eyes focused on Dr. Silva as she decided that quickly running up behind him and covering his mouth with the sock would work.

Phillips sped past the welcome sign to St. Clair and turned a corner at a high rate of speed.

In the kitchen of Dr. Silva, Jessica lunged at her target and wrapped the sock around his mouth. Bucking like a horse, he used the table in front of him to push up. As he righted his two legs and stood up straight, he used his arms and hands to try and pull the Isoflurane soaked fabric away from his face. After four full breaths of trying to breathe, he began to lose consciousness. Falling to the left, both he and Jessica crashed into the big picture window, shattering the glass.

Now on the floor, Jessica immediately got up by placing her hand in a pile of glass and shifting her weight to get her legs underneath her before she stood up. Bleeding from her scalp and hand, she grabbed his hands and began to drag him through the kitchen, through the laundry room and then had to rest and recover her strength in the garage. Pulling her keys from her pocket, she ran to her car with the intention of pulling into the garage.

Phillips navigated the streets of a subdivision and made several turns before finding Dr. Silva's street. Upon pulling into the driveway, he saw the moving truck and the garage door was wide open. Pulling his gun as he stepped out of his cruiser, he walked into the garage coming upon streaks of blood.

"Jess?" he hollered out. He peered inside without stepping on the blood trail and could see that a window was knocked out and glass was all over the floor. He holstered his gun and ran back to his cruiser.

Dr. Silva was crumpled up like a wadded up newspaper in the backseat of Jessica's Honda Accord. His legs were up on the seat while his head was on the floorboard directly behind her. As she drove at a breakneck speed, Silva's eyes began to open. He could see the dome light above him and could hear the roar of an engine which was being pushed to its limit. He reached his hand up toward the driver.

Jessica was on Peach Mountain Road and could see the Adler farm on the horizon. Dr. Silva grabbed a handful of her hair and pulled her head towards the backseat. Screaming from the pain caused by hair follicles pulling her already lacerated scalp, she could no longer reach the steering wheel and the Accord ran off the road and into a fence. Silva lost his grip and her head slammed into the steering wheel, rendering her unconscious.

Phillips happened upon the wreck first and stopped his cruiser. Steam billowed out of the radiator and rose into the air as he approached the wreck. Looking inside, Jessica was slumped over the steering wheel and Dr. Silva was unconscious in the floorboard of the backseat. He opened the back door and dragged Silva to his cruiser and locked him in the back. Phillips then removed Jessica from around the steering wheel and carried her to the front seat. After hitting the siren and lights, he felt a hand on his arm. Jessica looked at him.

"Where are you going?" she asked in a tired and distressed voice.

"The hospital."

"Either drive to the house or fight me for the steering wheel," she replied as she reached for the painful wound on her scalp to check the flow of blood. Phillips exhaled and turned the wheel before he floored the pedal.

"I'm gonna miss this job, Calvert," he said causing Jessica to smile.

Once in the driveway of the Adler Farm, Jessica limped out of the passenger seat and opened the back door. Phillips came around and grabbed Dr. Silva's shirt and dragged him out.

She grabbed his legs and helped carry him to the front door.

"Now what?"

"Upstairs."

"How do you know?"

"I don't."

"How do you know we won't be hurt?"

"I don't."

Phillips did most of the work walking backwards up the stairs while Jessica held his legs. Once at the top, they shuffled into Tilly's room and set Dr. Silva on the floor. The Ouija board was in the corner with the power cord running out the window toward the operations trailer. The planchette began moving with no recognizable words. The door behind them slammed shut.

"Oh, shit," Jessica said under her breath. Phillips hurried to the door only to lose consciousness and collapse onto the hardwood floor. Jessica slowly closed her eyes and whispered, "Please don't." The force felt like it came from behind and pushed her against the wall, her head striking the plastered surface. She fell to the floor, blacking out.

Slowly regaining consciousness, she first felt the pain in her head followed by severe, throbbing shoulder pain. She took in a brief glimpse of the room before her eyes opened and closed. Waking to a darkened room, she could see that her head was on the hardwood floor. Her body was contorted in an arrangement similar to a marionette at rest. She moved her head, scraping her temple lightly on the floor as she moved.

Looking at a window, she could see that the sun had set and Dr. Silva was on his back and breathing rapidly. The top of his head was near Jessica's. His feet were furthest away from her and he was naked. His breath was hurried until he took a pause, seemingly gathering the ability to speak.

"He's coming back," Dr. Silva said in between breaths. He tilted his head back and looked at Jessica. "He is coming!" he groaned just before he saw movement and shifting behind Jessica. Silva began screaming as something began to rise up from the floor.

As she turned her head and looked, she could see the rising figure was Phillips, slowly standing up and towering over her. He looked at Silva with a grin and eyes that were not his own. His fingernails had grown into thick, yellow points while his mouth and cheeks appeared to be heavily bruised and slightly elongated with his mouth full of sharp teeth. Shocked and unable to move, she could see blue veins just underneath his skin as he stepped over her and stood over Silva who looked up at the man as he screamed. When Phillips spoke, his voice sounded deep and full of gravel. His teeth could briefly be seen, each tooth discolored and jagged.

"*Putrescet cadaver tuum subter pedes meos,*" each word spoken sounded as if an engine was roaring in his throat as he spoke. "*Corpus ponatur intra muros te autem adsumam et gallos in medio animalium tuus mortem.*"

Jessica felt her muscles seize up from fear. Her heart thumped in her chest causing the sound of each beat to resonate in her head. Unable to move, she watched as Phillips leaned over Dr. Silva, continuing to speak Latin. His fingernails slowly plunged into Silva's flesh. Blood began to seep out of the fresh wound as the old man screamed.

A grin came across Phillips' face as he emitted a high-pitched whine from his altered vocal cords. His hands dug underneath Dr. Silva's skin as blood oozed out. Jessica started to lose consciousness. Just before blacking out, she could see bony, disheveled hands begin to pull the skin free from the muscle tissue. More screaming as the odor of copper and iron wafted in the air.

Chapter 34

The next morning, the Adler farm was buzzing with demolition workers wearing bright orange vests and white hard hats. A large flatbed truck hauling a backhoe was backing into the gravel driveway ready to deliver the rented beast. Construction site foreman, Milt Joyce guided the delivery driver into the backyard of the Adler farmhouse. Waving his arms slowly, the beeping of the truck repeated obnoxiously as the driver backed in slowly while watching the guiding movements. The driver stopped the truck when Milt held up his hands.

"Right here's good," Milt yelled. The driver slowed the truck, applying the air brakes and shifted it out of drive. He exited the cab of the truck and walked around the back and began the process of unloading the key piece of heavy machinery that would ultimately demolish the Adler Family home.

Several members of the construction crew had arrived in their trucks with breakfast sandwiches and coffee, ready to take on the day of destruction and clearing. Standing in front of a parked Chevy Silverado, three workers told jokes as they sipped on coffee and took bites out of sausage biscuits. Milt walked up to the men hoping to hurry them up.

"You guys see that police cruiser and the Honda?" he said

as he pointed. One crew member spoke as he chewed his biscuit.

"Yeah. We thought the cruiser was here to keep photographers back as we tore the house down."

"What about the Honda?" A short statured crew member asked.

"I need a final walk-through that includes inspection of the crawlspace and attic. Need this done first thing before we start ripping this apart. Once you're done come see me and all three of you need to sign off on the order."

Milt had wandered off to speak with the operator of the backhoe while the guys pissed and moaned about going inside a haunted house. The three men angrily shoved the last of their sausage biscuits into their mouths and took a last sip of coffee before tossing their empty cups into the back of the Silverado.

The largest and thickest construction worker named Bruce pointed at the small statured man named Spencer.

"Spence, you take care of the crawlspace. Me and Rocky will do the house and attic."

The other workers who were scattered around the back of the house watched as Spencer headed underneath the house. Silence fell among them as they witnessed Rocky and Bruce open the back door and go inside.

"Nice knowin' ya Rocky," shouted a worker. Chuckles and whistles followed.

Milt hadn't ever worked with the operator of the backhoe

and introduced himself with a handshake. He began to lay out the day and explained what he wanted to do first. During his conversation, the sound of two men shouting and yelling as they tore out of the house turned Milt's attention to the back door. Expletives followed, mostly taking God's name in vain as they ran to what they felt was a safe distance. Milt ran over to the workers along with other crew members who gathered to see what had happened.

"Call the police. Get them here now."

"What? Why?"

Sheriff Haydon was sitting in his office combing through a file when Deputy Barnes ran in and spouted off in a nearly incoherent manner.

"A man is nailed to the wall in the Adler house. Deputy Phillips and the Jessica girl are unresponsive on the floor," he yelled just before running out of the office.

"What?" he asked as he stood up and ran behind Barnes to his cruiser.

Upon arriving at the scene, an ambulance with sirens and lights pulled in behind them. Two paramedics jumped out and ran behind both Deputy Barnes and Sheriff Haydon to the front porch, through the front door and up the stairs. Turning right, they saw an open door and a man nailed to the wall who had been skinned. Muscle tissue and bone were easily identifiable as well as Dr. Silva's bright white teeth and even his eyes seemed to glow white next to the bloody exterior. His intestines had fallen to the floor like ropes hanging off a cliff and blood dripped below him into a pool of crimson.

The paramedics pushed past Barnes and Haydon as they were the first to step into the room. They stood over Deputy Phillips first and checked his vitals. His fingernails were missing and his jaw was broken. Each tooth seemed to drip blood from his gums while much of his neck and face was heavily bruised.

"I have a pulse!" a paramedic shouted. "Get a gurney in here now!" Deputy Barnes ran downstairs and headed out the front door. The other paramedic checked the vitals of Jessica; he could already see her breathing.

"Pulse and respiratory!"

"Dispatch get me a second ambulance," Sheriff said into his handheld radio.

Movement came from the wall where the man had been skinned. The head turned slightly and the eyes began moving with the sound of breathing coming from his throat.

"Oh my God. He's alive," a paramedic said as he stood up. Deputy Barnes could be heard coming up the stairs carrying a gurney with the help of a construction worker. Once they reached the top of the stairs, everyone was looking at the man nailed to the wall as he moved, obviously in great pain.

"Holy shit!" Barnes said. The construction worker saw the gory scene in the room and dropped his end of the gurney and ran down the stairs.

"Uh, bring the gurney." a paramedic said in a dazed voice as Dr. Silva continued to make noises from his throat. Barnes shoved the gurney into the room, opting not to step inside. It rolled to the feet of Deputy Phillips. The paramedics took their attention off the skinned man and moved Phillips, strapping him to the stretcher.

Finally snapping out of the shock and horror of the man who was still alive, they began to move quickly, getting Deputy Phillips into the ambulance just as another arrived. In the room, Jessica's breathing became heavier and she began to move. Both Deputy Barnes and Sheriff Haydon ran to her side.

"Easy. Easy now," Haydon said.

"The paramedics are on their way." Jessica started to cough and open her eyes, Haydon moved so that he would screen her line of sight from the skinned man. Suddenly, Jessica began to hyperventilate and she quickly pushed herself up and crawled backwards until her back hit the wall.

"Take it easy, you're okay. You're gonna be okay," Haydon continued to block her line of sight.

"Jessssickahh," a voice moaned behind Sheriff Haydon. Deputy Barnes stood up and looked while Haydon kept Jessica from seeing the skinned man. Barnes watched as the man struggled to speak, only this time his voice was louder. "Jessssickahh!" Sheriff could hear the paramedics coming up the front steps and figuring that Jessica didn't need to see what was behind him, reached down and grabbed her arm and shoulder.

"Let's get her out of here," he said. Barnes quickly followed suit and helped her to her feet. Dr. Silva took in a deep breath, his lungs could be seen expanding just before he spoke for the last time. Now at the top of the stairs, Jessica was being held on both sides as Haydon spoke loudly to the paramedics coming up the stairs. "We're bringing her down to you." "Jessssickahh!' Silva said in the loudest voice he could summon. As they took the first step down the stairs, Jessica turned her head and looked at Dr. Silva nailed to the wall, skinless and in agony. As they went down the second step, she looked back in horror. Then, her face slowly changed from one in a state of shock, to one of realization that it was over. Just before she disappeared from Silva's view, he saw the corners of her mouth turn slowly upward as a slight grin appeared.

Chapter 35

While Jessica had gained media attention upon discovering the bodies of children buried under trees, she had now gained nationwide fame. In the mind of the general public, it was a gruesome and horrifying story that appalled them, yet the story held their interest for a solid week. In the mind of the paranormal community, Jessica became an answer to the question they had all been seeking. Outside Schuylkill Medical Center, reporters camped out to get Jessica on camera while paranormal enthusiasts waited to get a glimpse of her.

Sheriff Haydon walked past the gathering of reporters and cameramen, stepping inside the lobby and over to the elevator. Deputy Barnes was getting a cup of bitter coffee from a vending machine when he saw Haydon step into the elevator. He hurried over, careful not to spill his coffee and slipped in the elevator just as the door began to close. As they spoke, five other people around them could hear their conversation.

"How's he doing?" Sheriff asked.

"He's good right now. Hasn't woken up yet. Doctor said he has a laceration on each finger tip and all his fingernails are gone," two of the elevator passengers winced as they heard the gruesome detail.

"Goddamn! His fingernails?"

"He's in bad shape. I won't even talk about his jaw bone. It was broken in three places. Doctor said he'll pull through."

"Yeah, I got a call that he would make it through, but not without pain and discomfort. What about Calvert?"

"She refused medical services."

"What? Why?"

"She refused everything. Just walked into a bathroom, took a shower while one of the nurses laundered her shirt and jeans."

"Where is she?" Haydon asked. The elevator doors opened and three people gladly got off while two others stepped inside. The elevator doors closed and the conversation continued.

"In the room with Deputy Phillips."

"What about the man with no skin? All I heard is that they were trying to figure out what to do."

"They took him down, gathered up his intestines and put them in a bucket. You get that? A bucket. All them tubes still connected to his gunny works. Then they got him into the ambulance where he died."

"Why bother getting him into the ambulance?"

"They had to try I guess. That man was screaming all the way down the stairs, bleeding all over. At first they had his intestines piled up on his stomach," Deputy Barnes said as he held his coffee level while pantomiming a cluster of organs on his stomach. "But while they were moving him, the pile of intestines kept falling and hanging off the damn stretcher." The other passengers in the elevator looked on in horror.

"So that's why they used the bucket?"

"Yep."

"How did he not die right away?" Sheriff asked. The elevator doors opened. Haydon and Barnes walked out and headed down the hall.

"I don't know. Every paramedic said he should have died. One guy thought that haunted house was keeping him alive somehow. You should have seen them too. They were all scared shitless."

"Just the thought of filling out that paperwork has me considering retirement. How the hell am I going to explain this one? Can't wait till that house is demolished."

"You're gonna have to wait. The county was paying the demo crew triple, but after that they won't even come near it."

"I wouldn't do it either," Haydon said as he shook his head back and forth. The thought of filling out more paper work hit him again, pissing him off. "Aww hell, who do I charge with the murder of skinless Silva?"

"That FBI guy gonna have a shit fit when you tell him it was a ghost."

"I can't put that on the report. The assholes at St. Clair City Police would love that. I can picture 'em now, sending me Halloween cards all year long."

"Well you ain't gonna charge Phillips or the Calvert girl are ya?"

"Hell no. Neither of them could have skinned that man. Phillips couldn't skin a cat. He can barely help his mother paint a wall."

When they arrived at Deputy Phillips' hospital room, they found him with his eyes open and Jessica asleep in the chair next to him. His hands were wrapped in gauze along with each finger. The skin around his mouth and jaw was bruised like a ten day old banana and his eyes were bloodshot. Wires that were plugged into a heart monitor were attached to his chest under his hospital gown and an IV ran from a bag to his arm.

"How ya doin' big guy?" Haydon whispered. Phillips shrugged.

"Can ya talk?" Barnes asked. Phillips shook his head no. Jessica stirred in her chair and opened her eyes. As she sat up, she saw Haydon and Barnes before she saw that Phillips was awake.

"He can't talk yet, but doc says he's gonna be fine," Deputy Barnes said. Jessica smiled and stood up before leaning over the bed and hugging Phillips. Haydon took his hat off and nudged Barnes.

"Let's go get something to eat," he said under his breath. "Phillips, we'll see ya in a few." Phillips nodded. Jessica pulled the chair closer to his bed and sat down. She looked into his eyes and she placed her hand on his arm.

"Do you want to know what happened?" Phillips shook his head *No*.

"I wouldn't tell you anyway. I have been through too much and just the thought of replaying that shit in my head is out of the question. Do you feel any pain?"

No.

"Good. I'm going to see that you get outta here and then I'm headed back to Washington." Phillips held up his bandaged hand, waving forward, gesturing that she should just go on. "Hell, no. I'm not going anywhere. I feel responsible. I got you in this mess." Phillips shook his head. "Well, you can't get rid of me. I'm sticking around. You just take it easy and if you need anything you let me know. I'm right here. By the way, did you see your mom? Was she here when you woke up?" He shook his head *No.* "She said she was going home to sleep and she'll be back soon."

Robert Wood had just finished reading a piece from a new reporter he had hired only weeks ago and felt that he made a mistake giving this stupid kid a job. The piece was chock full of both grammatical errors and structural errors. He stood up and walked out to the bullpen and stood over the new reporter and dropped the proof onto his desk.

"Just tell me you're retarded. It'll make life much easier on both of us."

"I was told to lay it on your desk sir. It was the only way to get you out of your office."

"What the shit?" he said as he put his hands on his hips. The reporter opened his desk drawer and removed a cupcake. He grabbed a lighter and lit a candle while other staff members gathered around and began singing Happy Birthday. During the song, a member of the staff pointed to the TV.

"Hey! It's Calvert! Look! It's Jessica Calvert." Everyone turned around and looked at the TV. Reporters followed her to her car as they asked questions.

"What did you see in the house?"

"Was Dr. Silva involved in the murder of the Adler Family?"

The questions continued as Mr. Wood reached down and pulled the candle out after blowing out the flame. Throwing the candle in the trash can and grabbing the cupcake, he peeled down the paper and took a bite, getting most of it on the outside of his mouth. He watched as Jessica turned around and spoke,

"I will explain everything, but you're gonna have to read about it in *The Washington Post.*"

The report ended and Mr. Wood started to walk back to his office, ignoring the birthday gathering while continuing to eat his cupcake.

"I do like her," he said under his breath as he closed his office door.

After six days of being cared for, Phillips was discharged with the aid of an ambulance. His mother, Patty Phillips, hurried to his apartment and began cleaning and vacuuming in order to prepare for her son's arrival. Jessica opened the door for the paramedics as they rolled the stretcher inside and headed toward the back bedroom. Once situated amongst the posters of baseball and basketball players, both Patty and Jessica propped him up using pillows and covered his legs with blankets.

Once he was comfortable and situated, Patty left the room to divide up his medication into pillboxes. Jessica knelt down at his bedside and placed her hand on his bandaged arm.

"I'm headed back. Don't be a stranger and call me from time to time. You're even welcome to visit."

"Thank you," he mouthed as she leaned forward and gave him a hug.

"Well, you're welcome, but the biggest thank you comes from me. You saved my life and I will never forget it," she said with a hint of tears in her eyes. Phillips attempted to speak, but only a whisper would emit from his throat.

"Christmas cards for life."

A final embrace before she left his apartment and got into her car. The feeling of ending a chapter in her life invoked tears of relief. She shifted her banged-up Accord into drive and turned out of Annhurst Apartments, wiping away a few tears.

Chapter 36

Heather Vanderwheele, the education reporter at *The Washington Post* had been looking forward to her new room-mate's arrival. Upon knocking on the door while carrying a laundry basket, Heather unlatched the door and opened it to Jessica Calvert.

"You are famous," she said with a smile.

"Oh stop," she grinned as she set her laundry basket down.

"No kidding. You're all I have been hearing about the last week," she replied as they embraced. Entering the small apart-ment, Jessica and Heather caught up in the living room until the phone rang. When Heather answered, she was surprised to hear the voice of her boss.

"Hey there. Did she arrive yet?"

"Just now."

"May I speak with her?"

"Of course. Just a second," Heather said as she cupped the phone and whispered to Jessica. "It's Mr. Wood. I told him you were living with me when you came back. He's been calling every few days or so. Sorry," she said as she made an apologetic face.

"It's okay," Jessica whispered back as she was handed the phone. "Hello?"

"Hey kiddo. You back in town?"

"Yep."

"I need something from you. Not going to sugar coat it. Mr. Reinhardt wants to meet with you immediately."

"Tonight?"

"In this town important things are done over drinks and cigars. I want you to meet us at the Jefferson Hotel in the bar. Do you own a little black dress?"

"No."

"Holy shit, Calvert. You're hopeless. Go buy a dress now. Get to the hotel by 8 p.m. This is big. See you there."

Click.

Jessica hung up the phone already full of anxiety.

"He never lets up does he?" Heather said as she crossed her arms.

"Can I ask you a favor?"

"Sure."

"I know I just got here, but do you happen to own a black dress?"

⸻

Jessica had put her hair up with bobby pins and threw a shawl around her neck and shoulders. The dress was snug and she could feel the need to cease high-calorie food intake with every step. Sucking in her stomach nearly the entire cab ride, she watched the city zoom past her window and held onto Heather's borrowed clutch.

When the cab pulled up in front of the hotel, she paid him and stepped out looking radiant. A doorman who wore white gloves and a concierge jacket opened the heavy brass door for her as she walked inside. Once she found the bar, she struggled to see in the darkness who was who. Both Mr. Wood and Mr. Reinhardt stood up, signaling she was to come to the back of the bar. Seated at a table, both men were smoking cigars and sipping brandy from a snifter.

As she walked toward them, Mr. Reinhardt took notice of her youth and her slender, attractive appearance. Forty years her senior, his hair was gray and the wrinkles cut into his face were deep and carved with experience. His eyes were sharp and stern, but his smile gave him away. Once introductions were made, Jessica sat down and whipped out a cigarette and lit it. Unable to resist a cigarette in the wake of the cigar smoke wafting around the table, she exhaled the first drag into the empty space above her as she crossed her legs. A waiter approached her and asked for her order.

"Chimalhucan Tequila. No shots, but a glass. Neat. Three fingers."

"Jesus, Calvert. Cigarettes and hard liquor? I thought you only drank water and ate leaves?"

"I don't think there is a successful newspaper woman who doesn't smoke and drink," Reinhardt said with a chuckle.

"Inevitable I guess," replied Mr. Wood.

"I appreciate the opportunity to meet you, Mr. Reinhardt."

"I assure you, the pleasure is all mine. I wanted to meet with you as soon as possible," he started to say as the waiter brought her a glass of tequila. "First, thanks for your comment on the news about reading your story in *The Post*. Very loyal of you."

"I just hope I still have a job."

"Absolutely. I want you to know that you are always welcome," he said with a smile before sipping his brandy. "Quite honestly, I was hoping you still wanted to work with us."

"Without question."

"Good to hear. I am fortunate to own *The Post*, but as you may know I also own a publishing company."

"Reinhardt Inc.," Jessica said with a smile.

"Correct. We publish both fiction and non-fiction and because of this, I would like to personally ask you to do something for us."

"Name it," she said as she took a sip of her tequila.

"I would like you to come back and write one article for the paper. Then, I would like you to resign your position and focus on writing a book for us."

"A book?"

"Yes, but don't worry. I won't throw you to the wolves. I will assign a staff to help you with the book. Experienced editors. We want the article you write to be a teaser for the book.

Once it's published, the team will book you on several television and radio shows to promote it and then you're welcome to come back on staff at *The Post*."

"I am shocked. I never thought this is what this meeting would be about."

"Well, perhaps we should have briefed you beforehand, but either way you are informed now. You have one of the most interesting stories in America right now. We need to strike while the iron is hot."

"Well, I've never been one to mull over a decision. I accept. No reason to delay."

"Calvert," Mr. Wood said as he leaned forward with a look on his face which implied she wasn't doing it right. "You're supposed to ask about compensation before you accept anything."

"Right. Well, I am sure he will take care of me," she replied while nodding in Reinhardt's direction. "After all, I am not a one-trick pony. Treating me right the first time ensures my ongoing loyalty and I know in my heart that Mr. Reinhardt wouldn't steer me wrong," she added with a smile. She turned her head and looked at Mr. Reinhardt who began laughing. He looked at Mr. Wood who simply replied with a smirk,

"Told ya."

Jessica spent four days in a secluded office smoking cigarettes, popping pills and drinking coffee. Chinese food was delivered and eaten in great quantities. Her keyboard *clacked* as she typed out her experience in St. Clair beginning with the harrowing crash through the second-floor window.

The day the article came out, hundreds of news outlets began to spread the story. Catholic churches released statements that condemned her findings, claiming she was meddling with evil on earth. The public wrote in to *The Post* to explain their paranormal experiences, flooding the mailroom with thousands of letters.

Television stations called the paper asking to speak with Miss Calvert, who had already vanished. Locked away in a Manhattan loft in New York, she penned the book with the help of a small staff. The walls of the loft were covered in notes, documents and a white board which allowed her to write out sections of the book.

On a table near her computer were items like Father Abbott's book and Dr. Thornhill's logbook that ultimately became her own logbook. Once the first draft was completed, six more drafts followed. Upon a final combing by the editor and Mr. Reinhardt, the book was approved to go to press.

Chapter 37

The book was titled: *What Lies Inside.*

When readers opened the book, they saw a preface and it was the first line that caught their attention.

Many people died to make this book possible. James Extine from Allentown, PA worked for a coal mining company. We were both thrown from a window, which I survived, by sheer luck. He did not. Father Abbott was a priest who was on sabbatical so that he could continue his research to better understand life after death. Ray Turner was a very smart soldier who knew how to implement technology in a way that enabled the team to communicate with the paranormal. Mr. Henrik Frazier was a wealthy businessman who made it financially possible to uncover evidence of life beyond death. These individuals gave their lives for the knowledge that paranormal entities exist. What follows in this book is their legacy.

After piecing together the puzzle, Jessica concluded that Dr. Silva would kidnap children four and a half hours north of

St. Clair and bring them back to his home. For many years he had easily gotten away with his crimes by carrying out his deeds far from home. She created a graph in the book using dates of each missing child. Children in the early 1970s went missing at a higher rate than toward the end of the 1970s. Jessica theorized that as he grew older, traveling and shoveling took a toll on Dr. Silva and caused him to slow down. When he was no longer able to make the trip up to Rochester, he resorted to a local child by the name of Scott Adler.

Scott was athletic and Dr. Silva was too old and slow to catch him when he slipped the grasp of his kidnapper. The theory further explained how Dr. Silva possibly threatened to withhold the rest of Gordon D'Silva's inheritance unless he caught the boy and brought him back to his house. When it was discovered that the boy evaded Gordon, Dr. Silva killed his brother and then entered the home of the Adler family.

The day the book was released, a young analyst working for the FBI left his cluttered desk of empty coffee cups, a stack of paper work, a lamp and solar powered calculator that never saw the sun. He walked across the building and barged into Warren Ford's office. Thinking he was going to ask him about going out to lunch, he held up his hand signaling he was busy. Ignoring the hand, the analyst asked him a question.

"Did you get it yet?"

"Get what?"

"The book. It came out today."

Warren left the office with his raincoat and stepped out

into the lobby of the building. As it was pouring, he pulled the coat over his head and hurried out of the front doors and jogged down the street in his plain, blue suit and dark blue tie. His feet slapped the wet cement with each step until he finally arrived in front of Fox Books. He turned his head and saw a window display of newly released novels. After finding *What Lies Inside,* he looked at the cover art featuring an old photo of the Adler Farmhouse with a crop of wheat in the background.

Beads of water left wet trails as the rain ran down the fabric of his coat as he considered the real possibility of a dead girl communicating with a living person. While he was partially convinced, he felt that if he read the book, he would be completely convinced. Taking a deep breath, he left the window display and walked a few feet to the front of the door of Fox Books and went inside.

The book captivated the nation, providing Jessica with unwanted fame, but the trade-off was the money. She had the publishing company pay her father 75% of her compensation and she kept the rest. Bob put in his retirement notice and put his house up for sale. Unsure of where he would go next, he considered finding a small cabin near a lake where he could go fishing as often as he wanted.

The number of phone calls that Jessica received became such a hassle that a temporary, second operator was hired at *The Post* just to help field the calls. While none of the calls made it though to Jessica, one man who kept calling and asking to speak with her, garnered enough attention for the operator to finally take his message.

She then took it upon herself to walk over to Miss Calvert's office. She cautiously approached, not knowing what to expect as she had heard many rumors. Relief set in when Jessica spun in her chair and looked at her with a smile and spoke softly.

"Do you need me for something?"

"Yes. I'm sorry to bother you..."

"Oh please," Jessica interrupted as she waved her hand in the air and leaned back in her chair. "You're not bothering me. What can I do for you?"

"I have a message from this guy that keeps calling and after his, like, seventh or eighth call, it seems he really needs to speak with you," she said as she handed Jessica the slip of pink paper.

"Oh. Okay, I will return his call. Thank you!" she offered as she looked down at the message.

"You're welcome," the operator said as she turned around and walked back to her desk. Jessica looked at her handwriting and was easily able to decipher her notes.

Paul Emmett - Professor

University of Texas

Needs to speak with Miss Calvert

Jessica dialed the number and within moments, a man answered.

"Paul Emmett."

"Hello, this is Jessica Calvert returning your call."

"Oh, Miss Calvert. Thank you so much for calling me back. I was afraid I wouldn't have been able to get in touch with you."

"No problem."

"I have to thank you first, for your book. It uh, well, I don't know how to say this, but I have been working on a project for years with minimal funding from the university and due to your book, I was able to get a sizeable grant."

"Goodness. That's unexpected. What is your project, may I ask?"

Professor Emmett began his story with growing up in the city of Alberta, Canada. The town was known for a hotel named the Banff Springs Hotel. It had been known to be haunted for longer than he had been alive.

"...And I'm sixty-one years old so the hauntings have been known for decades. One of the things the hotel is known for is that hotel staff bricked up room 873 in the 1940s and for years they said it was a structural issue with the flooring. However, people who checked in next to 873 were either murdered or vanished."

"Is this documented?"

"It is...by me and the influx of researchers here at the University. We have made many trips to the hotel and we are getting ready to make another one, especially since we now have a sizeable grant thanks to you."

"I am glad it worked out."

"Well, I was wondering if there is anyway I could persuade you to join us?"

"Oh, I don't know. I'm not sure I could assist you with anything. This really isn't my field."

"Really we just need an outside witness, one who has experience and your presence would certainly help us in terms of legitimizing our efforts."

"I don't think..." she started to say until she heard four words.

"We could pay you."

"You could? From the grant?"

"Of course. After all you helped raise the funds."

"I'm interested, but I can't commit just yet. How long are we talking here?"

"Three weeks or so."

"I'm going to need to think about this. Can I call you back?"

"Of course."

—∞—

Jessica researched Banff Springs Hotel and discovered it was built in 1888 by the Canadian Pacific Railway and currently had more than 200 rooms. A phone call to the *Calgary Herald* confirmed that the hotel was known for being haunted and its legacy certainly intrigued her.

Next, she checked up on Professor Paul Emmett and even ordered a background check through *The Washington Post*. He

was clean and had published many papers on design development and application of bio-sensing and sensor technologies.
His focus was on analytical devices incorporating a biological
material for use in medical studies. Unable to fully understand
Paul Emmett's field of study, she considered him to be legiti-
mate and ceased her research.

The next day, Jessica walked into Robert Wood's office in
hopes of getting three weeks off for the excursion. Thinking
that she still had a bestseller circulating the globe, she would
be given a little leeway.

"I got a call from a professor in Texas. He wants me to be
part of a research team investigating paranormal activity in a
hotel in Canada."

"Okay."

"He is asking for three weeks. Any chance you'd let me
do this?"

"I wish I could say yes, but I can't. I am not your boss
anymore."

"How's that?"

"Mr. Reinhardt has taken that role. Says I give you assign-
ments, but ultimately he is now your direct supervisor."

"Good to know. So we're co-workers?"

"Yep."

"Can I borrow a cigarette?"

"Go get your own," he said while making a snide face.
Jessica smiled and walked out of his office. Sitting at her desk,
she picked up her phone and dialed the operator and asked for

Mr. Reinhardt's office. After three minutes, he came on the line.

"Miss Calvert, what can I do for you today?"

"I have an idea for a second book."

"You do? I was hoping to speak with you about that next month as a matter of fact."

Jessica explained the phone call she received from Professor Paul Emmett and the history of the Banff Springs Hotel and then asked for time to travel to Canada. With a firm and immediate approval, she thanked him and hung up.

The same day, Paul Emmett had received a phone call from Jessica and compensation was agreed upon. The team would be arriving at the hotel in three days.

Chapter 38

Jessica had been assigned a profile piece on Secretary of Transportation Samuel K. Skinner and ensured her article was wrapped up before she left. After the piece was fact-checked, she took the final version into Mr. Wood's office and placed it in a tray on his desk.

"I'm out. See ya in three weeks."

"Fine. Travel safe. Bring me back some peanuts."

"Peanuts?"

"From the plane."

"I'll see what I can do," she said as she left his office and closed the door.

Once in her apartment, she packed comfortable clothes with her notepad and tape recorder in her blood stained messenger bag. In her red, zippered toiletry bag she removed her bottles of Percocet and Vicodin and shoved them into her front jeans pocket. Before she left for the airport, she wrote a note to Heather explaining that her rent and her half of the utility bill was in the envelope on the kitchen table. She closed the door and jumped into the cab waiting for her downstairs.

After checking all of her luggage at the check-in desk, she waited less than a half hour at the gate before she boarded and took her seat next to the window. She watched the baggage handlers load the luggage into the plane followed by the sound of the airplane door closing and an announcement by the captain. Once they pushed away from the gate and taxied, Jessica was forced to watch the live safety belt demonstration just before they took off.

Once the seatbelt sign went off, the drink cart rolled down the aisle and finally to Jessica's row.

"Two vodkas with ice please."

Her order was filled and looks shot her way from nearby passengers. Two clear cups, filled with ice and vodka for one petite girl in Row 39 Seat A.

"Little thirsty are you?" a man sitting next to her asked. Wearing a white button up shirt and yellow tie, he waited for her response.

"A little," she replied. After removing two Percocets from her prescription bottle, she popped them both and downed the first cup. "I'm terrified of flying," she said, a complete fabrication which didn't seem to stick with the yellow tie in seat B.

"I see that."

She sipped on her second drink until it was down to ice and closed her eyes. The wave of calmness started to come over her like a warm blanket with a numbness that spread throughout her body. The vibration of the plane and the Percocet cocktail flowing through her system was entrancing enough to cause her to slip into a deep euphoric state.